Richard Dee.

Richard Dee is from Brixham in Devon. Leaving school at 16 he briefly worked in a supermarket, then he went to sea and travelled the world in the Merchant Navy, qualifying as a Master Mariner in 1986.

He has also worked as an Insurance Surveyor, Lockmaster, Harbourmaster and Ships Pilot, taking over 3,500 vessels up and down the Thames, passing through the estuary, the Thames Barrier and Tower Bridge.

Since the publication of his first Science Fiction novel, *Freefall,* in 2013, Richard has written another eighteen novels, a textbook and a selection of short stories. He has been featured in several anthologies, including *1066 Turned Upside Down* and *Tales from Deepest Darkest Devon.*

He writes Science Fiction and Steampunk adventures and also chronicles the exploits of reluctant amateur detective Andorra Pett.

Richard is married with three adult children and five grandchildren.

He can be found at https://richarddeescifi.co.uk and contacted at richarddeescifi@gmail.com

Also by Richard Dee

The Dave Travise Series
Freefall
Myra
Promise Me

The Balcom Series
Ribbonworld
Jungle Green
The Lost Princess

Steampunk
The Rocks of Aserol
A New Life in Ventis
Tales from Norlandia
The Sensaurum and the Lexis

Andorra Pett Mysteries
Andorra Pett and the Oort Cloud Café
Andorra Pett on Mars
Andorra Pett and her Sister
Andorra Pett takes a break

Stand Alone Novels
Life and Other Dreams
Survive
The Hitman and the Thief
The Syk'm
We are Saul

Short Stories
Flash Fiction
Flash Fiction 2

Non-Fiction
Creating a Sci-fi World

I Remember Everything

RICHARD DEE

All rights reserved.

Published in 2023 by 4Star Scifi

4Star Scifi, Brixham, Devon, England

www.richarddeescifi.co.uk/4Star

Copyright © Richard Dee 2021-23

No parts of this publication may be reproduced, stored in a retrieval system, or transmitted in any form or by any means, electronic, mechanical, photocopying, recording, or otherwise, without the prior written permission of the copyright owner.

This book is issued subject to the condition that it shall not, by way of trade or otherwise, be lent, resold, hired out, or otherwise circulated without the publisher's prior consent in any form of binding or cover other than that in which it is published and without a similar condition including this condition being imposed on the subsequent purchaser. Under no circumstances may any part of this book be photocopied for resale.

This is a work of fiction. Any similarity between the characters and situations within its pages and places or persons, living or dead, is unintentional and coincidental.

Cover by 4Star Scifi, created in Canva.

For the voices in my head,
who have taken me on such a literary journey.

Chapter 1

I remember the first day of this new life, it started with pain, the same way that the last day of my old life had ended.

I didn't realise that it was a new life, not to begin with. It seemed to start only seconds after the end of what must have been my last one. In my old life, I had slipped into unconsciousness, there had been pain. Now I was awake again, the pain was still there, although it felt different.

I opened my eyes, took a deep breath, filling my lungs. Where was I? The last thing I recalled was the grin on his face, the cold, dark warehouse, the flash of a blade. Where I was now was bright and warm. And noisy; there was some soft music in the background. I could hear people talking, male and female. Most of what they were saying was indistinct, voices overlaid on voices, the music accompanied by the bleep of machinery. Was Beth here?

"What's the time?" said one of the female voices, out of my sight. "Twenty-oh-eight," said someone else. Who were they? We had been alone; they must be paramedics.

The lights in here were too bright for the warehouse, it looked like I had been found and taken to a hospital. The response had been impressive, it had been nineteen-forty-five when I'd got out of my car. I must be in the Emergency department. That explained the number of people around me.

The noise would be the monitors, registering my pulse and vital signs. My squad would have been called as well. This was good, despite what had happened I was alive and once I got myself sorted out, I could tell them who my attacker was. I'd been looking for him in connection with a string of armed robberies, now he had another charge to add to his lengthy list of offences. OK, I'd been injured but I would recover, it would be worth it to see justice prevail.

If I'd only done things properly, this never would have happened. When I'd spotted his car outside the warehouse, I ought to have called in and waited for backup. That was my first mistake. I had known that I was in trouble as soon as I had been forced to retreat into the corner, dodging the thrusting blade until I had run out of room. But now, things were all going to work out.

There was a brief flash of light away to one side of me, it made me blink. They must be taking photographs of my injuries.

"Where am I?" I shouted. All that came out was an unformed cry.

"That's a good pair of lungs," someone said. Maybe, but why couldn't I make myself understood? I was starting to get worried now.

"Perhaps it's time for a meal," said another voice. What were they talking about? Food was unimportant, just get me better, so I can bring him to justice. I had his name, it needed to be told.

I must have been lying down on my back, all I could see was the ceiling, the white strip lights under frosted plastic covers. I tried to move my arms, it felt like I had no control over them. My legs were the same. Had the knife stroke paralysed me? I couldn't even lift my head.

"Here, let me," said the first voice.

I felt myself grabbed around the waist, another hand went under my head, at the back. I was rising, my neck had no strength, it was unable to support the weight of my head. Before I knew what was happening, my face was smothered in warm flesh.

"Isn't she a beautiful baby?" said the second voice.

That was where the panic set in. I tried to push myself away, so that I could see what was going on, my arms and legs refused to co-operate.

I howled in frustration, what had happened to me? I wasn't a baby, never mind a girl. Less than thirty minutes ago, I'd been a twenty-seven-year-old male detective. I'd been investigating a criminal gang and, unfortunately, I'd been stabbed by their leader. What was I doing here?

I heard a woman's voice, she sounded tired but proud, her words defiant. "Her name is Suzan," she said, "my baby's name is Suzan Grace Halford."

All the experts tell you that babies don't understand. I see it differently. We understand everything, it's just that we can't tell you. At first, all I could do was scream.

"I'm Detective Ian Gisbon. I was attacked by Harold James Malvis, at Hendrix Metals Warehouse." I shouted it time after time. I was taken to a strange house, given food, warm baths, lots of shiny things and as many cuddles as a grown man could handle. But I still shouted it, so much that it made me sick.

I couldn't understand why the noises I made were not the same as the words I was trying to say. All that anyone around me heard were screams, they thought I was hungry, wet, dirty or suffering from indigestion. I was pushed around dark streets at all hours of the night, just so that one or the other of the two new adults in my life could get some rest. More adults came to see me, I thought that I might have better luck with them. When I was passed around for admiring noises to be made, I shouted louder. All that happened was that I was given back.

My new parents and most of the other people I had anything to do with thought that my screaming meant that I was sick. I was taken to see doctors who poked and prodded me and assured them everything was fine. They explained that all babies cried, they were just worried because they were new parents. In return, they doubled their efforts to solve the problems they thought I had. They cuddled me, fed me, changed me. I could feel their love and kindness but they weren't my family. My wife and son were who I wanted, my real family, my friends. Even the people that I'd worked with. It bothered me that everyone I had known would think I was dead, although in a way I suppose I was. I might as well have been.

My new parents persisted. Through all the anguish, I could feel their concern for me. In the end, thanks to their obvious distress and a kindly doctor, I was sent for brain scans. I knew what the scanner was, I hoped it would prove that I was in there. I lay quietly, as I knew I must, while it bleeped and clanked.

Then there was the wait for the results.

"There's a lot more brain activity than we would normally expect," said the doctor.

I tried to shout again. "Of course there is, I'm in here and I have a story that needs to be told."

"But nothing out of the ordinary, nothing to concern you," he added. The disappointment was like a physical thing, I was sure that my presence would have been revealed.

As time passed, I gained control of my arms and legs, could hold my head up. In frustration, I thrashed my limbs around, repeating my tale, even though I had realised by now that it was futile. The memory was starting to fade anyway, as my mind filled with so many other things. Some brought back memories, like the solid foods I was starting to be given, others were new to me, wearing dresses and having ribbons in my hair felt particularly strange.

And one of the strangest things was Suzan, the name I had been given. There was another personality developing in what I thought of as my brain.

To begin with, we fought, for possession of the right to speak, to think or to act. Over time an uneasy truce developed, I wanted to tell my tale, she wanted to be left alone to grow. She couldn't understand what I was doing in what she claimed was her body. Neither could I but as I told her, there had to be a reason and perhaps it's just not obvious yet. For a time, we agreed that I could tell my story but as she got older she became stronger, she wanted no more to do with me and my desire for justice. She didn't care about what I had suffered, was still suffering. *Leave me alone to grow*, she said, *this is my life, my body*. And I found myself less and less able to resist her.

All this inner turmoil and the compromise that followed meant that, as time went on, I (or should that be we) quietened down. Instead of trying to force the words out, I concentrated on trying to keep the memory alive in Suzan's head until the day when she would be able to tell everyone what I knew, maybe even act on my behalf. The people who were her parents were relieved that their daughter seemed to have settled. Now they called us quiet. People who saw our thoughtful expression when we were wheeled around our town told my parents that we had the look of an old soul. If only they knew; I still couldn't tell them.

Our shared body learned to walk and by that time I had given up on trying to force Suzan to do anything. Instead, I helped her to co-ordinate and achieve, so that she became known as a fast learner. By the time Suzan could actually speak, all she would let me say was Harold. Except that when her mouth said it, it came out as Haral. It became a family joke, Suzan's mother and father wondered where such a word had come from.

Suzan couldn't tell her and I wasn't strong enough to make any more words of explanation come out. Suzan and I might have occupied the same space but I could feel myself slipping away as she became her own person. I decided to bide my time; after all, it looked like I wasn't going anywhere. I would have to change tactics.

Instead of using force to try to get her to do what I wanted, I would be a voice in her head, a friend to help her navigate the world. I'd enjoyed helping her to learn how to walk and run, I could show her so much more.

That would have to do, at least until I was able to convince her to speak out. And to act. I still wanted revenge, justice for the man who had done this to me. I hoped that, if we could work together, one-day Malvis would never know what was happening.

Until it was too late.

Chapter 2

Suzan

If you're going to understand what follows, it's important that I start at the beginning. When I was growing up, I never thought that I was different or strange.

From the first time that I can remember, I had what I can only describe as an imaginary friend. Not in the physical sense, I didn't see someone that nobody else could, it was more like there was another person in my head. I have no idea where they came from, I don't ever remember a time when they weren't there, as an internal monologue, a whisper in my ear.

It was so much a part of my life that I just assumed that everyone must have one. At first, it was reassuring, helpful and wise. Even though it was a boy's voice, it had to be mine. Because it was in my head. I never even thought of mentioning it to my parents.

As I got older, the voice changed. Looking back, knowing what I do now, I can see that it was thanks to the voice that I was so quick to learn how to read and write. The voice made the squiggles on the page make sense to me and helped my hands shape letters and words of my own. It guided my arms when I drew and painted.

When I went to school, the teachers were annoyed that I could already read and write, they told my mother off for teaching me, 'you should have let us do that', they said, 'we have a system and it helps nobody if one child in the class does things differently to the others'.

My mum shrugged, 'we never taught her', she told the teacher, 'she just picked it up on her own'.

I didn't want to be thought of as different; anyhow, I was too used to it to tell them about the voice. So I kept quiet and spent my early school days at half speed, waiting for everyone else to catch me up. That was when I became best friends with Peta, she was a girl about my age, who was also referred to as gifted.

One of us was always top of the class, we lived next door to each other and did everything together. Our fathers were business partners, each half owned the tenancy on the farm where we lived, our mothers were good friends. We were both only children and we became inseparable. But even though we shared each other's secrets, I never told Peta about the voice. If she had a voice of her own, she never mentioned it and I never asked.

We spent all our free time running and playing with the other local kids in the fields that our fathers rented and farmed.

I had first gone to the fields when I was about three, sitting on my father's shoulders. Up there, I was tall enough to be brushed by the leaves when he didn't duck. They tickled and made me laugh. He knew all the names of the trees and plants, and he shared them with me. As I got older, I helped at lambing and shearing times, it was in many ways an idyllic life.

He encouraged me to spend time in the woods, showed me secluded places to sit and made me wait in stilled silence, so that the wildlife got used to our presence and came to join us. From when I started school, Peta and I would go over to the woods in the summer evenings and at the weekends, sometimes the other local kids would come too. We were allowed to use the farm as a playground, as long as we didn't annoy the sheep or make too much noise or mess.

There was a wooded glade, in a fold in the land, with a stream and deep pools to swim in. It was where we used to have all our adventures, making dens and playing until it got dark.

The local boys were awkward around us, knowing that, although we were girls, we could play football, run and swim or climb trees as well as any of them. If not better.

The voice was my constant companion, as much as any of the other people were. It meant that even when I was alone, I was never lonely.

When I was about seven, I heard an item on the news one afternoon. It was about a man who had done something really bad, he had blamed it all on voices in his head that he said had made him do it. Mum tutted, 'turn that off, Keith', she said to Dad. 'You don't want Suzan to hear about things like that'. It worried me because I had a voice in my head and it told me what to do. Would it make me hurt someone one day? If I told my mum or dad about the voice, would they decide that I was bad?

Almost immediately, the voice was there, sounding as calm and relaxed as ever. "I can tell you're upset," it said, "but don't worry. I'm not like that, what they have is a different sort of voice, one that people only get when they're ill."

I thought for a moment, I wasn't ill. "Will you tell me to do something bad one day?" I asked.

"No," it answered. "I'm not that sort of voice, I only want to help you. You don't need to tell anyone about me, they might not understand."

I had been planning to ask Mum, despite what the voice had said but my dad's reaction had scared me. The next day, he was reading about the same thing in the paper, while he was sitting in his chair after tea. "They knew he was possessed," he said, his voice angry. "Yet they didn't lock him up or try to stop him. It would have been for his own safety, as much as anyone else's."

Did that mean that, if I mentioned my voice, even though I hadn't been bad, my dad would say I should be locked up? Surely I was safe here, with them?

Since my voice wasn't telling me to be bad, I decided to think of the voice as no more than my brain's way of keeping myself company. And to keep it as my secret. I was careful, in case I let it slip and people laughed at me or told me I was crazy. If I was with other people, when the voice said anything, I tried not to listen to it and never answered out loud.

When it was there, the voice would suggest ways to do things. It would tell me if I was about to hurt myself. I ignored it a couple of times, at which point, as I was nursing a scraped shin or cut hand, it said, *I told you*, so I listened after that.

The thing was, it wasn't always there, sometimes I could go for ages with nothing from it. At other times, it would be really talkative and try to run my life for me. When I got fed up and tried not to listen, or told it to leave me alone, that was when it would vanish.

One day, I must have been eight or nine, I was outside on my own. Peta was ill with something or other, she rarely had any illness and I missed her. All the other school friends who normally came over to explore the woods with us hadn't showed up, so I went out on my own.

I knew our farm and the woods like the back of my hand, as long as Mum knew roughly where I was, she wasn't bothered. Anyway, I was looking at the newly green canopy of spring when the voice said something strange. It started off as a normal conversation, just like all the ones I'd ever had.

"That's a lovely oak tree, *Quercus Robur*," the voice suddenly announced.

I had known that for ages, even before we had been taught it at school. My dad had told me all the names of the trees on our walks, he had shown me how their leaves were all different.

"Tell me something I don't know," I replied, not in words, that would have been weird, just in my head.

"Touchy," came the return thought, as quick as lightning. "I was only making conversation. I remember sitting under one like that, a long time ago."

That scared me and made me stop walking. It was the first time the voice had suggested that they were anything more than a part of me.

"What do you mean, a long time ago?"

There was silence for a moment, it was slightly unsettling.

"Are you there?" I asked, out loud. It was a good job I was on my own, that would have sounded weird.

"I'm here," the voice was back.

"Well, what did you mean? You can't have been sitting under a tree, a long time ago. I'm only seven, I'd have remembered it."

There was another silence, as if the voice was considering a reply. "It was when you were a baby, your mum took you out on a sunny day. I'm surprised you can't remember it."

The voice was so reassuring, it sounded sincere, after all, it was me. We were part of the same person. The voice was right, I must have forgotten it.

"What are you? Just a figment of my imagination?" I thought. I'd wondered about this before but never actually asked myself the question.

"I'm part of you," it said. "A part that helps you work things out. If it makes you more comfortable, you can give me a name. But don't tell anyone, you know why. Remember what your father said. People will think you're crazy and it will cause you all sorts of problems. You could climb that oak tree, easy."

"Don't change the subject, I don't want to climb trees today."

From that day, the voice was Dave. And I could tell that the voice was right. I never told a soul. Until the day it suggested that I tried eating black pudding. I'd tried it once before and hated it. Now Dave suggested that I eat it again. It was another weird thing for the voice to say.

"But I don't like it," I said.

"You might this time," he suggested. "Just try a piece." Dave kept on and on about it until, in the end, it was easier to go along with it. I hoped that there would be plenty of sauce available, just in case. "Alright," I said, "next time Mum cooks it." I didn't have to wait long.

"Can I have some of that black pudding," I said to my mum while she was dishing up the fried breakfasts on the next Saturday morning.

"You wouldn't like that," said my father. "You tried it once before, when you were little. You were nearly sick. It's much too spicy, you said."

Dave was still talking in my head, it was hard to concentrate on two conversations at once. "I love black pudding," he said. "Tell him you weren't old enough to appreciate it. Tell him you'd like another go. Believe me, it's really delicious, go on try it."

"I know, Dad. But maybe I was too young to appreciate it. I'd like some, please. Dave said it's lovely."

Immediately there was a change of atmosphere. "What do you mean, Dave said it's lovely, who's Dave?" said my dad.

"Lie," said Dave in my head. "I'm supposed to be our secret, remember?"

"Oh, just a boy from school," I said. "He loves black pudding. I said I didn't like it and he said there must be something wrong with me. Can I try it again, please?"

"That's alright then, of course you can." Mum put a piece on my plate and I took a mouthful. It was gross, disgusting, just like last time and it made me feel sick. It was all I could do to stop myself from spitting it out. As I covered it in ketchup, hastily chewed and swallowed it, all I could hear in my head was Dave saying, "Ahh that's lovely, oh have another bite, that's gorgeous."

Somehow, by covering it with sauce and eating it along with the things I did like, I managed to eat it all, my thoughts were not charitable towards Dave. How could he like something that I hated, if he was no more than a part of me? I couldn't ask Mum or Dad, they'd say I was crazy. Who could I turn to?

"Well?" said my father. "Was Dave right?"

"No," I muttered, rushing from the room to brush my teeth. I could hear them laughing, *boys*, said Mum.

"I want a word with you, Dave," I thought. "That was disgusting. Never ask me to do that again."

"Thank you," said Dave, he was laughing too. "I enjoyed that more than some of the food you eat. And well covered. Is there anyone at school called Dave?"

"Yes, he's ugly and a geek."

"Your dad will think he's your friend now." He was still laughing while I scrubbed to get rid of the taste. "Just be careful, you don't want to give the game away about me. Remember, they'll think you're crazy if they know we talk."

"Then don't make me do things I don't want to; I have to lie about you and I hate it."

"OK," Dave said. "I won't do that again, promise."

"Good. If you do, I'll tell someone about you."

Dave was silent for a minute. "I'd rather you didn't tell anyone; it's supposed to be our secret."

"Can't you see what I'm thinking?" I asked.

"Not always; anyway, it would be rude. It would be more polite to ask." Like the thing about the tree, that reply seemed like a really weird concept to me. Surely Dave could see everything that I could?

"Then you don't know what I'm going to do now?"

"No…" he said.

"How about if I give you permission to look?"

There was a pause. "Oh, do you think that's wise?"

It was no good asking me that, he'd pushed me too far. I was so angry that I'd been talked into eating the black pudding. Not only that, I was getting fed up with Dave keeping on that I mustn't say anything. And hinting at a past that I didn't remember. I just had to tell someone. I went straight around to Peta's house. It was only next door, the rooms were a mirror image of ours.

"Oh, hello, Suzan," said her mum as I walked into the kitchen. "Peta's in her bedroom, go on up."

She was still in bed, surrounded by magazines. "Thanks for coming to see me," she said.

I perched on the end of the bed. "I'm going to tell you something and you have to promise that you won't think I'm crazy."

She gave me a strange look. "I think you're crazy anyway, but it's what I love about you, go on."

"I'm being serious. It's been bothering me for ages. Peta, do you have a voice in your head all the time?"

She shook her head. "No, it sounds a bit weird to me, you mean like another person?"

"Not exactly, it's more like a part of me that I'm not in full control of, it talks to me, gives me advice. It made me eat black pudding this morning." In my head, Dave was saying, "No, be quiet, you promised, just like I did about the black pudding."

Peta looked shocked. "It MADE you? What, it forced you, like in some sort of horror movie?" She shook her head, waved her hands around and *ooh'ed*, as if she was a ghost. It made me laugh. "Stop messing me around, Suzan. You're winding me up. I would have told it to shove off. I hate black pudding."

"I know, so do I, but the weird thing was, the voice said that they liked it. It never made me, just asked me if I would have some, so I did. It wasn't that I felt unable to resist, it freaked me out cos... well, how could they like it when I didn't? I mean it's part of me, isn't it?"

"Don't you think that's just a little bit wrong? Now you're starting to scare me. Do you think you might be possessed?"

"Don't be daft. It's always been there, ever since I can remember. I mean, I thought it was normal, like everyone has one. I started calling it..." I stopped for a second "...Diana, recently." I think I must have been starting to sound slightly hysterical.

She hugged me. "Don't stress, it'll be alright."

Peta's mum brought us squash and biscuits. She was what you might call an old hippy, wise and caring.

"Guess what, Mum," Peta said.

I nudged her. "I told you not to say," I whispered.

"What's that, dear?" Peta's mum said. "What are you not supposed to say?"

"Suzan's crazy, she says she has a voice in her head." I was ready for a laugh, instead she looked serious.

"What does it say, Suzan?"

I could feel myself going red. "Nothing much, just stuff. When I'm alone, it talks about what I'm doing and if I'm about to do something it might say, don't, or why not do it this way. And it told me to eat black pudding, which I hated."

"Oh," she said, "well I don't know but it sounds like it might be your conscience, that's your brain helping you to decide between good and bad. And it can be nice to try new foods, you never know what you might like."

"So I'm not weird?" Her matter-of-fact attitude was a contrast to how I had imagined a grownup reacting. Or how my father had reacted to that man having voices in his head. It made me feel better.

"Of course not, just about everyone can hear their own thoughts in their head, you're a sensible girl, it's nothing to worry about."

"There you are, Peta, I'm not crazy."

"But I don't have a voice in my head, telling me to eat things," she said.

"We're all different, Peta," her mother said. "When you're about to do something, do you get a feeling whether it's good or bad?"

She nodded. "Yes."

"Well, it's the same thing, you just see it differently, some people call it gut instinct, some call it conscience. It's a hangover from when we lived in much more dangerous times, it's your brain's way of evaluating danger. It's just a way of helping to keep you alive."

I had been frightened to tell my mother, she always seemed to get so anxious about me, having Peta's mum tell me I was normal meant that I was less worried about her finding out.

Dave was annoyed. I could hear him. "I told you to keep me secret," he said. "And Diana. Really?"

"I didn't mention your name, it sounded better than Dave. Anyway, you told me they wouldn't understand. Peta's mum does."

"That's not the point. You promised me you wouldn't tell anyone."

"Why not? They didn't think it was weird. Anyway, you're only a figment of my imagination, you're my conscience, my gut instinct. You can't tell me what to do; or make me."

There was no reply. Good. I was tired of having two conversations going on at the same time. It was hard enough keeping up with the one in real life, without being distracted by the one in my head. And I was fed up with having to be so careful that I never told my parents, I knew what my father thought about voices in the head, his probable reaction terrified me.

After that, hearing what Peta's mum had said, I wanted to take a look online about voices in the head. I couldn't help it. I had to know, did other people really not have them?

Dave must have noticed my intention, this time he hadn't asked if he could look. Instead, he tried to talk me out of it. "Reading about that'll just scare you," he said. "You'll only see all the horrible stories about people who did terrible things. Doctors decided that they were mad, they were taken away from their home and their family and made to live in a nasty prison, surrounded by bad people."

Even though I was annoyed with him, thinking about that frightened me. I could feel the dread in my stomach, so I didn't look. Now Dave sounded like a scary teacher. For the next few days after that, he left me alone. My mind was filled with happy thoughts and I started to forget he was there as I got on with school and all the other things in my life.

That meant hanging around with Peta, having fun. We were always together, a team, more like sisters than friends. We sat next to each other at school, could wrestle and fight, climb and run as well as any of the boys could. Nobody messed with us. We weren't bullies, the boys who tried to fight us, or picked on the younger ones, soon learned that if you took on one of us, you got a reply from both.

As I got older, I was relieved to find that the voice was becoming more selective in my life, as if it was trying to let me take more control and be less of an influence. It was easier to ignore it and I stopped worrying that there was something wrong with me.

By the time we were ready to go to secondary school, Peta and I had both become tall and lean. On the first day, one of the teachers called us the two string beans. After that, I became Stringy and Peta was Beano. We sat together in all our lessons; we might have mucked about a bit but we did the work too.

Life was good.

Chapter 3

Looking back, I can see how I was a solitary child. Apart from Peta, I had no other close friends. Since the time my father had got upset about voices in the head, I'd grown more distant from him. I was more cautious about admitting that I might have the thing that he was so angry about. Maybe that was illogical; to my young and impressionable mind, it was the right thing to do.

I just hoped that Peta's mother hadn't told my parents about it. When they never mentioned it, I assumed that she had thought it was unimportant.

The day my life changed started like any other.

On that day, in the summer holidays after my first year at secondary school, it rained. Stuck in the house, Peta and I were exploring our junk room, up a flight of rickety stairs in the loft. Our parents were outside working with the sheep. In a wardrobe, behind all the winter clothes and books was an old box, it had *Memories of Suzan* written on it.

"Let's have a look, Stringy," said Peta, snatching it from my hand. She dodged past me and went to sit at the desk facing the bay window. She pulled the box open, the contents spilling out onto the surface, among the other rubbish. There was a knitted blanket, a pair of baby socks and a whole load of greeting cards, tied with a pink ribbon. The whole collection smelled of baby powder.

"That's lovely," she said, "look at all these congratulation cards." I grabbed the bundle and flicked through them, they were from aunts, grandparents and people whose names I didn't recognise. While I was doing that, Peta continued her examination of the box. "Look at these," she said, waving a bulky buff envelope, marked *Hospital Notes*. "This will be all the grisly details." Right at the bottom was a folded newspaper.

"It's from the day after your birthday," Peta shouted out. "How wonderful to see what else was going on while you were busy being born." She pulled it from the box and held it up.

I peered over her shoulder to read about the other momentous events on the day I started my life. A man's face stared up at me, smiling.

Policeman killed in warehouse mystery was the headline. I suddenly felt cold and dizzy. The room spun and I must have fainted as I slumped over Peta's shoulder.

I woke up to her slapping my face. "Stringy, wake up, are you OK?" she asked me as I pushed myself upright. I was laying on the floor.

"Yes, I think so." My head was aching and I felt like I'd been sick.

"What happened to you?" she asked. "You were looking over my shoulder and you suddenly fainted."

"It was that picture, it just did something to me. I felt cold and it all went dark. I felt dizzy for a moment and blacked out."

"You had me worried there," she said. "I thought I was going to have to call your mum. What was so special about the picture? It was just a man's face; he's a bit old for you, not exactly handsome enough to make you swoon like that either." Peta had discovered an interest in boys a couple of months earlier. To me, they were still silly, boring people who couldn't keep up.

I punched her shoulder. "I guess not, there was just something familiar about him."

I looked at the article by the side of the image, it said the detective, whose name was Ian Gisbon, had been found stabbed to death in a warehouse. The article said that it was a mystery why he was there, as it wasn't on his normal route home. A police spokesman was quoted as saying that he hadn't told anyone where he was going. His body had been discovered when his car was found outside the premises.

The story went on to say that he had left a wife, Beth, and a young son called Tommy. There was nothing else.

"Creepy," said Peta, "him dying at the same time as you were born."

"It must happen a lot," I said. "People die and are born all the time. It's his wife and son I feel sad for. I wonder what happened and why he was there?" I had a sudden, overwhelming feeling of sorrow and started to cry.

Peta noticed, put the paper down and came to hug me. "That's you all over, you're so soft hearted. It's why I like you."

"I can't help it if I care, it's called empathy."

"But why care about people you don't know, things that happened years ago, that's just weird."

"I don't know, there's nothing I can do about it, it's just the way I am."

"Why don't you ask Diana about it?" she suggested, the sarcasm rich in her tone.

That was a good point. Dave, so quick with a reply was lost for words this time. I waited for a second, but there was nothing.

"Don't take the mickey, Beano. What would she know about it anyway? She's only as old as I am. She was busy being born too."

"Exactly, it's just another crime. Sad but over. It will have been solved a long time ago, whoever did that to him is probably in prison. Anyway, who cares, it looks like the rain is stopping. Let's go back outside."

We stuffed everything into the box, put it back where we had found it and ran downstairs.

That night, I had a dream.

Chapter 4

Ian

To say I was shocked would be an understatement. To be honest, my existence had been drifting along. When I saw my face looking back at me from the old newspaper cutting it woke me up with a jolt and rendered me speechless. I think that the shock I felt caused her brain to overload and she passed out.

My life, if you could call it that, had settled into a pattern. Suzan did all the important stuff; I was just there. I could feel every sensation but only in a remote kind of way, it was difficult to explain how it all felt to be happening without my control. And very strange to witness and experience all the female emotions. Although Suzan was young, she was quite different to how I had remembered being when I was that age. All I could do was watch and try to be the small voice in Suzan's head, helping her out with her schoolwork and her coordination in sports, suggesting the best thing to do when she was unsure.

Thanks to me, she was ahead of her peers in most subjects and was developing into a good all-round athlete. Fortunately, she had accepted me as a part of her, the earlier conflicts were long forgotten. I wasn't so pushy, even though there were little victories, I'd managed to get a taste of my favourite food and I had thought about trying to get her to visit the places in the countryside that I used to enjoy, back when I had been Ian.

Although it would be sad to be there without my family, perhaps I wanted to go in the faint hope that they might be there. Maybe I thought I could get Suzan to say hello or even get close, just so that I'd see them one last time. Before I could suggest it, I found that Suzan lived a long way from where I used to. For her to ask to visit would have been strange, so I forgot about the idea.

Of course, we argued. Suzan got angry if she felt I was becoming too overbearing, so I would back off a little and give her room. I told her not to tell anyone about me. I was worried that they would think she was mentally ill and make her visit therapists or put her on drugs. I had no idea what effect they might have on me, perhaps I was being selfish but I reckoned that denial would be the best path for both of us. As if I would be some kind of threat to her. The last thing I wanted was to cause her pain or give her a difficult life. Because of my help, the adults in her life seemed to think she was gifted, maybe a little quiet and reserved but basically normal. I was proud of the part I'd played in her life so far.

After I'd upset her, I'd always retreat for a while, try not to be too enthusiastic. I knew it was a long game, I needed her to get to be old enough to live independently before she could do what I really wanted her to. I felt a pang of guilt; had I lied to her when I said I would never make her do anything bad? She was too young to know all the details of my plan, but I didn't see my ultimate aim as bad. When I finally explained it to her, I was sure she would view it in the same way.

Seeing myself in the newspaper changed things, perhaps it was time to step it up a bit. I could show Suzan a scene from my memory, while she slept.

It would be interesting to see what happened.

Chapter 5

Suzan

I didn't know I was dreaming, it felt so lifelike.

It was cold and raining that night. If I hadn't been told about the accident, I would never have gone that way. All I wanted to do was get home, it had been a long, miserable day. I had nothing to show for it and I needed to see my family and unwind.

The street was deserted as I drove past Hendrix Metal's disused warehouse. There was an empty car outside the small door in the wooden gates, parked half on the pavement with the side lights still on.

I recognised the number plate immediately; it was the car that I'd been hunting for the past six weeks. The owner had to be around somewhere. I drove past it and turned down the first side road I came to, parking out of sight of the car, under a streetlight.

I could hardly believe my luck. Harold Malvis was close, perhaps he was inside the warehouse. I'd spotted that the gate was slightly open.

Goodness knows what he was doing there. I had been looking for him for months, for his part in a string of armed robberies, among other things. An informant of mine had told me about the car, but according to our records, that particular number plate didn't exist. Now was my chance to nab him. It looked like his car was the only one about. I was already imagining the commendation, my theories about him were less than popular with my seniors, it would be good to have been proved right.

I should have called for backup. I was in my own car so there was no radio. I had my phone, looking at the screen showed me there was no signal. I had no choice; I was going to have to do this on my own or risk him leaving while I drove around looking for a callbox or a signal.

I pulled a cap on and jumped out of my car. In my eagerness, I completely forgot about the stab vest, baton and handcuffs laying on the back seat.

I ran across the rain-soaked street to the door in the entrance gates, the wind blowing rain hard into my face. I was right, the door was already partially open, it resisted as I slowly pushed it wider and peered cautiously around the edge.

I could see across the yard, past rows of stacked pallets, covered in plastic sheeting, to the building itself. The rows of grimy windows were lit by an orange glow. I pulled up my collar and crept across the yard to the main door. I was expecting it to be locked, it opened easily. Cautiously, I peered around the door frame. There was a long corridor, the light came from an open door at the far end. Slowly, I moved towards it. The room beyond was a store, rows of shelving stretched away from an open space by the door.

There was a figure, sitting alone with his back to me. He seemed unaware of my presence. As I tiptoed towards him, I felt a rising tension in my body. And a moment of apprehension. I was alone, in a flash I knew that I had left my equipment in the car. How exactly did I intend to subdue him? I knew that I was in danger, that unless I was very careful, I was done for.

I was shaking when I woke, in my room, in the dark. The dream had felt so real, as if I had been there, on that night. The scary thing was that it felt like I had been seeing things through the eyes of the man in the picture. I knew he was a policeman, my waking mind told me that my dream must have been brought on by seeing the newspaper in the box and reading about him in the article. My imagination had made a story up and the dream was my subconscious mind acting it out.

I lay in bed and shook; I could feel myself sweating and suddenly felt cold.

I guess I must have shouted something as I woke; the door crashed open, making me jump again and my mother came rushing into the room. "Suzan, are you alright?" she shouted, her voice full of concern. She lay on the bed and hugged me. "You called out, you're sweating," she said. "Do you feel ill?"

"I'm OK, Mum," I said. "It was just a bad dream."

She stroked my hair. "Poor you, do you want to talk about it?"

The idea of going through it all again scared me. "No, I'm OK now."

"Well, if you need us, you know where we are."

She hugged me for a moment, kissed my head and went back to her bedroom. I could hear a muttered conversation, my father asking what was the matter, my mother's reassurance that it was just a nightmare.

I was almost frightened to go back to sleep, the power of the mind to make a story out of a picture on a scrap of paper had amazed and frightened me. But I must have; the next thing I remembered was the sun shining on my face through a gap in the curtains and the smell of bacon frying.

At breakfast, the dream wasn't mentioned. I said nothing about it to my parents, I was still trying to process the information. Mum put her arm around my shoulders. "Did you get back to sleep?" she asked.

"Yes, and I'm fine."

Dad muttered, "Are you alright?"

When I said, "Yeah," he just grunted.

I was alright though. I'd gone back to sleep and I hadn't dreamt about it again. The details were starting to fade and now it almost seemed as if I hadn't even had the dream at all.

I decided that I would mention it to Peta and see what she thought it all meant. She knew about the reaction I'd had to the picture.

I went around to Peta's house; her mum was in the kitchen.

"Hi, Suzan." She welcomed me in. "Have a seat, Peta's in the bathroom. You look tired. What have you been up to?"

"I had a bad dream," I said, reluctant to tell her more, she was good friends with Mum and it would be bound to get back. Although she hadn't mentioned the voice to her, which meant that she might be able to keep another secret.

"Dreams are messages," she said, "it's your mind's way of making sense of things in your waking life. Do you want to tell me what it was about?"

I decided against it. "No, thanks, I'm good. I think I know what set it off. It was something I saw."

"Alright, but if you ever want to talk, I'm always here. Perhaps I could help you unravel what your mind is trying to tell you."

"Not more of your airy-fairy nonsense, Mum." Peta had bounced into the room. "We're not all into that spiritual stuff you know."

She smiled. "You'll see, one day. Where are you going?"

"Just out, over to the woods. We'll be back for tea."

As we walked across the fields, towards the woods, Peta dug for information, not that she had to, I was bursting to tell her.

"What was my mum on about to you?" she asked.

"Remember that newspaper we found? I had a really weird dream. I was in the warehouse, the one in the article."

"Wow," she grabbed my arm, "that's freaky, after you fainted when you saw the picture too. What happened?"

"It was so detailed. It was raining and I felt cold and wet, there was a man I was looking for, a criminal, I saw his car and followed the lights into the warehouse. Just when I found him, before anything else could happen, I woke up."

"That's just your mind working overtime, your imagination making a story up from what you read. You knew the policeman was killed in a warehouse. That's why you had the dream."

"I guess. The thing was, it felt so real, it was spooky. In my mind, I was frightened, I knew that something bad was going to happen."

"That's cos you knew the ending, the real policeman probably wasn't frightened, he knew what he was doing."

"But he didn't," I said. "I could tell what he was thinking. He was so determined to get the man that he never told anyone what he was doing. Not only that, he left his stab vest and stuff on the seat of his car. He had no weapons to defend himself with." I realised that my voice was rising, why was I was getting hysterical about a dream?

Peta grabbed me and shook me. "Listen," she said, "calm down, or you'll be fainting again. None of what you saw or did was real, it's just your mind making it up. How could you know things like where his stab vest was, things that weren't in the newspaper? It was only a dream. You shouldn't keep thinking about it, I bet you'll be dreaming about something else tonight."

I hoped she was right. "But I have to know. I'm going to search the internet this evening," I told her. "I'll see what I can find out about Ian Gisbon."

"Well, I wouldn't," she said. "Leave it alone."

In my head, I heard Dave, he was agreeing with her. "It was just a dream," he said. "I could tell that it frightened you. Don't get too obsessed with it."

"A little search won't hurt me," I replied. "It'll put my mind at rest if I can find out more." Dave was silent. As I got older, he had been less obvious in his presence and less threatening when I disagreed with him. Instead, if there was any conflict, he would disappear for a while, as if he was giving me time and space. His advice was mostly good, he had stopped trying to make me do things. It was almost as if he had acknowledged that I had grown up.

I said nothing more about it and after tea, I had a quick look. First, I went to the loft and found the box again. I copied down the name of the place where the murder had happened from the newspaper. Then I went to search the Internet.

To my surprise, there was a lot about Ian Gisbon and his murder, but little about the crime. What there was mostly confirmed what I had read in the newspaper, the rest told me a bit more about Ian's life. There were details about his career, Beth, his wife, and Tommy, his son. I read some glowing tributes from his colleagues, *he was a brave officer*, said one, along with pictures of his funeral, showing lines of uniformed police in a churchyard, his wife in black, surrounded by family.

I felt sad to know that Tommy would never remember his father, he had only been just over a year old at the time of Ian's death. The warehouse where it had all happened was still standing, it had been converted into an upmarket shopping centre. There were pictures of it, inside and out, but it was impossible to be certain if it matched my dream version. As I searched, I couldn't find anything to say that anyone had been arrested for the murder of Ian Gisbon, there were no details of a prosecution. There were anniversary articles and appeals for information, but as the years passed, even these stopped.

It's so sad, I thought, expecting some sage remark from Dave. Instead, there was only silence.

That night, I had the dream again. It was exactly the same as before, starting with me seeing the car parked outside the warehouse. It replayed all the same scenes again, I saw all the same things and felt the same emotions, just like before. This time, it didn't stop in the same place. I got a little closer to the seated man. I must have made a sound, either that or he knew somehow that I was there. He turned his head to look at me, I almost saw his face for the first time as I woke up.

Chapter 6

This time, I realised that I didn't feel so frightened by what I had seen and felt. In a way it only made me want to find out more about what had actually happened. I'd seen half a story, now I wanted to know the rest. Nothing could hurt me; it was only a dream. It wouldn't be what had really happened, just a version of it constructed by my imagination. Perhaps I could write it all down. I recalled that my English teacher had suggested writing dreams in a notebook before they faded. This dream might make a great story, if I changed the names around.

Before I drifted back off to sleep, I decided that I needed to look online again. There were still some pages I hadn't looked at. I had no idea if what I saw in my dreams was anything near the reality. I wondered if I could find any more pictures of the inside of the warehouse. Because I wanted to see what happened next, even if it was only a story, more searching might prompt the dreams to continue.

Would I see the murderer's face? I knew that was a silly thought, it wouldn't be his real face. How could it be? It would be the face of someone I knew, or one I had seen in the street.

Something else about my dream wasn't right. In the paper, it said that Ian's car was outside the warehouse when it had been found. In both my dreams, Ian had parked it in a side street, the criminal's car was the one outside the warehouse. In a way, it proved that what I was seeing was just a made-up version of events.

Dave was absent. I tried thinking about what had happened, asking him in my mind but instead of the usual replies, I got nothing. In a way, that was more unsettling than the dreams. He must be annoyed that I had done the opposite of what he suggested. He'd done this before; he would be back in a few days. When I got up, I was distracted and couldn't focus.

My mother could tell that something was going on, in that way that all mothers can. "What's the matter, dear?" she asked me over breakfast. Dad was out working; Peta would be around soon. "Are you still thinking about the dream that you had?"

"Yes, I think I know what started it all off." I explained how Peta and I had found the memory box, how the face of the policeman had made me dream that I was him. All the time I was telling her what I had seen, I was expecting to get told off for looking in the box, either by her or by Dave.

She looked sad. "We forgot all about that box, hid it away, because of the other memories it brought back, not the good ones. We wanted to remember your birth as a happy day for the right reasons but all we could hear on the news was the story of that poor policeman's murder. It was everywhere, hard to believe that while I was having you, all that was going on. Somehow, it didn't feel right that we were celebrating in the midst of all that upset."

"I guess it must have spoiled the day. I can imagine it overshadowing your happiness."

"It was such an awful thing. While I was carrying you, we had decided that we were going to make a memory box, for you to have when you were older. And for us to look back on, a memento of the day of your birth. We thought that a newspaper would be a good idea, so that the older you could see what else had happened on that day. We hadn't expected them to be full of such a horrible thing. All the papers had the same story, the one Dad chose was the least gruesome of them all. In the end, we kept it all but put it in the back of the loft. In a way, we wished that you had been born the day before."

"I understand, it must have been awful," I answered. "I know these things happen but it was still a shock when I saw it, almost as if I knew the face."

Mum shook her head. "But how could you? It's just an ordinary face?"

"I know, Peta said it was nothing to swoon over." Mum laughed.

"It was the dream," I continued, "it felt like a memory. Even now, I can feel it pushing through my mind. It was so realistic, as if I was the policeman. And it was happening to me."

As I told her more about my dream, the rain, the car and the warehouse, her face changed. I could see that she was shocked and agitated by my words. I was hoping to get a sympathetic hearing. Instead, I got a reaction I'd never expected.

"Your imagination has made all of that up. How could you remember it?" she said. "You weren't there, it was just a horrible story. There are lots of nasty things out there in the world. Why couldn't you have been born the day before?"

"But I dreamt it again last night," I told her. "I saw the same details. The man who must have been the murderer. I almost saw his face. I felt the policeman's regret. I could tell that he felt stupid for not calling for help and then sad as he knew that he was in big trouble. The worst thing was that there was nothing I could do to stop it from happening. Then I woke up."

She hugged me. "You poor thing, it's just your imagination," she said. "You've always been full of stories like that. You need to get it out of your head, go and have a lovely day with Peta, fill your mind with happiness. Stop looking for answers, just let it rest."

Peta arrived and Mum had a serious word with her. "Peta," she said, "I want you to talk to Suzan. Can you tell her to stop thinking about her dreams? The past is the past and it can't be changed."

"I will," she said. "Or at least I'll try."

We spent the day exploring the woods, like we did every day. Peta kept chattering but I didn't hear her, it was all very well to say forget it, the trouble was, I couldn't. Maybe if Dave had told me to leave it, I might have listened. But he was nowhere to be heard. To keep Peta quiet, I promised that I wouldn't look any more, but they were only words.

"Be good," she said as we parted. "I won't see you till after lunch tomorrow; we're going to the town to get me some new school uniform in the morning."

That evening, I kept on digging. After tea, I was straight back on the internet to see what else I could find.

All that did was tell me less than what I already knew. Before I went to bed, I put a notebook and a pencil by the side of my bed. If I had another dream, I would be ready to write it all down.

The figure turned and looked up at me. "Hello, we meet at last. You must be Ian Gisbon."

"Then you're Harold Malvis." I'd never seen him in person before; as far as the official records knew, he had no criminal connections. I thought that I knew better, I had linked him to a web of organised crime. It did make me wonder if he had protection, some corrupt policeman on his payroll, keeping him hidden and safe. He must have heard my name somewhere.

He smiled. "That's right, fancy meeting you here." The way he spoke was as if he had been expecting me.

"You're unlucky," I said. "If it hadn't been for the accident making me come this way, I'd never have found you."

He shook his head. "If that's what you think. I know that you've been looking for me. Well, here I am, but whatever it is you want to say, you need to be quick."

"Really," I said. "There's all the time in the world. You're under arrest."

He laughed, he was relaxed, and in control of the situation. "No, I'm not. I'm on my way to Spain. A new life awaits me. It's all set up. You aren't going to stop it."

I moved towards him, intending to put him into an armlock and restrain him. I couldn't cuff him, the handcuffs were still on the back seat of my car. I felt a rush of panic, while I was distracted, I saw the glint of a blade and jumped back as it slashed across my body, missing me by inches.

"Don't be a silly boy," Malvis said. "I know all about you, your wife and son. Beth and Tommy, isn't it? They're expecting you home. Call them, oh-eight-three-six, seven-four-four-two-one eight. See, I know it all. Go now, run away, you'll never see me again." The knife slashed and I retreated, in a daze. While I tried to stop thinking about how he knew my wife's mobile number, I realised that I was being shepherded away from the door. I knew then that I wasn't going home, ever.

I struggled to put on a brave face. "Can't do that," I said, "my backup are on their way, they're probably outside now. It's only a matter of time. You might as well give up, make it easier for you."

"I don't believe you," he said. "There's no backup. I would have known. The streets are deserted, my men would have called me. They told me you were coming alone. Just like I intended." Purposefully, he moved towards me, the blade swinging. As I backed away, I desperately looked on the shelves for anything I could use to defend myself. I threw pieces of wood at him; he dodged them easily. "Is that all you've got?" he taunted me.

I grabbed a handful of dust and rubbish and threw it up in the air. "Very good," he said. Then he coughed as the dust reached him. He stopped for a second. I turned and ran. If I could get to the end wall, I could choose another gap between the racks and head for the door.

As I lay there, in the dark, I realised that I had some new information, things that weren't mentioned in the pages I had read online. Did that mean they were just my imagination? Quickly, I turned the light on and wrote them down. There was a name, one that wasn't in any of the papers. Harold Malvis. And there was something else. I wrote down the phone number, surprised that I could remember it. The thing was, it looked wrong to me though, not like the number on the phone I'd been given when I'd started at secondary school.

In the morning, I could feed this information into the search engine.

Chapter 7

"Aren't you seeing Peta today," asked Mum, after I'd spent most of the morning on the family computer. "Have you two fallen out?"

"Of course not," I said. "She was going to the town with her mum, uniform shopping. I might see her later. Anyway, I have to do this for school, I've been putting it off." I'd lied again without thinking.

After lunch, I'd read through just about all of the search results for my new information. I was starting to see the same thing again and again. There was absolutely nothing about Harold Malvis, the name threw up no plausible results, just a few foreign language sites about people in South America from years ago and an obscure German mathematician. The phone number didn't exist either, *oh-eight-three-six* was marked as an old prefix. All UK mobile numbers start with *oh-seven*, said a site I'd found. What it didn't tell me was how I could modify the number I had to make it work.

I left the computer and went to spend the afternoon with Peta. I had the feeling that she wouldn't want me to but I had to tell her about what I had found. "I saw more in my dreams last night," I said. "Ian was chased by the man with a knife. I got his name and a phone number. I've been trying to find out more about them all morning."

"I wish you'd leave it alone, Stringy," she said, she seemed worried that I was starting to get obsessed with Ian Gisbon. I told her that I couldn't find much else; she was right, I was going to leave it. I also told her that Diana was absent, the first time I'd mentioned them for ages.

"That scares me more than anything else," I admitted. "She's always been there. Now, just when I could do with some advice or reassurance, she's not." I was beginning to wish I hadn't said Diana, it was something else that I had to remember to be careful about when talking to anyone.

"Radical thought," she said, "have you considered that she's gone quiet because she's got something to do with it all? Maybe she's the part of your brain that makes things up?"

"No, it can't be, the last thing she said was telling me not to get obsessed, just to leave it."

"Then perhaps she's annoyed that you haven't?"

Now she was starting to treat Dave/Diana as a separate person, when they were only a part of my conscience.

"Don't be silly, it's just a voice."

"I'll say it again, you really should leave it, Stringy. Life's too short to get all worked up about things that you can't change."

Peta was leaving for a week's holiday. Before she did, she made me promise that I wouldn't do any more digging while she was away.

"I won't," I said.

"I'm pleased to hear it, see you when I get back."

I was determined to be good. When I got in, I didn't go anywhere near the computer. As I watched TV, Dad came and sat by me.

"Mum's worried about you," he said. "You've been on the internet a lot recently, you're having bad dreams, you found the memory box. Is there anything you want to tell me?"

"No," I said. "I'm alright, Dad, really I am. There was something I wanted to research but I've looked and looked. I can't find much out."

"Do you want to ask me?" he said. "I might be able to help you."

"It's fine, it was an idea I had but I can't be bothered anymore."

"I've looked at your internet search history," my dad said. He sounded worried. "You're on the internet a lot more than usual in the last couple of days. You're half asleep and distracted. You're looking at websites about crime, murders and criminals. It's no good telling me it's schoolwork. I find that hard to believe. We're in the middle of the holidays and you've never mentioned it before, it's not the kind of thing you'd be learning in school. I don't know what you're doing but it's having a bad effect on you."

I was angry. "You have no right to look at what I've been doing, that's private."

He sighed. "Maybe, but you're only twelve and I wouldn't be much of a father if I didn't keep an eye on you. I know we haven't always seen eye-to-eye but you have to believe that I'm trying to help you. What's so important about Ian Gisbon? Why are you looking into his life and death? It has to stop."

"He's who I'm dreaming about, I told Mum, I saw his picture in the memory box and it did something in my mind. I'm seeing his life in my dreams. It all feels so real."

"No. It's your imagination, you've always made-up stories. Your teachers all say how talented you are at creative writing. Look, you saw the newspaper cutting and had a dream. Then you started researching and guess what, you had more dreams. They're realistic so you believe them. But it's all in your head."

"I know things, things that weren't in the newspaper in the memory box. Things that aren't on the internet. I have to find out what it all means."

"No, you don't. None of what you think you've seen is true. Your mind has filled in the gaps, made up bits of a story to string it all together. There's nothing new to discover, you're not being shown anything that someone doesn't already know. It's not possible that you can know any more than they did back then."

"I know a name," I said. "One that wasn't in the papers. What about that, what about Harold?" There was silence.

"What did you say?" said my mother, she had come into the room while I was talking.

"That's the name of the man who killed Ian, it's not in the newspaper cutting," I answered.

"Come into the kitchen, Keith. Suzan, stay here," said Mum. They shut the door and there was a whispered conversation, while I wondered what they were talking about. I'd obviously struck a nerve although I couldn't think what it was.

After a couple of minutes, they came back out, both looked serious. "When you were little," Dad said, "Haral was your first word, or at least the first sound that you made that had any sort of meaning. You said it over and over, till it wore us out. We couldn't work out where you'd got it from, we didn't know anyone called Haral."

That was both exciting and frightening. I felt myself shiver.

"Then why can't you see," I said, "that something is going on? I need to understand why I'm getting these dreams. I'm sure that I'm connected to it all. Leave me alone to find out what it all means." I got up and left the room. "I'm going to bed," I shouted as I ran up the stairs.

That night was the first time that I'd ever heard my parents arguing, it was a new experience for me and I found it unsettling. It was all my fault, I wished I'd never found the memory box.

Then as I slept, the dream came back. This time, it started from where I had thrown the dust at Malvis and sprinted for the exit. I saw the way it all ended.

I raced down the aisle, the door was thirty feet away. Just as I thought I was going to make it, Malvis stepped out in front of me, blocking my way. He had dust in his hair and an amused expression. He laughed, as I skidded to a halt. "Nice idea," he snarled, "but not quick enough." He calmly walked towards me, the blade swinging and I had no choice but to retreat again. This aisle was the last one, I hadn't realised that. When I reached the wall, instead of going left, I went right and found that there was no exit. It was all over, Malvis had backed me into a corner. I moved towards him, he blocked me. He could have finished it quickly, instead, he toyed with me, almost letting me pass, then stopping me with the blade. Every time I tried to get past him, to head for the door, his knife stopped me. I had nowhere to go. He finally tired of the game, the next time I moved, he lunged and I felt the knife slide between my ribs. It was a weird feeling, sort of hot and sharp, like an oversized injection. At the same time, I knew it was the worst thing that had ever happened to me. There was no excruciating pain, just a dull ache, spreading across my chest. I coughed and felt the strength going from my legs. The room spun, the last thing I saw was Malvis's face, he was laughing. "So long, Ian Gisbon," he said.

Then it all went black.

Chapter 8

Ian

I would hate it if you thought that I was a nasty man, abusing my place in Suzan's mind to show her things that a young girl shouldn't see, all to make her do what I wanted. The thing is, I must be here for a reason, which means that I must do what I think my purpose is.

In my other life, Beth said that I was the gentlest person she had ever met, even if I was a murder squad detective. I told her that was working me, away from it I could afford to relax. And that it was a good way to channel my emotions, all the bad ones came out at work.

I was shocked at how much the first dream had affected Suzan. That was why I told her to leave it alone. I thought that maybe she was too young to see what came next. The second dream, where she saw a fraction more, wasn't my doing, it was a product of her own mind. Although I had wanted to stop it, she seemed OK with this new information, so I let it go and showed her more. Right up to the end and my demise.

I showed Suzan the way my life ended and fed her all my feelings, not to be cruel but because I thought she could cope with it. Not only that, I have to admit that I was becoming angry and frustrated at being trapped in her body. I was impatient for her to grow and help me, it felt like I was wasting my time. I hoped that seeing my death would clear the way to an honest conversation, where I could reveal myself and we could make a plan.

When she started searching, I was amazed at how much information was out there, surely there would be something useful in all of it? Time was going on, it had been twelve years. Malvis had got away, I needed Suzan to find him and bring him to justice for all that he'd done. I didn't necessarily mean prison either, although that would be a good first step. I was never in favour of capital punishment but, for what he had done to me and my family, I could almost feel myself changing my mind. Suzan was going to be the vehicle for me to achieve that. Then I could rest.

Perhaps she wasn't old enough to see the truth, it has set off her imagination, the thing I had so carefully fostered, now it was forcing me into the background, her brain was protecting itself as it tried to process the sensations of my death. I knew then that I had gone too far, set a train of events in motion that Suzan wasn't equipped to handle. I hadn't allowed for the fact that she wasn't me. She didn't react as the twelve-year-old me would have.

I tried to calm her thoughts, but they were too powerful for me to have any effect. Things were all getting out of hand, it was too early in her emotional development for her to cope with it all.

That was why I kept quiet. I didn't trust myself not to reveal the full story. There was nothing I could say that wouldn't give the game away about who and what I really was. If she knew all of it now, it could send her over the edge, that would do neither of us any good.

Chapter 9

When Peta came over, just after breakfast on another hot, sunny day, I was already on the internet. I'd told my dad that I wasn't looking for Ian Gisbon, he'd allowed me to use the computer again. The first thing I did was learn how to delete my search history.

I was in a rush, Peta was due back from her holiday and I wanted to get it all out of the way, so I could be honest and tell her that I'd finished with Ian Gisbon and moved on. She seemed to be home a day earlier than she had said, then I realised, I had been so engrossed that an extra day had passed.

"What are you up to now?" she asked. "I haven't seen you for ages. It's a beautiful day, let's get down to the woods. I want to tell you all about my holiday."

"Not today," I said pointing at the screen. "My dad says I've got to leave it alone but I can't. There's so much more to tell you, things have happened while you've been gone. I have one more thing to do, if it doesn't work then I promise I'll never look at it again."

I had been trying to find out more, going over the same old websites, following links and finding little. Instead of giving up, the fact that I'd seen what had happened at the end had made me want to carry on, in the faint hope that perhaps I could find someone who would listen to my story.

Then I found a website, it claimed to tell the true story of what had happened to Ian Gisbon. It was filled with *maybes* and *might haves*, but one thing gave me a real jolt. It asked why he had left his stab vest, his handcuffs and his baton on the back seat of his car. I remembered that I'd seen that in the first dream. I was sure that it wasn't mentioned in the newspaper that I'd read.

"Look at that, Beano," I said. "I saw that in my dream."

"And?" she sounded disinterested.

"Well, how did I know? It wasn't in the newspaper that started all this off."

"Search me," she said. "What do you think it proves? That you were there, well you weren't. That you have a good imagination? Maybe."

"But there's that, and the car being in the wrong place, how do I know it?" I was starting to shout again, why couldn't she see that I had some kind of connection to the dreams?

"It's a coincidence, look at the article," she said. "There's so much conjecture, none of it is probably true. Newspapers print the wrong thing all the time, my dad says it's all lies. You really ought to leave it, no good will come from all this."

"Don't you want to know what else I've seen?"

"Not really, but if it will shut you up, go on."

I told Peta about the last dream. When I had been stabbed, she shivered. "That's horrible," she said, "but I suppose I can sort of understand why you need to know more. Even if it's just your mind making it up."

"There's more, in the dream I had before that one, I got a name."

"That's more interesting," she was getting into it again. "What did your mind call the murderer?"

"Harold Malvis."

"It sounds like an evil name," she said.

"And there was another strange thing, I told my parents about the dreams and about the name. Apparently, when I was little, I used to say Haral all the time."

Peta was underwhelmed. "So, you heard the sound when you were younger and copied it. That's just coincidence, in fact it's probably why you got it as a name in your dream, because you said it so often when you were young."

"That's sensible, my mum and dad were shocked and didn't know where it came from. I suppose it makes more sense that way around."

"It's simple, more logical than some connection between you and a dead policeman."

I saved the best bit until last. "One thing I didn't tell them, I have a phone number," I said, "for Ian Gisbon's widow, I don't know if I should call it?"

"How did you get that?"

"I heard it, in the dream, that man Malvis said it, to prove to Gisbon that he was in control of his destiny. That he'd been lured to his death by someone that knew all about him. It freaked him out and made him feel helpless. It must have been important because I could remember it when I woke up. I wrote it down." I showed her the piece of paper.

"That number's wrong," she said. "All mobile numbers start with *oh-seven*."

"I know, that's what I was going to do when you turned up. I need to find out how to use it, there must be a way."

I went back to the internet. In the end, I found that the number was a really old one, to make it work, all I needed to do was add a seven before the eight.

"Should I call it?" I needed her approval. I wanted her to be with me when I did.

"You're probably wasting your time. It will have been disconnected, it's twelve years old."

Even so, I made sure I blocked my number before I dialled it. I put the call on speaker so Peta could hear what happened.

It rang twice. "Hello, who's calling?" It was a woman's voice, that was a start.

"Is that Beth Gisbon?"

"Where did you get that name? How did you get this number?" she sounded frightened.

"I found it," I replied.

"Who are you and what do you want?"

"My name is unimportant, I have a message for you, from Ian." There was silence, then a muffled sob, followed by angry words.

"You BITCH, I'm sick of you people. Will it never stop? You sound like a child, what can you know?"

In the background, I heard a baby cry, a male voice shouted, "Who is it, Beth, another one of those cranks?"

"Don't you call this number again," she hissed as she ended the call.

I sat and shook. Peta came and hugged me. "That was awful," she said as I sobbed. What had I done, how was it possible? This was tearing me apart and now I was hurting other people as well. Beth Gisbon must have a new partner, a new child. From what she had said, I was just another in a long line of callers not letting her get over Ian's death.

"I don't know how you got that number," Peta said, "but you have to stop this, right now," there was real concern in her voice.

"I know, but I can't," I said. "I don't know where the number came from, I'm as surprised as you that it was the actual number. What's happening to me?"

She shook her head. "You must have seen it on one of those websites and remembered it, that's the only explanation."

I was fairly sure that I had never seen it anywhere, but I had looked at so many. That had to be where it had come from. "This is driving me crazy,

Peta, going round and round in my head. I've told you, I was there again, last night, I'm seeing more and more. I felt the knife go into my chest. I know that Harold Malvis killed me."

"Can you hear yourself? Killed me? It's a dream, you're not being killed."

"But it feels so real. When I'm having the dream, it feels like it's happening to me."

"But it's not, you wake up."

"Yes, but everything that I can check is real, the place it happened."

"What do you know about the place?" she said. "Have you looked for it on the internet, is it the same inside?"

"It still exists, it's not a warehouse now, I checked, it's an upmarket shopping centre. It said on the website that they kept all the original fittings; all the cast iron pillars and brickwork. It was impossible to tell if it matched what I get in my dreams."

"I'm getting worried about you," Peta said. "You need to leave it all alone or you're going to have a serious problem."

That was easy for her to say, it wasn't happening to her. The thing was, I knew she was right. Worse was to come, despite my hiding my history, Dad noticed that I had been on the computer a lot again. He never asked me what I was doing but simply forbade me to use the computer. He told me again that I had to stop looking at things I didn't know about and couldn't control.

I suppose he was only looking out for me, but what my parents didn't understand was that while that might stop me when I was awake, it was too late. In my dreams, I'd died last night.

On the few times that I spoke to Dave, he was distant, it almost felt as if he was hiding something. That played on my mind, how could a part of my brain be hiding things from me? Unless it was trying to protect me. From what? I might have got the name Harold Malvis but I couldn't find out anything about him. Apart from the fact that I had kept saying it, or a version of it, when I was little, there was no other connection.

It had to stop. With no internet activity possible, I allowed Peta to distract me. I started doing the things that I had neglected in my rush to make sense of what was happening in my head. After I did that, the dreams started to go away, first for a night, then for longer periods.

As they did, Dave returned. I asked him what he thought was going on. "You got over stimulated, your imagination went wild," he said, "I told you to leave it."

He was right, of course he was, he was always right.

Finally, it was time to go back to school. I asked Peta not to mention my dreams to anyone. I really thought the secret of what I had experienced would be safe.

Chapter 10

When I returned to school, I was devastated to find that Peta and I had been separated into different classes. It was the first time since I had started school that she wasn't sitting next to me and I didn't know how I would cope.

To make matters worse, I had found myself saddled with a new girl, and she wouldn't stop talking. Her name was Rebecca. "Please call me Bec," she said and then proceeded to tell me her life story. It was so involved and *me, me, me* that I lost interest pretty quickly and just said *Oh* and *Yes* every now and again. She didn't seem to notice, nor did it stop her from babbling on.

At lunch on the first day, I sought Peta out in the fields surrounding the school; there was a place where we always used to go and chat. Bec tagged along with me, even though I hinted that I wanted some alone time with my friend. What was I going to have to do to shake her off?

Peta was already there and I hugged her. "Hey, Beano, what have you been up to?" I asked her, while Bec stood around.

"Who's she?" Peta asked. Bec took that as an invitation to speak.

"Hello, I'm Bec," she gushed. "Pleased to meet you. I'm new here, my dad has got a job locally, so we all moved out from London. I love it here..."

she kept going, I'd heard it all before and tuned it out. She must have shut up for a second.

Peta was polite and diplomatic. "Great, that's a fascinating story but would you mind if I talked to my friend for a while?"

"Sure," she said and wandered off. She grabbed some poor innocent as she walked back towards the classrooms and we could hear her telling the same story again. We both collapsed in fits of giggles. "She's been plonked next to me, in your old seat," I told her.

"It could be worse," she replied, "my replacement Stringy has spots and the worst BO ever."

Even though we had only spent a morning apart, we had no trouble talking until the bell went.

The next day, Bec was just as annoying. She put her hand up for every question and kept up a flow of whispers that made me lose concentration. That earned me a telling-off for not paying attention. At least it would be lunch soon. Peta would laugh when she heard how I'd got stuck with the class nuisance.

When we broke for lunch, she raced away towards the queue for school dinners. I had sandwiches so I headed over to our usual meeting place, relieved to be free from her for an hour. To my surprise, she was already there, but Peta was missing.

"Hi," she said, "your friend hasn't turned up yet, what shall we talk about?"

In my head, I heard Dave. "Get rid of her," he said. "She's one of those people, if you let her worm her way in, you'll never get her off your back. Do it now."

This was not my idea of how things should be going. "She must be somewhere else," I said. "Anyway, this is our private spot, you have to be invited to join in."

She looked annoyed. "Why? Do you have some dark secret you sit here and discuss?"

I must have gone red because her eyes lit up. "You do, tell me all the juicy details, I can keep a secret."

"There's nothing to tell," Peta had arrived. "We've been friends since we were little, this is the place where we hang out. Sorry, but we'd like a bit of privacy."

"I get it." She looked annoyed. "You sit here in your own sad little club. I know where I'm not wanted. I'm off to make some real friends." She flounced off.

"Beano, she's a real pain," I said. For some reason, Peta thought it was hilarious. "Seriously, she's starting to wind me up, she keeps whispering in lessons, putting me off."

"Still," she sounded thoughtful, "you don't want to upset her, she's new here, just trying to fit in."

"That's fit in, not barge in," I reminded her. "She could ask, not presume."

"Well, you've got to sit next to her, good luck with that."

The thought filled me with dread. When we got back to class, I was surprised to find that the space next to me was empty. There was a fuss on the other side of the room, Bec was trying to sit somewhere else. Sophie, I girl I vaguely knew, came over and sat beside me, she was flushed and I could see she was upset.

"What's up, Sophie?" I asked her.

"Can I sit here?" she said. "That new girl reckons you're a horrible cow and she doesn't want anything to do with you. What have you done to upset her?"

"Nothing," I said, "she wouldn't take no for an answer. When I met Peta at lunchtime, she hung around; all I did was ask her to give us some privacy."

"She said it was just like the same at her last school, nobody would be her friend. I told her you and Peta were alright but she's got it in her head that you hate her."

"Well, I don't." Perhaps I should go over and try to make peace. I looked across, she saw me and glared. Maybe I'd be better leaving it for a while.

The chance never materialised over the next couple of days. Bec kept out of my way. She had allied herself with a group that I was not that friendly with and they seemed to take up all her time. Peta and I met every lunchtime, under the trees when it wasn't raining and nobody disturbed us.

Life was returning to normal. Schoolwork was keeping me busy; it had been several weeks since I had thought about Ian Gisbon. My dreams had stopped and Dave was keeping a low profile.

One lunchtime, we were sitting under the tree when Peta brought the subject of my recent obsession up.

"That was a wild summer holiday," she said. "I was getting worried about you."

"I'm feeling better; you were right, it was getting scary for a while. I'm glad it's over."

She gave me a look. "Are you sure it's over? You've told me that before. Have you stopped looking at stuff about Ian Gisbon?"

I said that I had, but she persisted. "How about those awful dreams about his life, his murder, have they stopped too?"

"Don't bring it all up again, please," I said. "I feel like it's all gone, even Diana has stopped talking in my head now."

I stopped talking as we both realised that there was a rustling noise behind us. It sounded like someone was hiding, they must have been listening to our conversation. Peta put her finger to her lips and made a circling motion with her hands. I understood immediately, got up and moved to her right. She went left, until we stood on each side of the brambles, behind the tree and before you got to the wall. The rustling continued.

"Come out!" shouted Peta. It all went silent. "Alright, we're coming in to get you."

Before we could, Bec's head appeared. Peta grabbed her arm and dragged her out.

"You're hurting me," she squealed.

"What were you doing in there?" asked Peta.

"I was just walking around the field," she said, "and heard you two talking. I was gonna come out and say hello then you grabbed me."

It sounded absurd. "Walking around the field, through the brambles and bushes? Do you think we're stupid? You were hiding in there and listening to us."

"No, I could only hear that you were talking, not what you were saying. Anyway, you're so full of yourselves, Peta and Suzan, the string beans, everyone's favourites. I just wanted to fit in. I was told that you were nice, good people to be friends with. But you're not, it's a myth. I might have guessed, nobody's that perfect. I wanted to know what was so important that you came out here and talked about it every day. And why you didn't want me in your cosy little club."

"Cos it's private, we have serious things to discuss. It's nothing to do with you, or anyone else. If you breathe a word to anyone about what you might have heard, you're dead. Whatever you think, people like us. One word from us, that you can't be trusted, it'll ruin you here."

She went pale and nodded. "Understood, I won't tell anyone." Peta let her go and she scampered away.

"Do you believe her?"

She shrugged. "I have no idea, we'll have to wait and see."

Chapter 11

A week later, as I walked home from the bus, alone, I heard a car behind me, coming down the lane.

Automatically, I stepped to one side into a gateway, to give it room. It slowed and stopped by me. There must be someone I knew inside. The window rolled down to reveal a man's face, beside him I could see Bec.

"Are you the girl who says she's lived before?" he asked.

Bec was nodding. "That's her," she smirked. So she had heard us talking about Ian. What was worse than that, she had made up a more sensational version of the story. I might have known that she couldn't keep her mouth shut.

I just stood there, I didn't know how to respond. "Were you listening to my private conversation, Bec?" I managed to say. The man ignored me.

"I'm from the local newspaper," he shouted. My heart sank. "My daughter told me about your story. I'd like to talk to you, about your dreams. I can help you find out more about Ian Gisbon. I remember the case. We're going up to your house. Can we give you a lift?"

"Run home," said Dave. I didn't need him to tell me that. I shook my head and turned. I had been betrayed. Worse than that, my dad was going to think that I hadn't stopped looking. As quickly as I could, I climbed over the gate and ran. Behind me, the man called me back, he told me not to be stupid, that it was all going to come out anyway. Then I heard the car speed up. I tried to run faster, across the field, cutting the corner to my house. But I knew I wouldn't get there first.

When I got to our front gate, the man and my father were ten yards apart, facing each other. Even from the other side of the garden, I could feel the tension. Mum was standing at the front door, I heard her shout, "I've called the police."

"There was no need for that," said the man, Bec's father. "I just want to talk to you about your daughter's amazing story. The publicity will be good for you. If the story gets picked up by the nationals and the video services, there might be a few pounds in it as well."

"I don't know what you're talking about. Even if I did, we've got nothing to say," replied my father. "So you can leave. Suzan, get into the house, we'll talk about this later." I had come through the field gate and stopped behind Bec's dad.

Bec stood off to one side, a sullen expression on her face. "Here she is, Dad," she called as she saw me.

I tried to run past her father to get to the front door. Quick as a flash he grabbed my arm and spun me around. Mum screamed, "Leave her alone!"

I struggled. "Kick out at his shins," Dave said in my head. I did, he dodged my feet, his grip tight.

"Let me go," I shouted, "you're hurting me."

"No chance. You can stay right here and tell me what you know about Ian Gisbon," he said. "This could be my big payday."

Out of the corner of my eye, I saw my father move towards me and heard him shout, "Don't you dare touch her." Then everything seemed to go into slow motion. As he ran towards me, Bec moved to stop him. I could have sworn that she stuck out her foot and tripped him over. He fell forward, arms flailing, as he hit the ground his head jerked from the impact and there was a loud cracking sound. His body went limp. My mother screamed again. I could hear a siren in the distance as Bec's dad let me go and we all rushed to his body.

My mother tried to lift Dad into a sitting position. As she did, his head lolled. His eyes were wide open and unfocused. It was as if none of his muscles were working.

"Call an ambulance," someone shouted, it might have been me. Then a black feeling came over me and I fainted.

When I woke, I was in the back of an ambulance. I tried to sit up. "Take it easy," said the paramedic, a lady with a kind face. "You've been unconscious for a while. What do you remember?"

"Where's my dad? I want to see him."

"I'm sorry, dear," she said, "you'll have to talk to your mother."

"Suzan," Mum shouted, she must have been waiting outside, "are you awake?" She climbed into the ambulance and hugged me.

"How's Dad?" I asked. Her face fell.

Oh, Suzan, there's no easy way to tell you," she said. "I'm afraid your father's dead." Her voice was blank and I could see that she was trying hard not to cry.

It felt like my world was falling apart. "But..." I said, then I started to cry.

Mum held me tight. "It was such a silly random accident," she said. "If only he had managed to stop himself from falling. His neck was broken from the jolt when his body hit the ground. The paramedic said that he died instantly, he wouldn't have known what was happening."

As if that was a comfort. Whatever he did or didn't know, we knew, the sight of his lifeless head flopping as we lifted him would stay in my mind forever.

"Bec tripped him," I said. "I saw her, she stuck her foot out and tripped him over, she killed him." I was starting to shake, trying to get up, Mum held me tight, her tears wet on my shoulder.

"I didn't see that, I thought he just fell, we'll have to tell the police what you saw."

"I'm so sorry, Suzan," said the paramedic. "Are you in any pain?" I said that my arm hurt, where I had been grabbed. I looked, a large bruise was forming just below my elbow. She took pictures and rubbed some cream on it. She said that we could go and Mum and I got out of the ambulance.

I'd never seen so many people in our front garden. The worst thing that I could see was the lump on the lawn, covered by a black sheet. I knew it was my dad, or what was left of him. I started to sob again and Mum held my hand. "Be strong," she said. Dave repeated it in my head, "Be strong."

A man in a suit came over to us. "Mrs Halford?" he said. "I'm Inspector Guilman, I'm sorry for your loss."

"Thank you," said Mum.

"We will need to take formal statements from you down at the station but can you tell us what happened?"

"My husband answered the door," said Mum, "and that man," she pointed at Bec's dad with shaking fingers, "was outside. He said that he was a reporter and he'd heard a story about my daughter. He wanted to interview her."

"And his daughter is a pupil at your daughter's school?"

"That's right. She's new there this term."

"Did you know what the story was about?"

"I heard the man tell my Keith that Suzan had been saying to her friend Peta that she was living the life of a man in her dreams, a real policeman from long ago. She said that she'd seen him die and she knew who had killed him."

If that was a shock to him, you would never have known. "I see. What did your husband say to that?"

"He told him to get lost and told me to call you."

"Did you or your husband know about this story of your daughter's?"

"Yes," said Mum, looking at me, "partly, it's a long story. We knew Suzan had been having bad dreams, but not the rest of it."

He nodded. "Thank you, I know this is upsetting but we need to record it before the memory fades. Now, Suzan," he turned to me, "is that what you said to your friend?"

I shook my head. "No, it isn't."

He looked at me. "This is very important, are you sure?"

"Yes, I am, I wouldn't lie to you. I saw a picture, in an old newspaper report, of a murder and started having dreams about it. I did a bit of research on the internet and had more dreams. When I couldn't find out any more, I left it alone and forgot all about it. I was talking to my friend, Peta, about it when we found that Bec was listening to us. We told her not to tell anyone but... well, you can see that she didn't take any notice. She made up the bit about me having lived before, all I said was that my dreams felt so real that I thought I was living them while I was having them. And," I added, "she killed him."

"What did you say?" the policeman asked.

"She, that Bec, she tripped my dad up, while her dad was holding me. If he hadn't fallen, he'd still be alive. She killed him."

He nodded. "She has admitted as much, but killing is a bit strong, don't you think? She said she only wanted to stop your father from hurting her father." He changed the subject. "Has anyone examined your arm, where he held you?"

"Yes," I said, showing it to him, "the lady in the ambulance took pictures and gave me some cream to rub on it."

"Good. Thank you. As I said, we'll be in touch to get a formal statement."

He walked away and I looked across at Bec. She was being comforted by a female police constable. I could hear her sobbing and repeating *I didn't mean it, I just wanted to stop him,* over and over. Her father was sitting in the back of the police car looking ahead with a blank face. What could I do to make this right?

I had no idea what to do, I felt numb. It was like this was another dream. I just hugged Mum and hoped that somehow it would all go away. In the midst of it all, Peta's mum appeared and made tea for everyone. A black estate car arrived and three men put Dad in a bag and lifted him into the back of it. Mum tried to shield me from the sight. "You don't need to see that," she said but I pulled away from her. I needed to watch; it was the last time I'd ever see him.

When they drove away, the lawn seemed suddenly empty.

'He wouldn't have known anything', the paramedic and Mum had both said the same thing, it went over and over in my mind.

I listened for Dave; he had done his disappearing act again. Just when I needed him to talk to, to try to make sense of it all. I wanted to talk to him, even though he wasn't real. It would have given me somewhere to unload. My dad was dead and although I had blamed Bec, I thought that it was all my fault.

From when I had first seen the picture in the paper, things had gone wrong and it had all led up to this moment. If only it hadn't rained that day. If only we hadn't found the memory box.

Chapter 12

The next few days were a blur; before the police doctor left, he gave us some sedatives, so that we would sleep that first night. Mum and I cuddled up together and fell asleep in her bed, without eating. The pillow still smelt of Dad and his half-finished book was laying on the bedside table. Everything I saw reminded me of him. It was almost too much to bear while I was waiting for the tablets to work.

When I woke, at first I didn't know where I was, then I remembered what had happened. In a crushing explosion of emotion, I remembered it all. I started crying, which woke Mum. "What's the matter, dear, did you have another dream?" she said. Then her mind must have caught up, her face crumpled and she started crying too. We just lay in the bed, held each other and sobbed.

"It's no good us laying here," Mum said after a while. "We have to get up, there are lots of things that we need to get done."

"Does that mean I have to go to school?" I didn't fancy that, having to talk to everyone, relive it all, over and over. And see Bec, knowing what she had done.

"No," said Mum, "you can have a few days off. But I have loads to do, things to arrange, you get washed and dressed while I make a call and have a shower."

What did she mean? Was I going to have to spend the day on my own while she went and did 'things'? Shouldn't she be grieving, with me? Why wasn't she as sad as I was?

Five minutes after I came downstairs, Peta and her mum appeared. Her mum hugged me. "Hello, Suzan, I'm so sorry," she said. "Let me make some tea and get you breakfast, what would you like?"

Peta hugged me too. "Guess what?" she said. "Mum says I don't have to go to school today. She's going to help your mum and I'm going to help you."

After we'd eaten, we left the two of them together and went out to walk to the woods. I was still in a bit of a daze from the sedatives and couldn't stop sobbing. My parents had said that they loved each other, but it seemed to me that my mum was acting as if nothing had happened.

"Peta," I said, "why do you think it is that my mum is just pretending that nothing happened?"

"Is she?" she said. "Perhaps she's just as sad as you are but trying not to show it." She thought for a moment. "And she's an adult, they always have stuff to do, you know that. My dad said there are all sorts of things that you have to sort out when someone dies suddenly, there are solicitors and undertakers, wills and bank accounts. Everything changes and it all needs to be done at the same time. Meanwhile, you're struggling to come to terms with it all and I guess she's just trying to look strong for you."

That was a lot to take in, especially as I was having trouble thinking straight. "Anyway," she added, "I'm here to help. Just say whatever you like and I'll listen."

We sat under the trees, the stream bubbling and sparkling in the autumn sun and I told her all about what had happened. Even though it made me cry again. Every time I stopped, Peta waited patiently, her arm around me, until I felt able to carry on.

I told her how Bec must have made up a more sensational story to tell her father. "It was different to what we'd said before we caught her listening, so much more. All she got right was the name, Ian Gisbon. I suppose that her dad, being a reporter, knew the story from all those years ago."

I told her how they had stopped me in the lane, raced to the house and what happened when I got there. "I thought that there was going to be a fight, Bec's dad grabbed me, my dad came to get me and Bec tripped him up." I could see it all in my head again and it started me off.

Peta gasped at that point. "The cow," she said. "You mean, she tripped him up, and he…"

"I think she was just trying to stop him from getting to her dad, I don't honestly think she wanted that to happen. The trouble is, it did and now I hate her for it."

"I can't blame you for that, I would too," she said. "So what are you going to do?"

"I don't know, every time I shut my eyes I can just see him falling and hear that noise, it's much worse than the dreams about Ian Gisbon were. I know those dreams are sort of what happened, they might seem real but they didn't happen to me."

Her brow furrowed. "I get what you mean, it's just a weird way of looking at it. Didn't the doctor give you something to help you sleep?"

"Oh yes, I didn't dream at all while I was sleeping but now, if I just shut my eyes and even if I don't shut my eyes I can see it all happening again in horrible slow motion."

"You probably need a few more days' rest," she said. "Can I ask you, is the voice still in your head? Is Diana still there?"

"It is and it isn't, if that makes any sense. Occasionally I get a random thought but most of the time there's nothing. There hasn't been much at all since I saw the photograph."

We went home to find that Mum and Peta's mum had gone into town. There was a note on the kitchen table, 'help yourself to food, we've had to go and do some things. I'll explain it all later, Love Mum xxx'.

When she finally came home, she looked tired, and I could see that she had been crying again. Peta's mum offered to stay and cook; Mum said that she needed to keep busy. I offered to help her but she asked me just to let her do it.

I sat at the kitchen table and watched her as she peeled vegetables. It was such a familiar sight, I half expected Dad to come in and ask her what she was cooking.

"Mum," I said, "we need to talk. I feel abandoned by you and it hurts." She stopped peeling and came over to hug me.

"I know what you're going through and I understand," she said. "The trouble is, there are just so many things that you have to do when someone dies and you have to do them within a certain time. It's wrong because you're full of grief and you just want to be still and come to terms with it all. I'm glad to say I've done most of it now. Your dad was organised; we had a book where we kept a list of everything important and everything that needed to be done. I've seen our solicitor and he's going to organise a lot of it for me. The undertakers are arranged, we can't set a date for the funeral until the police have finished their investigations. I've been to the bank, there are just a few bits of tidying up to do. Now I'm all yours, I'm sorry but it had to be done."

"I was so angry," I said. "I thought you were dumping me with Peta and you didn't understand my grief."

"Don't be ridiculous," she said. "That's so far from the truth you wouldn't believe it. As I said, it all had to be done and I didn't want to drag you around and keep repeating it all. I thought a day with Peta would be better for you. Oh, one more thing, I've also spoken to Dad's sister, your Auntie Anne, and she's going to come up and help us for a few days."

"I just feel like everyone's left me to it. I know you had things to do but I can't help it. Dad's gone and then you left me. Peta was great, she's so kind, but I can't help how I feel."

"I understand totally," she said. "We'll have a proper day out together tomorrow. The only thing is we have to go to the police station in the morning and make formal statements but after that the day is ours and we can do whatever you want."

"Thank you," I said, "that would be good."

"You know, the doctor left us enough tablets for tonight, to help us sleep. I'm going to take some and I would suggest that you did the same."

I was dreading sleep, since I had stopped dying as Ian Gisbon, my sleep had become deep and untroubled. Now I was faced with watching a new death.

"I can't stop seeing him," I said, starting to well up again. "I can't stop seeing him fall and hear that noise. It's awful, every time I shut my eyes."

"Can I ask," she said, "is it the same as the dreams you had after you saw the newspaper?"

"No, I'm not having them anymore and I know and understand that they were different, just a product of my imagination. This is real, I know it's real and it's a proper memory so it's a totally different thing."

She nodded. "I see, I'm glad that you're not having both at the same time. If you were, that would worry me. I could tell the dreams about that poor policeman really upset you and, in a way, we both felt a little bit responsible for them."

"I thought that you'd think I was crazy, that's why I had to talk about them to Peta and that's when the girl overheard. She made so much more of it, though, enough to convince her father that he was onto the story of the century."

Mum looked at me. "It was all a series of events, I wish we hadn't kept the newspaper or had talked to you about it more, then none of this would have happened." She sighed and looked across at the pile of vegetables. "Why am I doing all these veg? It's just habit, your father was always so hungry after a day working on the farm. I don't need to spend all my time doing that anymore, I should be talking to you instead. Let's just have something easy for tea."

"I'm not hungry," I said, "but it's good to talk. I know what you mean about not keeping the paper but you weren't to know. You can't think like that, things happen sometimes."

"That's very adult of you," she said. "It's done now and we just have to get on and make the best of it. Dad wouldn't want us to dwell, he'd want us to carry on with life so that's what we have to do."

"Okay," I said, "it doesn't mean I'm not going to be sad or miss him though."

"No, I'm always going to be sad but it's a new reality and that's what we have to do now."

"Me and you, against the world?"

"That's right, always. How about beans on toast?"

While we were eating, I asked about Auntie Anne and when she would be arriving.

"The day after tomorrow," Mum said. "She has work to do and she couldn't get away." Her tone suggested that she was annoyed with her. I knew she was Dad's older sister but I'd never met her. Of course, I'd had birthday and Christmas cards from her and some nice presents, but I always got the impression that they didn't get on.

"I've only met her a couple of times," she added, "she didn't seem too bad, considering. Never mind why, before you ask. Just remember, it's very kind of her to come and help us so we should just be grateful and see what she's like when she gets here."

We finished eating and washed up together, there seemed little point in doing anything else so we both went to bed, I stayed in my own room, the smell of Dad was too much for me to bear. I took the tablet and fell asleep easily.

The next morning, Peta's mum dropped her at school and took us into town. She stopped outside the police station. "Deep breaths," Mum said. "This is the last big official thing we have to do so let's get it over with and then we'll go and have coffee and a cake."

We were shown into a room and the policeman from before came in, with a female constable. Tea was served.

"Now then," he said, "once again I'm sorry for your loss. I know it's a hard time for you but we need to get the paperwork out of the way."

He produced typed statements. "These are transcribed from what I recorded at your house, it says so at the top. Please read them and if there's anything you want to add, tell us now."

Reading it all back in the official-sounding language made me see it all again. It was all there, including the bit where I said I had seen Bec trip up my dad. Mum had a few things she wanted to be corrected and we had to wait while it was done. The detective made conversation.

"How about you, Suzan, is that a proper record of what happened?"

"I've got nothing more to add," I said. "What happens next?"

"Well," he said, "based on your statements, plus the ones from everyone else, and the evidence from a post-mortem, a decision will be made. I can't tell you what that will be yet."

"But she tripped up my dad, if she had done anything else he would still be here." I was starting to shout.

"Enough, Suzan," said Mum.

"It's alright," said the policeman. "I understand. He shouldn't have been pestering you, nor should he have tried to restrain you. That's assault. As for the trip, it remains to be decided if it was a deliberate attempt to cause bodily harm. That's above my pay grade, I'm afraid to say. But we will keep you informed. You should be prepared, if it comes to a court case, you may be called to give evidence." He thought for a moment. "I can tell you that he's been ordered never to publish anything about you or any story that he might have thought he had."

That was a relief, it meant we wouldn't be bothered by anyone else. I had a sudden thought, Ian Gisbon's wife had been hounded by reporters, far worse than we had been, yet she hadn't been able to stop it. I was guilty of harassing her, with my phone call. Surely what happened to Dad wasn't karma for that?

Mum's corrected statement arrived and after reading it, she signed it. The detective thanked us and showed us out.

"Time for cake, then a look around the shops."

We had a nice afternoon. I had almost forgotten about the reason for our visit until we were walking down the lane from the bus stop. We came to the gate where I had been stopped by the car; was it only two days ago? I suddenly felt sad. "Perhaps I should have got in the car," I said. "Maybe it would have all ended differently."

"Maybe," said Mum, "or maybe not."

When she got home, Peta came to tell me what was happening at school. Bec had returned and had been given the silent treatment, nobody was talking to her. Apparently, she was getting pushed around and bumped into or tripped up everywhere she went. I didn't want that, although I was still angry with her. She might have tripped my dad up but I didn't honestly think she had intended to kill him. I was touched that so many people had passed messages of sorrow and support on. Peta had a handful of cards, from pupils and staff. Even the dinner ladies had sent one.

The next day, a taxi deposited Dad's sister outside the door. Anne was older than Dad and looked as if the cares of the world were on her shoulders. She had a kind smile though.

She swept in with a business-like air. "You're not to do anything," she said. "I'll take the weight off. Now, how about getting a takeaway delivered, my treat?"

After I'd gone to bed, before I fell asleep, I heard her and Mum talking. Anne was sobbing, "He was my baby brother," she said, "I held him when he was five minutes old."

It broke my heart to hear that, it made me realise that it wasn't just me and Mum that were hurting. Then they talked some more. They must have shut the lounge door because I couldn't hear it too well. I thought I heard words like blame, guilty and prison. Who were they talking about, did they mean me?

I would have to try and talk to Mum about what they were saying, it wasn't fair to have secrets, there were only the two of us now and we had to stick together. I didn't need to feel any more guilt, Dave had already said that I'd overreacted to the picture, which hadn't been much help. I knew that and felt guilty about what I'd done. I needed someone to tell me that it wasn't my fault.

By the next morning, the whole atmosphere had changed. There was an air of tension and Anne was giving me sideways looks. Even though neither of them ever directly said it, I had the feeling that Anne blamed me for what had happened to her brother, which made it difficult to talk to her.

"Guess what," Mum announced after breakfast. "Anne wants us to stay with her in Devon after the funeral." Despite my misgivings, it seemed like a good plan to me, I hated it in this house now, it had far too many memories for my liking. I couldn't look at the lawn without seeing my dad, under the black plastic sheet. But, I realised, that would mean leaving Peta.

The three of us argued. Mum was bitter about the memory box and blamed herself for it all. This didn't suit me, I thought it was all my fault, for reading the newspaper and overreacting. Anne thought we were both being stupid.

And I found out something else. What I'd heard wasn't anything to do with me. It was Anne's husband, Martin. Apparently, he was causing her some problems, she never said what but it must have been serious. Not only that, Mum told me that we didn't have the option of staying here, even if we had wanted to. Dad was only a tenant, along with Peta's family. We didn't own the house, it belonged to the farm. The owner wanted a new family to come and work the farm with Peta's dad, which meant we had to go. Dad had life insurance, but it wasn't enough to buy us a new house.

"Houses are cheaper in Devon," said Mum. "We can live with Anne for a while, as long as we need, and I can get a job and you can go to school, we'll soon find a new house of our own."

"Will it be in the country?" I didn't fancy living in a town, I loved the fields and the woods.

"Devon is mostly countryside, it's quite different to here though. There are moors and it's a lot wilder, I think you'll love it. Anyway, we don't have much choice. The landowner has given us a month to get organised."

Chapter 13

At the funeral, there was an argument, between me and Mum. The service was in a crematorium packed with so many people that they spilt out into the porch. Family, friends and people from school all formed a long line to hug us and say how sorry they were.

A priest, who had never met Dad, spoke about how wonderful he was, I just sat there thinking how hypocritical the whole thing seemed. Then after the coffin had disappeared, we moved on to the wake.

Peta's mum and Anne had organised it at her house, ours was full of boxes. Surrounded by well-meaning friends and relatives, I found a bottle of something and proceeded to sit in the corner, ignore everyone and get drunk. I hated it, everyone was being so kind when they should have been as angry as I was. Somehow, it didn't seem right. In the end, I got up and stood on a chair, wobbling as I tried to keep my balance.

"Can I have your attention, please," I shouted and everyone looked my way.

"I wish you could just blame me for it all," I slurred. "I know it's what you all think, let's have a bit of honesty."

The room went silent. Mum came over to me. "Get down, Suzan," she said. "This will do you no good. You're being stupid. How will this help?"

"It'd make me feel better. I'm sure you blame me and I just want you to be honest enough to confirm it. My dad's gone, I'm being taken away to the wilds, leaving my friends." I swayed a little. "I hate you all."

"Come on, Stringy," said Peta. "Get down and come and talk to me, please."

I decided that returning to the floor level in a dignified way was probably the best thing to do. I only just managed it.

"Thanks, Peta," said Mum. She hugged me. "Suzan, you're my little girl and I love you. Things happened but to blame you would be wrong. You saw the picture, perhaps you should blame me for not throwing it away. Or your father for having the idea of a memory box in the first place."

"I think I'm going to be sick," I said and rushed for the toilet. When I'd deposited most of my stomach contents, I cleaned myself up and felt embarrassed. I couldn't face them all. I sneaked back to our house and went to sleep.

In the morning, I had my first hangover; it wasn't pleasant. I resolved never to drink again. Everyone who had stayed over was so kind about my outburst, maybe they put it down to grief. They all reassured me that it wasn't my fault, just one of those unfortunate things.

But I couldn't stop the feelings of guilt, they churned around in my mind.

I went back to school just once, not for lessons, just to collect my stuff from my locker and say goodbye.

The girls at school were pleased to see me, kind and sad. 'We've made Bec's life a misery', they proudly told me, 'Your dad was OK, he was good to us, let us play in the woods, he didn't deserve that'.

It was inevitable that Bec and I would meet and when we did, the other girls made a circle around us shouting and urging us to fight. I didn't want to but it looked like I had no choice.

"My dad's got a police record because of you," Bec hissed.

How dare she blame me for that. "Well, my dad's dead because of you not being able to keep your mouth shut, what you told him was all made up anyway."

"Freak," she said. "What's it like to be possessed?"

"At least I'm not a murderer," I answered, which was how I felt.

"Just get on with it, Stringy," said Peta. "Sort her out."

Bec made a grab for me. I backed away until I was stopped by the crowd. They pushed me forward. "Try to trip her up," shouted someone from the throng. In my mind, I saw it all happen again and although I had sworn not to be angry and blame her, I was suddenly furious, at how unfair it all was, how people trip over all the time, get up and carry on. In a rage I flew at her, taking her by surprise.

I had her in a neck lock, flat on the floor and was about to grind her face into the concrete when the teachers pulled us apart.

Sat in the head teacher's office, waiting for Mum, I knew I had screwed up and wanted to get away. I had been determined not to fight. Then someone shouted 'trip her up' and it had all changed. Bec's mother had already arrived and collected her, at least my mother wouldn't have to face her. She had avoided eye contact with me and practically dragged Bec away.

Fortunately, Mum was on my side. "We're leaving," she announced when she arrived, before the head could say anything. "I don't want to hear who started it, you're the head teacher, you know what's been going on. It's your job to make sure this doesn't happen. We're moving away for a new start and we won't be back."

Dave was suddenly in my head, it was the first time I had heard him in ages and he sounded worried. "Suzan," he shouted, "something's happening,"

Before I could ask him where he had been, or what he meant, I felt a tremor in my arm, something wet and metallic on my top lip, then my head snapped back and I fell to the floor. I could feel my body convulsing. It felt like I'd been plugged into an electric socket. My arms and legs were twitching and I couldn't stop it. My head banged on the floor. The last thing I heard was my mum shouting, "Call an ambulance."

I woke up in a hospital bed, wearing a mask. There was a strange taste in my mouth and as my eyes focused, I saw Mum and Anne beside me. As I reached for the mask, I could feel something stopping my arm from moving. I looked across, there was a plastic tube attached to my elbow. I needed to speak and used my other hand to pull the mask off. "What happened?" I croaked.

"Try and keep still, you've had a fit," Mum said. "You gave us quite a scare. Don't you remember?"

I recalled the strange feeling of helplessness, like I wasn't in control of my own body and I remembered Dave shouting. It had been a shock to hear him again after so long. "I don't know," I said. I tried to sit up and felt incredibly weak.

I heard a door open. "Lay still." A nurse came into view. She helped me to sit up, adjusting the bed to make me more comfortable. "Now you're awake, I'll get the doctor."

"What happened, Mum? The last thing I remember was arriving at school."

"You fought, with Bec," she said. "I've been told that she accused you of getting her father into trouble."

"I don't remember," I said.

"It's OK," Mum said. "You'll never have to go back there again, I told the school that they were supposed to be looking after you, keeping you two apart. I was worried this might happen."

I searched my memory, it was scary, the whole day was gone from my mind. The last thing I could remember was feeling nervous as I approached the gates with Peta holding my hand and whispering support. "Did I hurt her?"

"Not as much as she hurt your dad," said Anne.

"Really, Anne," Mum said. "There's no need for that, she shouldn't have done it. The school will be making a note on your permanent record, it will go with you to your new school. But don't worry, I will make sure they know the full story."

"Well, I think you did the right thing," said Anne, immediately going up in my estimation. "If it had been my dad, they would have had to prise my hands from her throat with a crowbar."

Before Mum could say anything more, the door opened and a doctor came in. He introduced himself and consulted my notes.

"What happened, Doctor?" said Mum.

"It seems like Suzan had some sort of seizure," he explained. "You needed emergency treatment at the scene, with a drug called Midazolam. As well as stopping the seizure, it's also a sedative, so you will feel tired and weak for a while. We need to do a brain scan to see what the activity is in your head before we can decide if it was a one-off event or symptomatic of anything else."

"Do you mean epilepsy?" asked Mum.

He nodded. "Possibly, but it's important that you're not alarmed, epilepsy is very treatable these days. It's not curable but it can be so well controlled that you'd never expect a problem. Tell me, Mrs Halford, has your daughter ever had anything like this before?"

Mum shook her head. "No, but when she was a baby, she had brain scans. She seemed over-active." That was the first I'd heard of it.

"I see, I'll have to take a look at them, they should give me a baseline measurement. What did they show?"

"Nothing to alarm us, the doctor at the time said there was a lot more activity than he would have expected, but he never said she was epileptic or had any other condition that required treatment."

"Thank you, I will review her notes, get her scanned in the morning and decide what to do next." He shook Mum's hand and left.

"Sorry, Mum," I said, "for messing up our moving plans, and that I shouted at the funeral."

She smiled. "Your dad used to say that it wasn't a proper funeral without a drunk, a fight or an argument. We had two out of three. If he had been there, it would have amused him. We aren't moving without you, the place is just about packed up, we can go when you're fit enough to travel. You know, I wonder if whatever's going on in your head is a result of stress activating whatever it was we thought you had when you were young."

"I never knew," I said, "you never mentioned it."

"There was nothing to say, until now. You were a highly active child, always shouting and very agitated. We took you to the doctor because we thought there was something wrong. Everyone said we were over-protective, that you would settle."

I wondered if that was when I was shouting Haral, I didn't like to ask Mum with Anne listening, in case we got into the whole Ian Gisbon thing again.

Visiting ended and I was left alone to eat my hospital tea. Before I went to sleep, the nurses took the tube out of my arm,

I was tired and slept right through the night. When I was woken for breakfast, I felt like I had another hangover, I asked the nurse why my head hurt when she bought my food.

"That's from the sedative," she said, "drink lots of water and you'll be alright."

Mid-morning, a wheelchair arrived, pushed by a young porter. "Miss Halford," he said, "I'm Ron, your driver today. Your chariot awaits for your trip to the scanner."

It made me laugh. Mum had said I had been scanned when I was younger; I didn't remember it. I climbed in on my own, my legs were a bit shaky but at least my headache was going.

Ron and I chatted on the way to the scanner, he had a good sense of humour and cracked lots of jokes, I guess he was trying to relax me. It felt nice to be the centre of someone's attention for a while. "I'll be right back for you, soon as you're cooked," he said as we arrived. The nurse looked at him disapprovingly, "no need to frighten her," she said. He just grinned and walked off.

"I'm fine," I said, "Ron has cheered me up today."

"A lot of people don't like him," she said.

"I think he's cute," I said it before I thought about it.

"You're going red," the nurse replied, "never mind him, can you climb up here and lay down."

The scanner was a thing like a doughnut with a bed in the middle of the hole. I got myself comfortable, a nurse put a small box in my hand before retreating. I heard the door shut behind her. Then a voice said in my ear, "Keep completely still, there may be a bit of clicking from the magnets but don't worry. It will only take a couple of minutes to complete what we need to do. If you feel frightened and want us to stop, press the button in your hand."

I tried to think happy thoughts of Peta and me in the woods. Before I knew it, the nurse had returned. "Well done," she said, taking the box from my hands. "That wasn't too bad, was it?" The nurse told me that the doctor would tell me the results of the scan. "He'll wait until your mother arrives to visit you," he said, "but don't worry."

I felt sad when it wasn't Ron but an older man who came to collect me. I asked where he was, "tea break," he said.

I got back into my wheelchair and was returned to the ward.

Peta came in with Mum for visiting after lunch. She hugged me. "Are you alright, Stringy?" she said. "We've all been really worried about you."

"Hi, Beano, tell me, how's Bec?"

"She's OK, more's the pity. She reckons the teachers saved you. According to her, she was just about to roll over and punch your lights out."

"In her dreams! She was saved from me, I was going to push her nose through the tarmac." We high-fived.

"That's enough," said Mum.

The doctor returned with a brown file. "Peta, would you mind waiting outside," said Mum. She got up and left.

"I have your results here." The doctor opened the file. "I'm pleased to say that it's not all bad news. Your scan shows abnormal synaptic activity. Similar to what was noted when you were a baby. It bothers me that nothing was done back then, perhaps that doctor was concerned about medication at such a young age. Suzan, you will need to adjust your lifestyle a little and take regular medication but there's no reason to be pessimistic about the future."

It sounded ominous, despite what he was saying. "Do you mean that it could happen again?"

He didn't answer directly. "Let me explain a bit more," he said. "I've looked at this scan and compared it to the old ones. I'm moderately concerned about what they both show. I wouldn't normally diagnose medication after one episode but in your case, based on your past, I'm going to make an exception. I think the stress and shock of your father's death triggered a long-standing problem in your brain, which had been dormant since you were very little. I'm concerned moving forward that the aftermath of recent events might trigger more, so I'm putting you on a low dose of a drug called Topamax."

"How long will she be on that drug?" asked Mum, she was looking worried.

"We can't say. We'll need to review her every six months," said the doctor, "with brain scans. If the drugs are causing problems, we can modify the dose or try a different one. Maybe a combination of therapies. We can adjust your diet as well, if we need to."

"Thank you," I said. "Can I go home now?"

"As soon as you've got your drugs and the social services have seen you."

"Why do they want to see Suzan?" asked Mum.

"The school made a referral when they were informed of your father's death. I assume that it's for bereavement counselling."

He left us alone and five minutes later, a nurse came in. "There's a man from social services who wants to see you," she said. "When he's gone and your drugs have arrived, you can go home."

The man who arrived was short and bearded. He looked scruffy and like he needed a good wash. With thick glasses and bad breath, he asked if he could speak to me on my own. Mum said that, as I was recovering from an epileptic event, she would rather be present.

He shrugged. "Of course," he muttered.

He pulled papers from a tattered briefcase. "I'm sorry about your father," he said, "we're here to devise strategies to help you cope with the emotions produced by an event like this. How do you feel?"

I thought that was a stupid question but decided to play along. If I was honest, I was tired and drained, I just wanted to go home. "I'm upset and angry," I told him. "My life has been turned upside down, how would you feel?"

"Would you like me to arrange for you to talk to someone, a professional grief counsellor?"

It seemed like a good idea; I'd only spoken to people who were close to me. A different perspective might be a good thing.

"I don't know, maybe it would help me make sense of everything."

I looked at Mum. "It might help you," she said.

"Alright, but I'm moving house soon."

"We can arrange it quickly for you," he said. He stood, "I'll get right on it now. Good luck." He left, which meant we were almost free to go.

An hour later, a nurse, came in with my tablets. "Can you walk to the door?" she asked, "or shall I get Ron to push you?"

I could feel myself going red again, Mum noticed and gave me a look. "He's cute," I said. "But I want to try and walk."

It took me a while to make it to the entrance, I had to sit and get my breath back while we waited for a taxi.

Two days later, with less than a week to go before we moved, I was in a counsellor's office. Mum offered to come in with me, but I'd decided to do it on my own. He talked to me about my feelings and the state of my mental health. I explained a little about seeing the picture and the dreams. I told him I felt guilty for what had happened. All the time he nodded and wrote notes. I explained how I'd been told by my father to stop looking for answers but hadn't. He stopped writing and looked up.

"Guilt is a very powerful emotion," he said, "it can override most things and put you in a spiral. In the end, you can convince yourself that you're to blame for just about any set of random circumstances."

"But... if I hadn't," I started. He waved me to silence.

"Stop right there, never mind *but*. In all these things, there are a sequence of minor events, if they had occurred in any other order the result would have been completely different. You can't attribute what happened to a single cause, each one of those minor events has its own trigger. You have to accept that you might have done something completely different and got the same result, or done the same things on another day, even another hour and what happened would have been different. For example, if your father hadn't tripped, if he had broken his fall, if the man hadn't grabbed you, or if you had broken free before your father moved."

That was all true, but it hadn't happened any other way. I couldn't see the point of trying to think of it differently. "But none of those things happened. I still don't understand how you can help me."

"I want to change the way you think, break that habit of automatically looking for a way to ascribe blame to your actions when they were not the only ones. I'm putting you on a course of antidepressants and arranging some more sessions. If we can quieten your thoughts, we'll be able to help you to change them."

"I'm already taking a tablet," I said. "Topa, something."

"I saw that in your notes," he said. "These are called Escitalopram, they're safe to take together with the Topamax. They will make you feel a little strange at first, but after a month or so, you should start to feel the benefit of them."

Although he tried to find out more, I never told him about Dave, or too much about my dreams, which had been absent since before my father's death. I didn't want to make more trouble for myself or Mum than I already had.

"But I'm moving to Devon soon," I told him.

He handed me the prescription. "That's OK, perhaps it will help you to have a new start. I'll send your doctor a letter, it will go with your notes. When you see your new doctor, they'll have it, they'll be able to carry on helping you."

The last few days before we moved were hectic. Anne had gone back to get her house ready for us and resume her job. As well as all the stress of moving, there was saying goodbye to everything, the people and all the memories. At the same time, the tablets were starting to kick in and to be honest I wasn't feeling any better. I was feeling tired and groggy, I had a constant dull headache. I remembered that the doctor had said it would be at least a month until things improved, so I put up with it. I talked to Mum; she said if it hadn't gone by the time we moved we would have to see our new doctor as soon as we arrived. She'd already registered with Anne's surgery and had arranged for our notes to be sent on.

Packing up my room was a real wrench. Mum said I couldn't take everything because where we were going was a lot smaller. We were storing all our furniture in one of the farm outbuildings until we had a place of our own.

I asked Peta if she would look after some of my more treasured things, so I knew that they would be safe.

"Of course I will, silly," she said, "then you'll have to come back and see me if you want them."

"I'm never losing touch with you," I promised her. "I'll call you every night."

"You make sure you do," she said.

So I packed up a lot of the things I remembered from my younger days into a couple of boxes and gave them to her. She said she would put them in with her stuff and they would be safe until I wanted them back.

While we were sorting through the loft, Mum found the memory box. "I don't want this anymore," she said. "Let's just get rid of it."

I was shocked. "But you can't," I argued. "They're all the things in there from when I was little. I might want to show them to my children one day."

"Well, alright," she said, "but the newspaper goes. I don't want another reminder of what happened that day." She pulled out the newspaper and I got a last look at Ian Gisbon's face before she threw it into the black plastic bin bag.

I thought that Dave might have had something to say when he saw the picture again, but he wasn't there. In fact, he'd been there less and less since I started on the tablets. It felt strange not having him there, it was just another thing that wasn't there like Dad and soon this house. His absence made me feel just as bad as losing the rest of my world. If the tablets were making me feel less upset. I just wondered what on earth I would feel like if I wasn't taking them.

The saddest thing about that final day was leaving Peta. At least we could still communicate on our phones and video call. We promised that we would always be there for each other.

"Come back and stay with me when you're old enough," she said. "We mustn't stop being friends."

As we got into the taxi to take us to the station, I turned my head for one last look at the only home I'd ever known.

Peta and her mother stood arm-in-arm by the gate, both looked upset as they waved, until we turned a corner and the high hedges of the lane shut them out.

"Going somewhere nice?" asked the taxi driver. "A holiday away from winter?"

Mum was sitting next to me and she gripped my hand. "A new start," she whispered.

"Me and you," I said, it had become our mantra.

"Against the world," she answered.

"I don't think you need me to talk to you anymore, you're old enough to manage now," Dave said, unexpectedly. He had been less and less active in my head since the whole Ian Gisbon thing had started.

"Of course I do, I've missed you and I wanted to ask you about the things that have been going on in my head. When I needed you, you weren't there for me."

"I'm sorry, but I can't talk to you about all that," he replied. "I've been thinking, it's not that simple anymore. If you bring up all that stuff about Ian again, if we churn it around in your head, you're going to investigate more. In the end, you're going to tell someone about me and they'll think you're crazy. Hasn't there been enough turmoil? I'm staying in the background from now on."

"But I want to know, I need to know. Was this anything to do with you?"

There was silence.

Chapter 14

Ian

Long before Suzan's father hit the ground, I knew that I'd screwed up. And it made me feel bad. This was all my fault. I'd been impatient, once I'd seen the picture. The whole cascade of events that followed was the result. If only I had waited, like I had said I would. I had pointed Suzan at my old life, retreated and left her to it, when it would have been better to talk to her, to explain and persuade. Now it was too late to go back, I felt guilty but unwilling to tell her the real story.

The tablets that Suzan was on were a powerful mixture that made it a lot harder to communicate with her, even if I had wanted to. Just saying goodbye in the taxi took all of my strength. I was stuck in her body, with nowhere to go. All I could do now was wait, until a time when I could try to repair the damage I'd done. I still had a job to do, only now there was less chance of me being able to do it. That angered me.

The stress I had put her under had grown until it was too much for her. I could feel it building; all through the funeral, the alcohol she was consuming reminded me of my days as a person and it made me feel good. I know she was too young but I prodded her to have more, until there was the obvious problem that it loosened all her inhibitions. I worried that she might blurt out something about me but she never did.

At the school, the other girl, the one I had seen trip Suzan's father, deserved a lot more than she got. I did a bit to help there, I was angry at myself but what she had done was unforgivable, she needed to be taught a lesson. Suzan was upset enough to do what she did without my help but I stoked it a little and in the end, the two sets of emotions caused a bit of an overload, just like it had done when she was a baby and I was still trying to adjust to my new existence. The brain scans revealed my presence, just like they had all those years ago, except that nobody knew what they were looking at.

None of this was helping, it was time to retreat. Hadn't I done enough to her?

Chapter 15

Harold

On the Mediterranean coast of Spain, near the cement works at Alcanar, a large villa stood on the hillside, overlooking the sea. Surrounded by a high wall and fitted with stout gates, it was the home of a British man and his entourage. The locals viewed the place with some suspicion, remembering his sudden arrival several years ago. Maybe he was one of those English criminals, on the run, they thought, yet though the Guardia Civil were regular visitors to his house, it was never suggested that he was anything other than an honest, wealthy man, living in a foreign land.

To be fair, he ran a thriving business, exporting fruit and vegetables, spent his money in La Rapita, employed locals as cleaners and gardeners on good wages and never caused any trouble. And, unlike a lot of the British people living in the area, he flew the Catalan flag and had taken the trouble to learn Spanish, proper Catalan too, not the *Bastardo* slang the elite spoke in Madrid.

The owner was currently sitting on the terracotta tiled patio by the pool with a tall glass of wine, with an even taller blonde woman, currently kneeling in front of him.

In the house, the phone rang. He tried to blank the sound out, "keep on doing what you're doing," he muttered to the woman.

He was just getting back into the moment when there was a shout. "Sorry, call for you, boss." His bodyguard, Blue Tony, was one of the last links he had with the old days and the man who organised all his less-than-legal activities in England.

Life here in Spain had been good to him. The man formally known as Harold Mavis was now known to the locals as Harold James. It was near enough to his real name, and thanks to a friend of his, who had produced the necessary paperwork, he could prove it had always been his name. Should anyone be careless enough to ask.

"Who is it?" he shouted. They were just getting to the crucial part and he didn't want to get up from the pool and walk inside. It would mean breaking the moment, with Christina working her magic, breaking the moment was a bad thing.

"Harry, come on," Tony said. "It's Fitz, from Blighty, apparently it's important."

"Sorry, Christina," he said, getting up and adjusting his shorts. "Hold that thought, we'll have to continue this later." Christina nodded, her dark eyes sparkling with excitement. She wiped her lips with the back of her hand and took a drink as Harold headed inside. She knew that a call from Fitz, his right-hand man in England, was the only thing that could make him forget pleasure for a while.

Tony was wearing a shocked expression when Harold pushed past him. "I didn't want to disturb you, Harry," he said. "Fitz thinks we have a problem."

Harold picked up the phone. "What is it?" he snarled. "After what you've stopped me doing, it'd better be important."

"Sorry, Harry, I got wind of a report from somewhere out in the sticks from one of my friends, a journalist was investigating a weird story, something about a girl who had dreams."

Harold couldn't see the connection. "So, what can that possibly have to do with me? I'm clean in the UK now, I ceased to exist there a long time ago."

"Well, her dreams were about Ian Gisbon. Something about her being born on the day Gisbon died. She was having dreams of him, being killed by you, at Hendrix's old place."

There was a name Harold hadn't heard for years. If he thought back he could still remember the man, young and keen, so keen that his foolish enthusiasm had been the death of him.

"Ah, it all sounds interesting but how could a kid know? Only you and me know what really happened. There were no witnesses."

"I know, boss, it sounds impossible but there it was. I didn't get all the details but there must have been something. This journalist went to see the girl. Her father objected. There was a fuss, he fell and broke his neck. The police arrested the journalist and gave him a caution. I heard about it and managed to get a block put on publishing the story."

"Why bother me with this, Fitz? There's no way I can be linked to it, just get it sorted, it's what I pay you for. Find out who knows what and shut them up. I don't care what you do, who you have to kill, just make it go away."

"Will do, boss, leave it to me. I just thought it would be better if you heard it from me first. I have an idea of what to do. I'll get it organised."

The call ended and as Harold put the phone down, he wondered why Fitz was bothering him with a little local difficulty. It had been more than ten years since he had disappeared, without a whisper of a problem. Perhaps Fitz was getting careless in his old age. Surely he could arrange a couple of unfortunate accidents? Honestly, you couldn't get the staff these days.

Fitz would sort it, Harold was sure of that, now where was Christina, perhaps he could get the moment back?

He walked out towards the patio, hearing a splash from the pool. Christina was taking a dip, maybe he'd get in and join her first, anticipation was already building. After all, there was nothing else he had to do today.

Chapter 16

Suzan, seven years later

As I took another swig of cider from the plastic bottle, a few drops spilt down my chin. I wiped them away with the back of my hand and passed the bottle on to Frog.

"That Ian Gisbon, he messed my life up," I said, to anyone who would listen. *Not to mention Dave, the voice that used to be in my head,* I thought, except that I didn't say it. Both thoughts of Ian and Dave had been absent for a long time, but the resentment at what they had caused remained, like a festering wound. If I tried hard enough, I could blame one or the other of them for everything that had gone wrong in my life in the last seven years.

There were about fifteen of us, sat around a shelter in the park, drinking cheap cider and passing the joint around for a toke each. The October night was still warm, not yet time to huddle up or light a fire.

"Who's that Ian wossisname then?" said Frog, the man sitting on my left. His real name was Frankie but everyone called him Frog because of his croaky voice. He was after me but I was playing hard to get. Officially, I was Donnie's girl. Keeping Frog at arm's length kept both of us safe from his outbursts. We weren't officially an item, but we did make out. Donnie, when he was sober enough, wanted me to be his exclusive property, he had a temper if he thought I might not be. Absent-mindedly, Frog put his hand on my denim-clad knee. I knocked it off.

"A bloke where I used to live," I said, not wanting to tell him the whole story. "He's the reason I'm here and why I'm out of my mind."

"I thought that was the booze and the weed," said Donnie, sitting on my right. He was my cousin. I could add him to the list of people who had messed my life up after things had seemed so promising at one point.

As I said, I'd been in Devon for about seven years, today was my nineteenth birthday, not that I had much cause to celebrate. My mother was off with Roy, her new fella. She was always off with Roy lately, when she wasn't working. As a result, I had been dragged deeper and deeper into Donnie's world, more by default than anything else. He might have been three years older than me but he had been the only one who ever listened. I hadn't told him everything though, I'd learned my lesson about doing that.

"Not someone round here then," he sighed. "I thought I might be able to sort him out for you."

Bless him, in his own way, he was on my side. At least someone was. Sorting people out and supplying me and the rest of his followers with booze and weed were about the only things he was any good at.

I had been living in Devon since we had left our farm, but I couldn't remember much about a lot of my time here. My teenage years had all passed in a kind of haze. Everything that had happened since my dad died had been part of the same blur. I guess it had been caused by shock, then guilt and the tablets that I'd accepted to try and stabilize my brain, then the realisation that I was alone.

I'd been taken from my friends and deposited in a strange town, where I knew nobody. Even Dave, the voice in my head, had deserted me.

I hated life for what it had done to me. I'd thought about trying to come off the tablets so many times, but I didn't want the dreams again, so I never did. Being constantly tired and disinterested was in some ways better than feeling that knife slide into your body every time you slept. Then, thanks to Donnie, I discovered cheap cider, vodka and weed. And other things, but that was nothing to be proud of. Before I knew it, the years had rushed past, with hardly anything to show for it.

The weed was working its magic. As I closed my eyes, I got the familiar jumble of memories, snatches of the life I'd come to hate.

Chapter 17

The day we arrived in Devon, it was cold, dark and raining. Mum didn't drive so we travelled down on the train, an awkward journey that seemed to take forever. The trip across London, on the Underground, was like being in some sort of science fiction nightmare. With all our bags we were jostled and pushed around by a rushing mob.

I slept most of the way from Paddington to Ivybridge, the tablets that I'd been given made me feel so tired, I had trouble staying awake at all. Oblivion was nice though, it gave my thoughts a rest, which was what the counsellor had told me was important. Most of our possessions were in store, the things we needed that we couldn't carry with us were arriving when Peta's father could bring them down. Every time I woke, we were a little further west, until eventually, we got to Ivybridge and found Anne waiting for us.

We all climbed into her tiny car and she took us to her house, just outside a place called Tavistock. "It'll be nice to have some company," she said. "Martin, my ex, has just come out of prison, again. I told him I didn't want him back this time, I'd had enough. He's shacked up with some tart and Donnie has decided that I was wrong to throw him out. He lives with him most of the time. I'm on my own a lot."

That explained why she had been so funny, what they had been talking about that night when I'd thought they meant me. It seemed a little bizarre, choosing one parent over another. Donnie was lucky that he still had that choice. I had already decided that living with Anne could be difficult, so I thought it would be best to keep my mouth shut, at least until I knew a bit more about what was going on.

After living on the farm in the country, moving to Anne's house was a real shock to my system. It was a smaller house than ours had been, in the middle of a modern estate. The front garden was mostly concreted over for her car to sit on, with a small lawn in front of the door. Just one of a row of identical dwellings. Inside, it was tired and shabby. Anne had the biggest bedroom, with its own bathroom. Donnie's room was on the same level; even though he wasn't living there, it still contained a lot of his things. Mum and I took the others, up another floor and each side of a shower room. Mine was no more than a cupboard. I had a bed, a new flatpack chest and a wardrobe, that was it. There was hardly room to turn and thin curtains closed out a streetlight that was ten yards away. At least I had no trouble sleeping. It seemed like I could take the tablets and have no dreams but feel dead and unable to function.

One of the first things I did was to go to see my new doctor, by then it was nearly a month since I'd started the tablets. I still wasn't feeling much better, it was true that my thoughts had slowed down but the cost was tiredness and lethargy.

He looked at all my notes and listened to my story. "Well," he said, "it's good that you feel calmer but you need to be able to function. We can make some minor adjustments, I don't want to reduce the dosage of the Topamax until you've had another brain scan. I'm a little concerned that you were put on Escitalopram, it's not recommended for teenagers. So changing your antidepressants is something we can do that might help. As you've only been on these for a month, we can do what's called a direct switch.

Don't take any more Escitalopram, start the others tomorrow. The new one, Sertraline, is a slightly lower dose too, so you shouldn't feel so tired. It might be a bit strange for a couple of days, as you change over and your body gets used to it. Don't worry, if you have any problems you can always come and see me."

He scribbled out a prescription form. "Here you are, see how you get on with those. There's also a note here that says you should be seeing a counsellor. I'll arrange that and they'll be in touch. Come back and see me in a month anyway and we'll see how you're doing."

I hadn't been given a school to go to yet. Mum was out every day looking for work and houses, she was surprised to find that they weren't as cheap in Tavistock as she had expected. "I'm going to have to get a proper job," she said, "to make enough to be eligible for a mortgage. I've put our names down at the council as well, but there's a huge waiting list." It looked like we would be staying at Anne's for a while.

After a week, Anne managed to get Mum a job at the same local shop where she worked, which meant that every day, I was left at home on my own. Going back to school was never mentioned; anyway, I was too ill from the drugs to think about that.

While I swapped the tablets, I lounged around, feeling bored. As the Escitalopram wore off, before the Sertraline kicked in, I started to get the dreams again. I saw the warehouse and the knife, I felt the pain. I had no choice but to persevere and hope they went away again, even though I was frightened that these new pills wouldn't be any better, I had to try them.

I wanted to explore the local area but I'd been inside for so long that I was frightened to go out on my own, scared that I'd get lost or attract attention because I was different.

I needed someone to talk to. Mum was never about for a serious chat, I didn't know Anne well enough for a heart-to-heart and Dave was absent, no matter how much I asked him to appear and help me out. At least I could talk to Peta. She was about all that kept me going through those first few weeks. We called every night, in turn, spending hours just chatting about what had been going on in our lives. Although we talked about everything, I made it clear that I didn't want to discuss the voice in my head or what had happened because of it. It wasn't a subject I wanted to revisit.

"The voice in my head has never come back," I told her, in one of our first calls. "If you don't mind, I'd rather not be reminded of it."

"Fair enough, I can understand that," she said. The subject was never mentioned again. Instead, we shared details of each other's lives in our calls. She was doing so much more than me, but she never made it sound boastful, instead, she listened and sympathised with what I was going through. At first, I had nothing much to say, apart from how ill I felt and how lonely, then, after I'd seen the doctor, I had some better news.

"I'm still waiting to be given a place in the school," I told her. "The doctor has changed my tablets, I felt so tired and disinterested on the last ones. The only trouble is, I'm getting funny dreams again, as I change over."

"Poor you," she said. "I hope the new ones suit you better, and the dreams stop. Are they, you know, like the last ones?"

I didn't want to start that conversation again so I told her a lie. "No, they're about moving down here and weird versions of events from when I was little."

"Then I guess that's progress," she said. "Talking about bad dreams, it's a nightmare at school, since you've been gone. There're a lot more rules. Bec has left, thank goodness. I couldn't bear to see her and not you. It's just not the same anymore."

I felt like I was missing out, but had no energy to get annoyed, it just made me feel sad. "I miss you so much, Beano," I said.

"I know. How's your mum?" she asked.

"She's OK, working all hours. We want to get a place of our own. My Auntie Anne has been kind but it's not home."

It was conversations like that, every night, that kept me going. If it hadn't been for them, I don't know what I'd have done. On another, I told Peta that I was waiting for counselling. I confessed that I wasn't looking forward to it. She seemed unsure that it would help me, "I suppose you'll have to dredge it all up again," she said, "it can't be easy, to keep getting reminded, when all you want to do is forget."

She was right, I wasn't looking forward to reliving it all. To be honest, I must have been feeling better because I almost wanted to get back to being with people. Especially people who knew nothing about me, who would only know what I told them. I could reinvent myself and be what I wanted.

Because I wasn't at school, it was easy to go to the counsellors when the appointment came through. Anne took me in her car and waited outside for me. The counsellor was an older lady and over several sessions, she got me to talk about my feelings and about my guilt over what had happened. I was getting fed up with repeating my story, I just gave her the heavily edited version that I'd told everyone else, expecting to get the same responses.

She told me that the new tablets should help me to function and that as I was more able to do that, I would feel better about myself. She said that over time the guilt would go away in the same way that the grief would fade. I suppose it was all sensible stuff. She asked me what my hopes for the future were.

I said that I just wanted to have a normal life, I'd had far too much excitement so far and I just hoped things would calm down. I said I was looking forward to starting at a new school and making some friends. It was lonely sitting in the house all day while everyone else was out doing things. I mentioned that I was feeling anxious about going out.

She sympathised; told me that I seemed like a nice enough person and that she was sure I'd soon make lots of friends. She said it was a friendly area and that I ought to try a few walks or bus rides.

I just hoped she was right; we would just have to wait and see. At least the dreams had stopped now that I was settled on the new medication.

I went back to the doctor when I was running out of tablets. He was pleased that I seemed happier on the new medication. I told him that, apart from the occasional headache, I was feeling about ninety per cent better.

"That's pretty good for less than a month," he said, "considering where you were, we'll leave it like that. You'll get an appointment for your next scan; I don't need to see you again until then."

He arranged for a regular prescription of both my tablets. I left feeling positive, perhaps the counsellor was right and things were looking up.

I had walked to the doctor, it was a fine day, the views of the moorland in the distance were beautiful, everyone I'd met had smiled and most of them had said hello. I went into a café and had coffee and a cake, then got the bus home.

Chapter 18

And then there was school. After another two weeks, when the new tablets had settled and I was feeling so much better, the letter arrived.

"You're going to Donnie's school," Anne said when I told her. "Of course, he'll be three years above you and leaving this summer, perhaps he'll introduce you to some nice people."

I'd almost forgotten about Donnie, he had a room in the house but I'd never seen him. Anne rarely mentioned him, I got the impression that she was angry with him for choosing her husband over her. I thought it made him sound interesting.

I was looking forward to going, to getting back in the swing of learning and making friends.

When I first arrived, I was surprised to find it was a mixed school. I was used to a girl's school and it was a bit of a shock to find myself the centre of attention from the boys in my class, at least to begin with. Not being local, everyone wanted to know all about me. I wasn't too keen, I told them we'd moved here after my dad had died and of course that prompted all sorts of questions.

At least I wasn't too groggy from the drugs, I didn't tell them about that part of my life. I could function well enough to tell them that I didn't want to talk about it. I just clammed up. I told them it was too upsetting and that the police had told me not to discuss it. I thought that would make them shut up. All it did was make them ask me more.

The last thing I wanted to do was tell them the full story, that wouldn't do me any good. It all came to a head one lunchtime, I was surrounded by a group of kids who all started shouting questions. Was I saying nothing because I'd killed my dad? Was it a lie and he'd really run off with someone else? In the end, it all got too much for me, and I just stood there and let them push me around.

It was getting more violent and I was considering which one to try and punch first when there was a lull. "Do you know who this is?" said one of the boys. They stopped for a moment, still surrounding me. Nobody answered. "This is Donnie's cousin," they said.

"So," answered one of the bigger kids, "who cares about Donnie, he's all washed up anyway."

"Leave her alone," shouted a male voice and the crowd opened. A boy about three years older than me was standing there, looking at everyone.

"Listen you lot," he said, "this is my cousin, she's had a rough time of it. You're all to leave her alone unless you want to answer to me." He turned to the one who had said he was washed up. "As for you, Eddie Phillips," he said, "do you wanna come round behind the classrooms with me? I'll show you just how washed up I am."

"Sorry, Donnie," he muttered. "I'll make sure she's left alone now."

"That's good. Now clear off and remember what I said." There were mutterings of 'sorry, Donnie, whatever you say', as they dispersed, leaving the two of us. Donnie stuck out his hand and in a daze, I shook it. So this was the mysterious Donnie

"Thanks," I said, trying not to cry.

He dropped my hand, grinned, moved in and hugged me. "It'll be OK," he said. "They'll listen to me. If anyone gives you any grief, just let me know."

"I will," I said. "It's good to finally meet you."

"You're welcome," he said. "Everyone here knows who I am. Not only that, I know where they all live." He made it sound like a joke but I wondered if he meant it, after all, his father had been to prison, perhaps he could be violent.

I was grateful to Donnie for getting me out of trouble but it meant that nobody in my class wanted to be my friend. Because I'd been away from school so much, I found it hard to concentrate on the work and just did the bare minimum to keep me off the teacher's radar. There was so much catching up to do, so much I hadn't been taught. The teachers were mostly understanding, they must have been told to make allowances.

With nobody to talk to, I had no choice but to be friendly with Donnie and the people who hung around with him. They were a bit creepy and sycophantic, but they treated me OK. I found that being associated with them kept the pests off my back too, the bullies and the ones who kept asking me about the grisly details of my dad's death backed off when they saw me with Donnie.

Peta was quite shocked when I shared the information with her.

"It seems so different where you are," she said, "maybe it's because it's a mixed school."

"It's a weird place here, nobody seems to like people who aren't local. The school's a nightmare, too many bullies. My cousin has been sticking up for me."

"Is he handsome?"

"No, to be honest, he's a bit of a creep." But he's all I've got, I thought.

Despite Donnie's warning, one lad thought he would be abusive, not about my dad, just in general. According to him, I was all skin and bone.

Which was true, so it didn't upset me like he thought it would. I just laughed at him. Although I had filled out a little, I was still a different shape to most of the other girls of my age. I never told Donnie about it. I thought I'd dealt with it pretty well, he must have found out from someone else. Next thing I knew the boy had been beaten up on his way home from school, which shocked me. I asked Donnie if it was him. He just grinned and denied any knowledge of it. But he started walking me home.

Then Donnie introduced me to more of his mates, I started hanging around with them after school. They were older than my peers and their behaviour wasn't appropriate for someone of my age but nobody seemed to care and neither Mum nor Anne ever asked what I was doing.

So my life carried on. I took the tablets, did the schoolwork, went for scans and reviews, and was relieved when everything seemed normal. At the end of the school year, Donnie left but his influence remained. When the new school year started, people were still nervous around me and left me alone. In a way, I felt just as lonely as when I'd been sitting in the house on my own.

Then Donnie started to come round to the house when I had finished school, while Mum and Anne were out. Even though he was sallow and weedy, he had a strange magnetic sort of personality. The first time, he only stopped for a few minutes. "I just popped in to get some of my stuff," he said. "How are you doing?"

"I'm bored," I said. "Fed up with being on my own, doing homework. I want to get out and explore the countryside." I thought that he might tell me some good places to visit. Strangely, he didn't seem to know much about the countryside, considering he lived in Devon.

The second time he came around, he brought snacks and soft drinks. We watched TV and talked. He had been hurt by his parents breaking up and said that he blamed himself for it.

"Mum told me that they never argued until they had me," he said. "So, in my mind, the reason they split up was me."

OK, his suffering was different to mine but I could relate to the painful feeling that everything was your fault. Then, Donnie told me something interesting. "My dad says that I've got to keep an eye on you."

"Excuse me?"

"I know what you're thinking, he's done some bad things but that's all in the past. He's told me he's reformed. He's learned that a life in prison is no example to set me. He met a bloke the last time he was inside who helped him get his life together."

"And he wants you to keep an eye out for what?"

"You've had a rough time, he knows about that and so do I. You're in a new town, all the usual stuff."

Despite the air of menace, Donnie seemed like he was trying to help me. I couldn't understand why Anne didn't like her son. I was about to find out.

She arrived home with Mum one day while we were sitting around the kitchen table chatting and drinking tea. "What's he doing here?" she shouted.

"Hello, Mum," said Donnie. "I've just come round to see Suzan, we were chatting about this and that."

"Well, you can get out," she said. "I don't want you around here upsetting her."

"He's not upsetting me," I said.

She turned to me. "I didn't ask your opinion. I don't want you encouraging him." I felt deflated. That upset my mum.

"Anne," she said, "there's no need to talk to Suzan like that, she's only being friendly."

"This is my house and I don't want him in it," she said, "he's not a nice person. I don't like his father or all the people he hangs around with.

Donnie, you're not to come in this house when I'm not here. If you want any of your stuff, you can call and arrange a time to pick it up. Now get out."

Donnie shrugged. "OK," he said. "I'll see you around, Suzan."

"No, you won't," said Anne. "You're not to speak to her."

"I work near the school," he said.

"Well, you can keep out of her way."

He slammed the door behind him.

"Anne," said Mum, "don't talk to Suzan like that. She's not your daughter."

"I'm sorry," she said, "it's just that Donnie winds me up so much. I don't think it's wise for her to have anything to do with him, that's all."

"But he's been so kind to me," I explained. "Some kids were bullying me at school and he told them to leave me alone and they have."

"I'm not surprised, they're all scared of him and his mates, he'll beat them up if they don't. Or get someone else to do it for him. Is that the sort of person you want to associate with?"

"I've had enough of this; it seems to me that you don't want me around. You're always too busy doing something else to take any notice of me. And, when someone does take an interest and tries and look out for me you don't want them around either. What *do* you want?"

I stomped off to my bedroom and slammed the door. I was fed up with it, nobody wanted me, my dad was gone and now these people just wanted to shove me away. At least Donnie had been nice to me, whatever he was supposed to be like. I just wanted someone who would treat me right, respect and understand me and that's what he had done.

Once again, I felt as if I was of no account, someone else had gone from my life. I was sick and tired of losing people and being told what I could and couldn't do. I wanted to talk to Mum but she was always at work.

I called Peta, it was my turn, we had slipped from calling daily to weekly and sometimes even longer than that. She was still pleased to hear from me though and every time we chatted it felt like it had hardly been any time at all since we had last spoken.

"There's been an argument," I said, when she asked me how things were. "Donnie was round here and his mum arrived and threw him out."

"I thought you didn't like him."

"He's growing on me, he's not that bad."

"Well, that's progress, I suppose. Will you see him again?"

"I might, even though I've been told not to, apparently he's a bad influence, but nobody else has had any time for me."

Chapter 19

The next day, instead of going straight home from school, I went to see Donnie, at his father's house. The area had a run-down tired air about it, despite the backdrop of stunning countryside. Donnie answered the door, the house looked like it was a bit of a dump, there was broken furniture in the garden and stained curtains at the dirty windows.

"I'm sorry about what happened with Anne, when I saw you last," I said.

He shrugged, leaning against the doorframe. "That's OK, nothing to do with you, I'm used to it from her. I just wanted to come and see you. My dad said that I ought to look out for you, because you're new here and it would be nice for you to have someone you could talk to. Why don't you come in and meet him."

"I should go home," I said.

He grabbed my arm, gently. "I know he's got a reputation and he's not necessarily always been a good man but he's trying to do the right thing."

Five minutes shouldn't hurt, it seemed impolite not to. He must have heard me at the door. I went into the lounge where a large man was sitting on an old sofa, drinking tea.

"Hello, you must be Suzan, I'm Martin, Donnie's father," he said. "Sit down and have a cup of tea. Rach," he called out, "make our guest a cuppa."

He was a bit scary looking but very polite. A blonde woman, who must have been Rach, brought me a cup of tea and left us alone. She didn't look much older than me. She was skinny, with bleached hair, dressed in designer rip-offs. She left us alone, we sat and chatted. I told him about me and my life, he listened and nodded, obviously interested. We seemed to be getting on really well.

"Donnie is a good lad," he said. "Because of me, he has a reputation. People don't like him but he's done nothing to justify it. I told him to look out for you. It's hard moving to a new town, especially after what you've been through. The most important thing is that you shouldn't feel frightened about living here. I heard about the bullies at school, that's not on. Donnie told me and I said to him, you gotta look out for her and that's what he's been doing."

Despite what Anne had told me, I quite liked him. I could sense an undercurrent of repressed violence in him, although, to be fair, he was never anything but polite to me. We chatted for a while, then he said that he had to go out. I left, after promising to keep in touch, and walked home.

When I got back, there was another argument. Someone who knew Anne had seen me going to Martin's house. Then they phoned her with the news. I think that Anne had been winding Mum up, she was fuming.

"I thought you were told not to go there," said Mum. "Do you know what his father has been in prison for?" It was clear that she was very angry.

"But I wanted to see Donnie," I protested. "He's the only one that's been nice to me since we moved down here and I thought it was unfair the way you talked to him yesterday. That's why I went round his house to see him after school."

"Then you lied, you said you were going to some sort of school club. And I suppose you met Martin as well?"

"I did, he seemed nice. He certainly didn't ignore me. In fact, he said that he understood how I felt. He said that he told Donnie to make sure I was OK at school."

Mum didn't say anything but I could see that the dig had been noticed.

"So it begins," Anne said. "He'll be all nice until he's convinced you then, watch out. Don't you trust him."

"Listen to your aunt," added Mum.

"He was nice to me, he said that Donnie should be looking out for me, because of the bullies at school and because of the horrible things that happened in my life. He said we were family and I needed someone I could trust, someone I could turn to."

Anne laughed. "And you think that's him? He's just a criminal, he's just out for what he can get."

"Well," I said, "there's nothing much he can get from me so why is he doing it? Why is he being nice? I want to give him a chance."

"That's what you think, you silly girl. You still don't know what he's been in prison for, do you?"

"Why don't you tell me then?" I asked. "Give me a chance to make my own mind up about him."

"Drugs," she said. "He supplies drugs and hangs out with young people, getting them hooked. So he can ruin their lives and make money off of them. Just how old do you think Rachel is?" Before I could answer, she spat the words out, "He's got lucky, found himself a legal one this time."

So she was younger, so what, that part of her rant sounded like jealousy to me. I ignored her. "Don't worry, Mum," I tried to reassure her, "I'll be careful. I'm not stupid and if I don't like what Donnie or his father is up to, then I'll keep right out of it."

"I'm not happy, Suzan," she said. "You should listen to us. I worry about you after everything that's happened. I know that you've been having a tough time of it. I just want things to get better. All I ask is, just be careful."

"I will, Mum," I promised her.

I told Peta, the next time she called. "I've met Donnie's dad."

"Isn't that the jailbird?" she said.

"That's right. He's called Martin, I don't know what he did but I think it has something to do with drugs. And girls."

She gasped. "You be careful, I'd run a mile. I thought you said he was some sort of petty criminal who appeared to be going straight."

"Mum and Anne are frightened of him but, although he looked scary, he couldn't have been nicer to me."

She shook her head. "You're just like your father," she said, "stubborn."

Time passed and I got older. A lot of the next few years were as boring as the first six months had been eventful. Anne, Mum and I had an uneasy truce, moving house seemed to be off the menu. Mum never had enough money for that. I decided that I would leave school and get a job to help out, just as soon as I could.

One day, unexpectedly, Donnie left Tavistock and I lost touch with him. By now, I'd found a few people to talk to, they might have been friends of Donnie and the younger siblings of his gang members but at least I wasn't lonely.

I had drug reviews and brain scans, all showing no change. My tablets were working properly and were left alone. I'd settled on the regime now. I went from six months between scans to a year, then when I was sixteen, I was told that it would be two years until they needed to check me again.

I left school at the same time as Mum got a job in the offices of the shop that she used to work in. We heard that Martin had been arrested for some drug deal and was headed back to prison. At the same time, Donnie returned and tried, unsuccessfully, to come and live permanently with us. Anne wouldn't have him in the house. He said that he was taking his stuff and moving it all over to Rachel's.

A week later, I bumped into him in the park, on my way home from town. Donnie was distraught. "Dad's been in a fight in prison," he said. "I don't know all the details but it sounds really bad." Donnie was in such pain, I hugged him and sympathised.

"I liked your dad, that day I met him."

"He said the same."

"Send him my best wishes, won't you."

We were still hugging when Donnie moved his head from my shoulders and kissed me, full on the lips. It was a shock and I was about to pull away when I found that I quite liked it.

Chapter 20

"What are you going to do now you've left school?" asked Mum.

"No idea, I want to get a job, to help pay for things. Then, maybe we can get a place of our own."

After a bit of searching, I managed to get myself a job in a local shop, selling clothes. It was a lovely place to work, the people that came in were mainly around my age and I started to get to know a few of them.

Donnie came in one day and found some stuff that he liked. "Can you get me these, please?" he asked. "I've left my wallet at home. I'll pay you back for them."

It seemed such a little thing, a favour for a friend. "Of course, I will," I said and I put them through the till at the end of the day as if I was buying them myself. Which meant that I got a staff discount. I took them around after work, he was still in the house with Rachel. He didn't invite me in, he just stood in the door and gave me the money, in new ten-pound notes. Since we had kissed, he hadn't done anything more to take things further, which kind of disappointed me.

I told him the money was too much. "I get ten per cent off, for staff," I explained.

"Thanks," he said, "keep it. That's done me a real favour." Over the next few months, I saw a lot of his old friends. They all said that he had told them to come in and I would get them clothes with a discount. Pretty soon, I was selling loads of clothes, the place was really busy and the manager was happy. Then, things started to go missing.

As a new member of staff, their fingers were all pointed at me. I knew that I was scrupulously honest and, as everything I did at the till was on camera, I thought I was safe. The manager took me to one side and explained that although no one could prove anything, I had to go.

"But why?" I said. "I've done nothing wrong; I've brought loads of business to your shop with my cousin and all his friends."

"That's another part of the problem," he said. "We think that your friends have been stealing."

"But I've paid for everything they've bought," I said, "and if it wasn't for me working here, they wouldn't have been shopping here at all."

His face fell. "That's as maybe, some of the other staff have been complaining about you using your staff discount for half the population of the town. To be fair I think they've got a point, the shop's not designed to sell everything at a discount. As that's all that seems to be happening now and with the thefts as well, I'm afraid I'm going to have to let you go."

I realised that I'd been far too generous. I was angry with Donnie for taking advantage.

When I told him, he was furious. "That'll be one of the other employees," he said, "jealous of you, so they've been stealing and blaming it on you. I'll make sure that everyone knows, no one will ever go in there again."

I told him it was partly his fault for promising everyone a discount on my behalf. He just laughed. "You should have said no then. Look, I'm sorry that you lost your job over it, that was never the intention. Why don't you come round to the park tonight, a few of my friends will be there, we're having a couple of bottles of cider and a chat. It's my treat, no need to bring anything, perhaps it will help make it up to you."

We had a pleasant evening, with drink and food, everyone was apologetic and I felt better when I got home. I never told Mum. I was embarrassed and I wondered if I hadn't brought it all on myself. The last thing I needed was another lecture.

I continued to leave every morning as usual, as if I still had a job. Instead, I spent the day looking for one. The word must have gone around because nowhere would take me, even places that I knew wanted people. I wasn't 'what they were looking for'. One lunchtime, I was sitting in the park, eating a sausage roll, when I noticed a group in the far corner. It was Donnie and his mates, sitting around and drinking. I thought I might as well join them; one drink wouldn't hurt me.

And that was how it all started, a one-off night with a couple of bottles of cider, followed by a lunchtime when I was feeling down soon turned into every night. Vodka was added and then the weed came out and before I knew it, I was spending all my time in the park, even during the day. I didn't even bother to look for another job. I didn't need money, everything was free, from Donnie and his gang, as much as I wanted.

That was when Donnie and I started fooling around. One thing led to another and we almost became lovers. But not quite, although we did quite a lot of pretty heavy stuff, we never went all the way. Something always seemed to stop us. I was afraid of the commitment, annoyed that Donnie was only amorous when I was drunk.

Not only that, I saw that Donnie got angry if he thought I was looking at someone else, which scared me. It was easy, when I was sober, to say that I'd walk away, that the relationship was abusive and doing me no good. But like a moth to a flame, I couldn't leave the booze and the drugs alone. Which meant Donnie, since he supplied it all. I learned to modify my behaviour to keep him sweet and do most of what he wanted.

Before I'd realised it, my eighteenth birthday came and went, uncelebrated. I didn't care, life was passing in a haze.

To make matters worse, Peta and I were drifting apart. Every time I talked to her, she was full of chat about boys or fashion or music, she seemed to be living the dream. She was moving to London, she had a job and a flat, while Mum and I were barely existing. It shouldn't have been but it made me feel resentful. That made the long-repressed guilty thoughts come back, that our situation was all my fault. Gradually, our calls became less and less frequent. Once I was drunk, I couldn't be bothered to listen to it all.

It was around this time that Roy appeared and Mum dropped her bombshell news.

I found him and Mum on the sofa when I sneaked in late one evening from a drinking session in the park, although I didn't know who he was. I crept past them, hoping I'd be able to get to my bedroom unnoticed. As it happened, they were too busy snogging to see me.

The next morning, Mum was sheepish. "There's something I need to tell you," she said. "I've met a man; he has a house of his own and he wants me to move in with him. You're included, of course. I told him, if you want me, you get Suzan as well, we're a team."

It felt like I'd been punched in the stomach, I had no idea that Mum was doing anything else but work. "What? When? What about Dad?"

"I'm sorry I've been neglecting you, but I deserve a bit of happiness. I'm not trying to replace Dad, I couldn't ever do that, but it's been years since Dad. Roy is a nice bloke. You should come and meet him."

"How long has this been going on?"

"A few weeks, you've been so busy with work and seeing your friends in the evenings that I haven't had the chance to tell you before."

Even though I was shocked, I was pleased because it meant that we could get away from Anne, who always had a bad word for me and Donnie. I could see why he would want to live with Rachel. I knew Mum was getting fed up with Anne as well. I'd told her that I'd noticed she did a lot more work around the house than Anne did. She told me that I wasn't to repeat it, but that Anne wasn't as good a worker in the shop as she was, so she had been given a lot more duties. "If I'm lucky, I'll be a manager soon, then we'll definitely be able to get our own place." Maybe Roy would be good for her. As long as he left me alone, we'd get along just fine.

"Don't go straight out tonight," Mum said. I was just finishing my tea, after another day of pretending to be at work while I sat in the park. Anne was out somewhere, I thought that Mum was looking especially nice, she had done her hair in a huge clip and put on smart clothes.

"Why? Looks like you're off somewhere," I said. "Anyway, I have plans."

"Roy's coming to pick me up soon, wait and say hello, please."

I considered it for a moment, an hour wouldn't hurt. "OK."

There was a knock at the door and Mum looked flustered. "That'll be him, be nice," she said.

Roy was a tall, vaguely handsome man, about Mum's age. He looked nervous as he said hello and shook my hand. At least he didn't try to hug me, he had sense enough for that.

"Hello, Suzan," he said. "It's nice to meet you, your mother says you're always busy doing something."

I smiled, he wasn't too bad, there was a friendly sort of energy about him. He wasn't my dad, but as long as he didn't try to become him I could put up with him being around.

"That's right," I said, "and I have to go, have a nice evening." I left them to it and headed for the park and my real friends.

I didn't see him for a few days after that, it was almost as if he was keeping his distance from me. It was good to see Mum happy, but it still felt wrong to me in a way cos he wasn't who my mum was supposed to be with. Then things moved quickly. I woke up one day as Mum came into my room.

"Why haven't you done any packing?" she said. "Roy is bringing a van around today and we're off to his place."

"Isn't it a little sudden?"

"Don't you remember? I told you it was today, a couple of weeks ago."

I didn't but then, I had been drunk a lot. "So that's it then," I said. "Is he taking you away from me?"

"Not at all." She looked sad. "He's never going to do that. I would be off like a shot if he tried. He wants to talk to you but you're never around. You can help us move; it'll be an ideal time."

He didn't say much as we filled his van with boxes. When we arrived at his house and before we unloaded, Mum left us alone and we had a serious chat.

"It's time we talked," he said. "I know I'm not your dad and I never will be. I like your mother but I don't want to take his place in your life. That would be wrong. I just want to be your friend."

"Fair enough," I said. "I'll be your friend, but if you hurt her, you'll answer to me."

"Where were you?" asked Donnie, when I arrived in the park.

"We've moved," I said. "My mum's moved in with a bloke called Roy."

"Good for him," he said, passing me the bottle.

Life carried on for a while, the worst bit about sharing Roy's house was that, at night, I could hear my mum and him through the walls. Listening to them upset me. It should have been my dad. Although Roy might have been nice, he was still replacing Dad in my mum's life.

I wanted her to be happy, but it felt like she was pushing me even further away to make room for him. Since we had moved, she had been busy and there was never any time for us, now life was better and she should have had more time for me; instead, she concentrated on Roy and there still wasn't. That was why I was spending more and more time with Donnie and his gang, at least they listened to me.

Then one evening, I heard him talking to Mum, about how he was worried that I was wasting my life. She said that I could do what I wanted. That made me feel even more resentful.

Things all came to a head when Donnie and I argued one evening. About the usual thing. We were making out and he announced that it was time to take our relationship further. I told him no and he got angry. I was not so drunk that I couldn't walk away, but drunk enough for it to be noticeable when I got home.

Roy was fuming. "You're only just eighteen," he said, "you shouldn't be drunk like that, wandering the streets."

"I'm almost nineteen," I said, slurring my words. "And there's no law against enjoying yourself. Anyway, what do you care, you've got what you want, nobody gives a monkey's if I'm alright. At least the people I hang with look after me."

"You need to shape up," Roy said.

"Piss off, you're not my dad. Donnie and his mates are looking after me."

"I'll talk to you in the morning," he said, "when you're sober."

"Whatever," I replied. "Hadn't you better get back to taking my mum away from me?" I stomped off to bed to sleep it off.

The next morning, Mum and Roy gave me a lecture. My head was thumping and all I wanted was for them to clear off and leave me alone but I was stuck in the house with both of them.

"Your mum's worried about you," he said. She said nothing, just sat there, holding his hand.

"I know what you're going to say, I can look after myself. You can't tell me what to do, you're not my dad."

"I know that, but I care about you."

"Why?"

"Because I care about your mum. I've been following you."

I gasped. "You bastard," I said. "How dare you."

He shrugged. "You're a girl, not an adult. You said you have a job, you got fired months ago. You spend all your time in the park with a gang, drinking and smoking weed. Do you know where they get the drink? They're criminals, Suzan. Donnie is a drug dealer. They're using you. Soon, it won't just be a drink in the park. They're grooming you for their lifestyle. Once you've started, you'll be a criminal too."

"You're wrong, Donnie's family."

"It's not too late, you can straighten yourself out, sort out your life. While you still have a choice. Get away from those awful people that aren't doing you any good. Clean up your act and get yourself a proper life. If you want to do that, I'll help you and support you every step of the way."

"Whatever," I said. "If it makes you happy." As far as I was concerned, he was only doing this to keep in with my mum. He didn't care about me. If I humoured him, he might leave me alone. "Can I go now?" It was nearly lunchtime; Donnie would be waiting. I needed a drink.

And that's just about all I remember, from those seven wasted years.

Chapter 21

Another long day in the park was drawing to a close. Most of the people were dozing, I was in that drugged-up state where I loved everyone. Suddenly, there was a commotion, on the other side of the fire from us. There was lots of shouting and then silence. Roy appeared in the firelight.

"Come on, Suzan, you're coming home with me," he said.

"Mind your own business," sneered Donnie.

"Shut it," snapped Roy. "Suzan, your mum is going out of her mind with worry about you, I'm taking you away from these losers. You told her you were going to sort yourself out yet here you are, getting wasted again."

"I'm family," said Donnie, struggling to stand, he was that stoned. "You're not, you're just her mum's bit of rough."

"Stay down!" said Roy. "Get up and you'll be going back down. Come on, Suzan."

"She stays with me." Donnie had got to his feet and pulled a knife. I didn't know he had one. I had a sudden flashback, a warehouse, a knife waving around and then the sharp feeling as it entered my body. In my drunk and drugged state, I couldn't remember why it was important or what it meant. Hypnotised by the blade, I watched as Donnie waved it around. Roy calmly looked at him.

"Really?" he said. "You're holding it all wrong if you think you can stick me with it, you'll have to change your grip." Donnie looked down and Roy was on him like a flash. He grabbed Donnie's wrist and lifted it, spinning Donnie around until he yelped and dropped the blade.

"You're breaking my arm," he squealed, suddenly very sober. "Help me, lads," he shouted, looking around for his sycophants to help him. For a group who talked so loudly about sorting people out, they had all vanished. Roy kicked the knife into the fire.

"Listen very carefully," he hissed into Donnie's ear, "if you or any of your rabble come anywhere near Suzan again, you'll be sorry. Got it?" Donnie nodded.

Roy pushed him away and as Donnie staggered to stay upright, Roy kicked his backside, somehow, he kept his balance and ran into the shadows. "Come on, Suzan," Roy said, pulling me to my feet. I didn't protest as he lifted me over his shoulder and carried me home.

I woke up with a headache and reached for my morning tablets. As I swallowed them, I realised that I was not alone in the room.

"We're doing what we should have done ages ago." My mother was on the other side of the bed. "You're going to see the doctor about your medication, you should have had a scan. Then, we're getting your life back on track."

I could vaguely remember the events of last night; Roy carrying me away. I cringed, I couldn't go back, it would be too awful to have to face them. But I'd never admit that. "Clear off and let me get washed and dressed," I croaked. "You took me away from my friends. Do you have any idea how embarrassing that was?"

"How are those losers your friends?" Roy said. He was in here as well. I was shocked at the invasion of my privacy. "I got the impression they were just using you."

"We'll be waiting downstairs," said Mum.

"Please let me help you," said Roy when I finally appeared. Mum passed me a mug of black coffee, which I sipped.

"It's time," said Roy, "to sort yourself out."

"You're not saying much, Mum?" I said. Did I have the energy to fight anymore? "You haven't shown much interest in me in ages, we were supposed to be a team. Are you going to let him tell me what to do?"

"I know I've not been there as much as I should," she said, looking very shameful, "and I'm sorry for that. When we first moved, it was hard, I was still in shock and I concentrated on the wrong things. I can see that now. Perhaps a part of me even blamed you. I wanted to talk but I didn't know how, you were always so confrontational. Like your dad was at times." I saw a tear form and roll slowly down her cheek. "Then it all seemed like it was too late and I didn't know how to begin. If I could turn time back, I would but I can't, so I have to start from here. Please let us help you, I'll try harder."

I thought about it, Roy was right, I'd been drinking far too much, it was only mid-morning but I wanted a drink. As for the weed, I didn't smoke it all the time, maybe once or twice a week. I never felt addicted to it, not in the same way as I did the vodka.

I hugged her. "Fair enough, I haven't been perfect myself. I'll try to get sorted out."

"I've been looking at some information about the drugs you're taking," Roy continued. "You shouldn't be drinking with them and you shouldn't be smoking weed either. I'm surprised you haven't had more fits."

Even though I'd just agreed to change, the casual way he said it annoyed me, as did my mum's lack of protesting at the way he assumed the role that should have been my father's. The old me resurfaced for a moment. "What do you care? You're just the bloke my mum's with. No one ever told me not to drink."

"Of course not, you were only twelve when you first went on them. You were only sixteen at your last assessment. You should have been seen every year or so, for review and adjustment."

I shrugged, that made sense, although I wasn't going to admit it. "Then it must be due soon. What do you care anyway?"

"That's not fair, I'm very fond of your mother and I want to look after you both. I can see that your life will be ruined if you continue to hang around with those losers."

"Why do you care so much?"

"Will you stop fighting me? I'm trying to help you. You're supposed to have regular checks, to make sure the tablets are working properly."

"If you must know, I saw the nurse practitioner, not long before you came on the scene, she said everything was fine, I didn't need a scan and the prescription was renewed. I haven't had a fit since I've lived here. I've fallen asleep a few times and had headaches but that's probably the weed."

"Your review was due a year ago," he said. "Only you never went. Do you realise that the combination of drugs and lifestyle could kill you if you don't change?"

That stopped me, I hadn't realised how the time had passed. I'd been so busy getting stoned to notice. Neither had Mum or the doctors. It was three years since I had been seen and they had just kept on dishing out the pills.

"If you don't need them," Mum said, "you can come off them. You need to speak to the doctor and get a scan."

I suddenly felt scared, perhaps I was living on borrowed time. "Fair enough," I said, all the fight had gone out of me. "How do I start?"

"First, we stop the weed and the booze," he said.

"We're both here to help you," added Mum.

The first couple of days were the worst, I wanted a drink, I needed one. All I got was soup and water. Roy and Mum took turns staying with me. They kept me in the house, out of the way of Donnie and his friends, out of temptation.

To my surprise, neither Donnie nor any of the others ever came around to see what I was up to. I felt disappointed, even though Roy had warned him off. Donnie had always talked so tough, I was sure he would have come to rescue me. It was definitely not because I fancied him or anything like that. As my mind cleared, I remembered more about what we had done in the park; it made me squirm. I could see that Roy was right and what my life was going to be like if I didn't try to change.

Maybe I was lucky or maybe it was the effect of the other tablets I was on but after a few days, I started to feel less bothered if I didn't have a drink.

When I could, I went to see my doctor, the one who had been giving me anti-epileptic drugs and antidepressants for years. Mum came too. I asked him if I could have a scan. He was shocked that I hadn't had one at my last review. "We've been busy," he said, "your care was passed to the nurse practitioner instead of me, she missed the fact that you should have been scanned a year ago. I can only apologise. Leave it with me, I'll organise it."

"If it's alright, can I come off the tablets? I'm feeling better and I want to see if I can manage without them."

"Let's get the results first, then we'll see," was all he would say.

I was scanned a week later. Roy took me and Mum to Plymouth. After I had been put through the scanner, we went down to the Hoe and had a walk around. I'd been here seven years but hadn't seen the sea in all that time.

Looking out across the sound, with the empty horizon in the far distance made me feel like anything was possible. We went into a small pub on the Barbican and had a meal, I didn't even feel like a drink, I just had fizzy water.

I had to admit that Roy was quite good company, Mum wasn't too clingy and didn't show me up by kissing him in public or anything like that. They bought me some new clothes; I had no cash on me. I still had some savings in the bank. I'd been planning on spending it on booze but as it was all free in the park, I'd never touched it.

"I'll pay you back," I said as Roy waved his credit card at the till.

"If you can stay clean, I won't expect you to," he said. "I'll even get you a card, on my account, so you can get anything you need. But no cars or foreign trips, OK?"

When I went back for my results, the doctor was pleased. "We seem to have got away with missing a year," he said. "In fact, this scan is an improvement on the last one you had. There's a note from the consultant, he says that, as it shows no evidence of anything abnormal, it would be safe to come off the medication, as long as we continue to monitor you."

I came off the tablets over a couple of months, with Roy's help. As I did, I found out he was a nice bloke and I could see why Mum liked him.

To my surprise, as the tablets left my system, the dreams didn't come back and neither did Dave. I had expected both of them too, as I started to withdraw. Perhaps it meant that I had finally moved on. I didn't need a voice in my head anymore, I could cope perfectly well without it.

I needed to discuss things with someone female and Peta was the obvious choice. It had been far too long since we had spoken, I felt guilty for losing touch, she had been a point of stability in my life. I'd missed one of those. It looked like I had gained a male one with Roy but I needed my old friend, she knew things I could never discuss with anyone else.

But first, I would have to pluck up the courage to call her.

Chapter 22

When I was feeling a bit more like my old self, Mum suggested that I ought to think about going to see a therapist. I realised that I had wasted my teenage years when I should have been learning about myself. Instead, I had spent it in a drug-induced haze and in being led astray by the wrong sort of people.

I had felt so isolated, after my father's death and moving away from my friends. Back then it felt like I had lost everything in my life.

I was so angry with Mum. Even though I could sort of understand why she would want to get away. Add to that the fact that, once we had, I never saw her, the only person who was nice to me was grooming me for a life of drunkenness and it felt like a new man was taking my father's place; it was a recipe for disaster.

Now I was on a more even keel I could see that I had been wrong to feel that way. Mum was just doing what she could to survive. Roy was proving to be a good man, never a new father. If it hadn't been for him, I would have been in a lot of trouble and possibly either in prison or dead. True to his word, he had got me a credit card, "Just in case," he said.

I needed to talk to someone impartial, to get an objective view of everything and perhaps even to validate myself.

The therapist was an older man called Justin. He lived and worked in a big house in the centre of Tavistock, on a side road near the Bedford Hotel. The first time we talked, he asked me if I had wanted Mum to come in with me. I said no. He raised an eyebrow but said nothing.

We sat in armchairs, which was vaguely disappointing. I'd been expecting a couch. I thought that it would be like in the movies, where you lay back on red leather and watched a swinging pendulum until you fell asleep.

After a bit of small talk, we got down to business.

"Are you going to hypnotise me?" I asked.

"No," he said, "that's not how this works. Just relax and get comfortable, tell me a little about why you're here. What do you hope to get from this."

I told him about how my life was a mess, how I'd been having a drink and drug problem. "But," I said, "I'm trying to turn my life around."

"I see. When you say drugs, do you mean medication or recreational drugs?"

"Both," I admitted.

"It's alright, I'm not here to judge, or to break confidentiality, you can tell me anything."

Everything except the cause of it all, the voice in my head, I thought. If only I could have told people about that, from the start, how different my life might have turned out. But was that true? Dave had been gone for years now, was I using him as an excuse, did he even matter? The strange things he had said, even the coincidences about Harold, were they just that? Perhaps Peta's mum had been right, he was just my conscience, I didn't need him anymore, so he had gone. It would take me an age to explain it. Instead of mentioning it, I told him about my brain scans, how they had been normal and how I was coming off the tablets.

"That's good," he said, "very positive. And what do you hope to achieve, after you're off all the medication?"

"What I want, is to get back to normal, where I don't feel so responsible for everything."

"That sounds fair enough, and it seems like you've made a good start. Do you have a good support network?"

"I pushed them away for a while but they stuck by me, so yes, I would say that I have."

"Excellent, you can rarely do these things on your own." He paused for a moment. "Suzan, you sound like you've been angry, can you tell me if you still are?"

What sort of question was that? "Of course I am." I didn't mean to but I almost shouted it.

He hardly raised an eyebrow at the strength of my reply, He merely nodded, making a note on a pad. "It would be strange if you weren't. Who or what are you angry with?"

I hadn't thought of it in those terms. Was I angry with myself, for getting obsessed with a picture in an old newspaper? Or was I angry with Bec for listening to my conversation and blabbing to her father? Or was it the seizure I had suffered, after the fight in school, which had led to the medication? I wasn't lacking any number of reasons.

"Everyone," I said, "including myself. It would take me a long time to explain it all, from scratch."

"That's OK." He sounded so calm and gentle, I wondered what I could say to produce any emotion. "We have plenty of time. Just tell me as much as you want."

"My father's dead and it was all my fault," I started.

"Hmm, that's a lot of responsibility to claim. How old were you when he died?"

"I was twelve."

"Then unless you killed him yourself, it's unlikely that it is, and as you're sitting here and not in a secure environment, the police clearly don't think you did."

"But..." I was going to tell him that it didn't matter what anyone else thought, it was what I thought that mattered.

"We all feel guilt," he continued, "for any number of reasons. Why would you think that? No, wait," he changed the subject, "let me put it in another way, is it because of something you did or didn't do?"

What should I tell him about the thing that had changed my life?

"It all started when I saw a picture," I said.

"Go on." He leaned forward. "Tell me more."

I told him about the memory box and about the chain of events that led to me being here. I told him about Bec and her big mouth, the lies she had told her father, my dad and the fight, having to see the counsellor and being put on the medication. It was the same story that I'd told everyone over the years. He scribbled notes, looking alternately shocked and sad but said nothing except "go on" every time I stopped.

Then I told him about moving, about how I felt alienated and forgotten, about how I'd fallen in with my cousin. How things got worse, with the drink and the drugs and all the other things I'd done that I wished I hadn't. I told him things I hadn't told my mum, about everything that had gone on in my life. I told him about everything except Dave.

Why didn't I mention him? He'd gone from my life over seven years ago, it was as if I'd left him behind with Peta and everything else. Even so, I still felt some sort of loyalty to him, the thought also occurred that nobody would believe me anyway.

Now that I was getting clean, if I wanted them to think that I wasn't crazy the last thing I should do is start bringing up the voice in my head that told me what to do. That was never going to help.

He listened without comment, just let me spill it all out. Then, when I stopped, he sat back.

"Thank you for sharing it all," he said. "It must have been difficult for you, to live through it and to tell me about it. I imagine you've had to repeat it more than once over the years. The thing is, our minds are incredibly complex. Guilt is a powerful emotion. Your mind can attempt to justify your behaviour or explain what happens in so many ways. I can understand why the doctors put you on the anti-epileptic medication and the anti-depressants, I'm sure at the time because of your age they wouldn't have told you that you shouldn't be drinking or smoking cannabis when you're taking them. They don't mix, the combination can give you hallucinations and they can also make you feel guilty and paranoid and all sorts of other things as well, I think a lot of that explains why you are like you are."

I didn't remind him that a lot of my problems predated the tablets. I wasn't going to stir all that up again, now that I finally felt free from it all. "I've stopped drinking and smoking weed," I said, "I'm coming off the tablets, too, over the next couple of months. My last scan showed less unusual brain activity than the one before, my doctor says he wants to see how I get on with nothing in my system."

"I think it would probably be a good idea if you kept away from the drinking and the drugs as well, clean yourself right up. Can you come back and see me in six months and we can sort out the next steps?"

It sounded fair enough, reasonable even. Because I hadn't heard from Donnie, I didn't even have to try and sell it to him, or anyone else that I hung around with. In my mind, I was convinced that this was the way forward. I'd changed and I'd had enough of that life.

Chapter 23

As I was walking back to the bus, I felt a strange sensation in my head. It wasn't like a headache, it was more like someone opening a can of Coca-Cola and pouring it across my brain, a fizzing, bubbling feeling. I started to panic. Was I having another fit, just when I was hoping to be clear of all the substances I'd been taking? It had been a while but this felt different to how I remembered the last fit I'd had, back at my old school, after the fight. I stopped walking and leaned against a wall.

"Are you alright?" A lady put her hand on my arm. "You don't look well."

"I'm OK," I said. "I just had some pain in my head, it made me feel dizzy."

"Oh," she put her hand to her mouth, "you're one of those addicts, from the park, aren't you?"

"Not any more," I replied, the pain in my head was pulsing. "I used to be but I'm getting myself clean." I sagged and she supported me as I slumped against the wall. "Wait there," she said, "I'll get you some water."

As she walked away, I thought about what she had said. I hadn't noticed that we were that visible, it struck home to me how right Roy had been, I had been 'one of the addicts from the park'. It made me more determined to stay away from them and off any sort of drug. Then, I heard something that I hadn't heard for a long while.

"Hello, Suzan." It looked like Dave had returned. It was the first time I had sensed him in years. When I had needed him, he was gone, now I had learned to manage he was back. As if there wasn't enough going on in my life.

I felt a combination of shock and relief, I wasn't sure what to say, it had been so long. "Hello," I said, "where have you been?"

"The medication you were put on, after your father..." he explained, "it made me very weak, I could feel myself slipping away. So, I stayed quiet to protect myself, but I never stopped watching and all I wanted was to one day be able to talk to you again like I am now."

This was unexpected, Dave was different, almost as if he wasn't a part of me. I wasn't sure how I should deal with it. "Why are you back? I've got used to life without you. I've learned to make my own choices without your advice. I might have made a mess of things, but I've done it on my own. Now I'm starting to get my life back on track and you show up."

There was a shadow in front of me. "Here you are," the lady had returned, she passed me a bottle of water. It felt cool to my touch; I opened it and took a long drink. "Thank you," I said. "It's so kind of you."

"That's alright," she replied, "your eyelids were flickering, are you sure you're OK?"

I smiled, if only she knew what had just been going on. "I'm fine, just a bit dehydrated I guess," I took another drink, I wanted her to go so I could talk to Dave, but I didn't want to be rude. "Thank you for the water. I'm feeling better already."

"Can you stand?" she held out her gloved hand and I pulled myself upright. I didn't feel dizzy at all, the pain in my head had gone.

She looked at me. "Can I give you a lift home?"

I shook my head. "Thanks but I'm fine, I have things to do, I'll pay you for the water."

"No you won't," she said, passing me a small card. "If you ever need help, call me."

I stuffed it in my pocket as she walked away and I continued walking to the bus stop. "Are you still there?" I thought. Immediately Dave was back. And he sounded agitated.

"I need to warn you, about Roy, he's not who he wants you to think he is."

"Is that all you can say? You disappear for years, leave me just when I needed to talk to you, then you come back and the first thing you say is something bad about someone who's been here and helped me. You gave up the right to tell me what to do when you vanished."

"I've already explained that, it's a good job I'm back, this is important."

"I wondered about him, at the start, on my own," I said. "I was suspicious of his motives. Now I've got to know him, he seems alright to me. My mum likes him and he's been good to us both, so far."

"Just don't trust him, please."

"How can you say that?" This was one of those freaky conversations when Dave seemed to know more than he should. "If it wasn't for Roy, I would probably be dead or in prison. He saw what was happening to me and got me cleaned up and off the drugs. If it hadn't been for him, we wouldn't be having this conversation. I'd still be on the tablets, you'd still be locked in my head, unable to speak. I thought you'd bailed out and left me like everyone else did."

Then Dave said another weird thing. "I can't do that," he said. "I have no idea how this works. I didn't choose to be here but somehow I am. It would be wrong if I didn't tell you how I feel. I can read people. I can just tell when there's something not quite right about them. And Roy is one of those that gets me nervous."

"What about Donnie and his father?"

"I don't know, I was never really awake enough to get an impression of them."

"Well, I'm not going back to them, just so you can tell me they're not nice people," I said. "I thought that they were OK, that they had my interests at heart. Now I can see the truth. Donnie wanted an accomplice, a drinking partner and who knows, a lover he could control with drugs and booze. But I wouldn't do that, so he just got me stoned instead."

I didn't mention that he'd managed to make me do some things that I wasn't proud of, while I was under the influence. To be honest, I was embarrassed by the memory. Dave didn't comment, perhaps he hadn't seen that bit either.

"I understand why you're grateful," he said, "but think about it, what does Roy gain from helping you? He gets your mother's appreciation."

This was turning into a surreal experience. The way Dave talked had changed, or was it because I had grown up? I decided that it would be best to just go with it and see what my mind came up with.

"That's cynical of you," I said. "OK, I'll be careful. What I want to know is, why did you vanish? Not when I took the tablets, I can understand that bit, how they affected you, I know the way they affected me. I mean before that. When I started dreaming about the policeman. Where did you go? Because you weren't always there, sometimes you were in my head all the time and sometimes you went away for days or weeks."

"There's not a simple answer," he replied. "It was like being asleep but I never knew for how long it was going to be. When you were younger, I was awake more in your life. Sometimes I would talk to you and other times I'd just leave you to get on with it – especially if you seemed to be annoyed with me. Because of the tablets, I've spent a lot of time asleep. It was probably something else but I don't know what. I can tell you that I don't exist anywhere else when I'm not with you."

"I understand, but you still haven't told me why you vanished after I saw the picture of the dead policeman and had the dream?"

"You're never going to believe it but that was because of me."

That was another strange comment, or did he mean that, as part of my imagination, he'd caused my dream? I was so confused by what had happened in the last few minutes.

Dave was still talking, "it was all a terrible mistake. I put that dream in your head. Then I ran away and left you to it. Which was wrong. I'm sorry."

Now I was getting angry, I didn't understand what Dave was saying, it sounded like a strange way for a part of my brain to behave. "Why and how? You're only a part of my brain, not a separate person. Aren't you just a reflection of my conscience, or my guilt?"

"No, I'm not." He was definite in the way he said it. What was he talking about? Before I could ask, he started again. "I stopped talking to you because I realised that I'd gone too far. I would have had to explain it all, at a point in your life where you weren't able to cope with it. I needed you to do something for me but I should have waited until you were a lot older and more able to help."

That was a laugh, I was older and I could hardly say that I'd coped with my own life recently. What could it be?

"What do you mean, do something for you? That makes no sense. You're me. There's nothing that I want to do for myself, apart from sorting my life out. And I'm not even sure if it involves you, after so long. I'm getting by on my own."

"Ahh," he said, "you don't understand, even after all you've seen. There were enough clues, enough times I slipped up and almost gave the game away. It must have made you suspicious. It's time. Are you ready for what I'm about to tell you?"

Chapter 24

I had no idea what Dave would say but I was intrigued to see what my mind would come up with. I'd been told once that I had a vivid imagination, it was time to see if all the vodka and weed had dulled it. If I didn't like what Dave was telling me, I knew that I had the tools to shut him up, I could just go back on the medication. Almost without noticing, I'd reached the bus station. As I sat and waited, Dave started up again.

"Listen to me," he said. "You need to get away from here, get back in contact with Peta and get her help. This thing needs to be finished and it might be more than you can do on your own."

"And what is it, this mysterious thing that I was too young to handle?"

"You're not going to believe me," he said.

"That's a joke, right? After what's happened in my life, I think I'm ready to believe anything that helps to explain what's happened."

"You think I'm just a voice in your head, a part of your imagination. Well, I'm not."

That wasn't what I was expecting. It was so preposterous that I almost burst out laughing. I stopped myself, the people waiting with me would think I was crazy. But as the shock of it wore off a little, I realised that it made perfect sense. It felt like a truth bomb, like dynamite going off in my brain. Everything I had ever known was suddenly cast in a different light. The voice had been there forever. People had told me it was my conscience; the voice had never suggested it was anything more than that. Then I understood what Dave meant, there had been a couple of moments when I was younger, the voice had said weird things and I had wondered about it.

"What do you mean, you're not part of my imagination? You always said that you were."

"That's because it was easier for me to do that. The truth is... well at the time you wouldn't have believed the truth. I did try and show you but that was where all the trouble started."

"And that was when you ran away, hid in some dark corner of my head. What on earth do you mean?"

"I told you, it was me who showed you the dream." Dave said it calmly but the effect it had was anything but. I froze. I almost dropped the bottle.

"Do you mean the dream about the policeman?"

"Yes, that's right, I showed you that because that was me. And, it wasn't a dream, it was how Ian Gisbon was killed."

The bus came at that point and I was too dazed to get on. The driver shouted across, "Are you getting on or not?" I waved him away, the conversation with the voice in my head was more important. I couldn't work out if I was making it up or if it was real, the facts fitted but that was all.

"It can't be," I said. "How could I know what happened? I was busy being born at the time. That's just ridiculous, you're my conscience, you're not someone else, in my head."

"Oh," he said. "If only it was that simple. I don't know how it happened but it has to do with the moment you were born being the same moment that I died. Somehow I ended up in your head. You see, I'm Ian Gisbon, or what's left of him."

That was almost too much for me to take. It was a good job I didn't find this out while I was on the drink and the weed. Or perhaps it was only happening because I'd been on them. I might be clean but it didn't mean the effects had worn off.

"That's impossible, I can't believe that you're another person, talking in my head."

"I am," he said. "Think back. Did you never wonder how you found Beth's phone number? And how come it was right? It's because I knew it, I'd never forget it. And how about Harold Malvis? I used to shout it when you were little, but nobody could understand me. Your parents remembered, didn't they?"

That was so true, then I recalled the oak tree. "Did you sit under the oak tree with..."

"Beth," he said, "and Tommy. He was only just crawling around and we had to stop him from putting acorns in his mouth." I could feel emotions like pride and sadness all mixed up. They must have been Ian's. Everything he was saying, it all made sense, whether I liked it or not.

Never mind how it had happened, it looked pretty certain that I did have someone else living in my head.

"You need to help me finish the job I must have been put here to do," Dave said. "You're old enough to help me properly now. I have to find Harold Malvis and bring him to justice. If you do that, I promise that I'll be gone from your life, forever."

It was all very well to just say find Malvis, Ian had been away from the real world for a while. He wasn't even mentioned on the internet the last time I'd looked.

"How do you propose we do that?" I said. "It's nearly twenty years ago, he could be anywhere in the world."

"I don't know yet, that's why I need your help. And your friend Peta too. Malvis said he was going to Spain, just before, well you know. So that's where we can start."

"If you think I'm flying to Spain, I don't have enough money or a passport."

"We don't need to go, we just find him and send him a message. Something so important that it will make him come to England. Then we arrange to meet him, with police backup. He arrives, I say my piece then he gets arrested."

"Isn't that risky? Look what happened to you last time you tried it."

"It's completely different," he said. "I won't make the same mistakes again. For one thing, we won't be alone, without anybody knowing what's going on. We'll have backup. I'm not going to risk your life."

"But we'd be alone, before the police came in, or he wouldn't go for it. He's not stupid, he'll be expecting a trap. What about if it all goes wrong? He might bring reinforcements. What do I do if he attacks me with a knife? I don't want to end up stabbed like you were."

"You might have to defend yourself," he admitted. "I can help you, but I'm sure that it won't come to that."

I wasn't so convinced. He wanted me to face Malvis, someone who'd killed at least one person. Me, Suzan Halford, reformed addict. The idea of it made me feel sick, I couldn't do that. Maybe I could humour Ian until I could work out what else to do. I would have to go back on the tablets to shut this voice from my head.

I was angry. "So now you want my help after you've messed my life up. You ruined my teenage years and killed my father, for what? So you can get even with the man who killed you. Why am I even talking to you, you're not a real person, perhaps Justin was right and I'm going crazy. I think I'll go back on the tablets to get you out of my mind."

"Look," he said, "I'm sorry about that, I know it was wrong, it was stupid. When you found the picture, you were too young but I saw it and just couldn't help myself. I felt like time was wasting. Malvis was getting away with it. He was having a life while I wasn't. I needed to stop him. I just snapped, I was angry and thought that I'd waited long enough. I figured you could handle it. I remember how I was at age eleven and knew that I could have."

"Well, you soon found out that I couldn't, didn't you," I said. "What you did set a chain of events in motion. It was like ripples spreading out in a pond. Those dreams became my obsession and in the end, they killed my father. Because of that dream, I had to move here. I lost all my friends, had seven shitty years, drugged up and taken advantage of. For what? What have you achieved so far? I tried to call your wife; I got that wrong. I was too young and you used me without a thought for my mental health."

There was silence, I spoke into it. "Another thing, it would be easy for me to think of you as a parasite, and the one thing a parasite should never do is damage its host."

"You know," he said, "you're right, and you're so much more adult now, I suppose you could think of me as a parasite, but I don't want you to. I want us to be friends."

"Now that you want something, you want us to be friends?" I laughed, a man walking past gave me a very strange look.

"Can you find out if your friend Peta is living in London?" Dave said. I suppose I should think of him as Ian, that was going to take some time to get used to.

"Don't change the subject," I answered. "As far as I know, she does. I haven't been in touch with her for a long time, things happened."

"This is important, you need to get in touch with her and you need to get away from Roy, as quickly as you can. He's with your mother to get to you. Go home, when Roy's not around tell your mum you want to go to London to see Peta. She can help, you used to be so close."

It was so much against my better judgement, but he had a point about Peta. I did need to get in touch with her, getting away from here for a while wouldn't hurt me either. "I don't want to, let me think about it."

"Fair enough," he said. "If you don't want to help me, I can understand. But it means I'll be stuck in your head for the rest of your life, the only way you can get rid of me now is by finishing the job."

That felt like blackmail, I was seeing a different side of the voice. "So you still get your own way, or else. Is that what you're trying to tell me? Just remember, I could always go back on the tablets and blank you out."

Dave was silent. There was just too much going on, I felt as confused as I had after Dad died. I could see that, if I wasn't careful, I would be right back where I started. The next bus arrived and I headed home.

Roy was at home when I got there, Mum was out somewhere.

"Hello," he said, "I thought you'd have been home by now, where did you get to?"

It sounded innocent enough but after what Ian had said, I was suspicious of him. I had to act casual and watch for clues. At least until I could decide if what Dave, or Ian, had said was true.

"I missed the bus," I said, "got talking to someone and lost track of time."

"Oh, right, I wondered where you were. I was worried about you, you haven't been out much on your own, since…"

"I'm not tempted to go back to the park," I told him. "I saw them from the bus, it's not my life anymore." I didn't mention what the lady had said, how she had recognised me. Even so, she'd been kind, got me water and offered to talk to me. "I'm going for a shower," I said, "what's for tea?"

"Your mother's getting something on her way home."

In my room, I took off my coat and remembered the card I'd been given. I pulled it from my pocket.

As I saw who the lady was, I realised that she might be the only person who could help me make sense of what I'd learned today. I would have to get in touch and take her up on her offer.

Chapter 25

Ian

I was back. In a way, it felt like I had just been dozing, in that half-sleep where you know what's going on but you're too tired to do much about it.

I had watched as Suzan's life had descended; from the day she'd seen my picture. It had been rough for her, my ability to help or talk had been limited. First with my hesitation, after the realisation of my culpability in all the bad stuff in her life. Then because of the medication that she was given to help her deal with it. It was frustrating to feel time slipping away and watch Suzan's life unravel while being unable to do anything about it. The relief that I felt when she started to come off the medication was incredible, I knew that I'd soon be able to communicate, maybe this time I could do it properly. As I adjusted to a fuller range of sensory inputs, I could tell that there was a deviousness about Roy, I couldn't tell what but I knew he was up to no good. Suzan needed to be made aware of the danger she was in, as soon as possible.

I hadn't learned from my last mistake. As soon as I started talking to Suzan again, I realised that I had overreacted. Once again, I let my enthusiasm get the better of me. Instead of just saying hello and letting her get used to the idea that I was still there, it looked like I had blurted out my feelings about Roy and upset her. Not content with that, I'd let the cat out of the bag about who I was straight away.

How she took the news was a bit of a revelation. I had expected some anger, and I had got it. What I hadn't been ready for was a kind of resigned acceptance of the way things were. There was no forgiveness, that was understandable. I hadn't wanted to threaten her, but I needed her to get moving. It seemed like this time, she was old enough and mature enough to trust with the truth, the knowledge made me happy. Although her suggestion that she could just turn me off again frightened me.

Then I saw that she had a plan, she was going to do the one thing that could prove to her that I was who I said I was.

She had said that she could manage her life without me, that she wasn't sure I was who I said I was. Her plan was a good one, she had thought it up all on her own. I was proud of her, it was the logical way to proceed.

Already, I was looking forward to working with Suzan again.

Chapter 26

Suzan

As far as Mum and Roy were concerned, I was just going into town to look for a job. Since I had cleaned up my act, Mum had cared a lot more about what I was up to, she was keeping to her side of the deal. Roy was good for her, I could see that. But I didn't trust him enough to tell him where I was really going, just in case Ian was right.

Naturally they had asked where I was going. Roy had made me promise that I wasn't sneaking out to see Donnie. I told him that there was no way I was going back to my old life. I'd not seen Donnie or his friends around since Roy had intervened, not that I'd been looking. I'd avoided the park and all their usual haunts.

I'd called the number on the card the next day when I was alone.

"Do you remember me?" I asked the lady when she answered. "You gave me your card, and got me some water, yesterday."

"Of course I do," she replied. "When I saw you there, I knew there was something about you, I could sense it in your aura. Although we never touched skin to skin, I was close enough to feel that you had a lot of unresolved issues."

"Can I come to see you?" I asked. I wondered if she would ask me why, the way she talked, like Peta's mum, it sounded like she thought she already knew.

"Of course, how about tomorrow?" We agreed on a time and she made sure I knew where Paddons Row was. "It's a little hard to find," she explained. I told her I knew where it was and that I would see her there.

In the morning, I took an early bus back to Tavistock, then walked past Justin's house into town. Paddons Row was a quiet lane, through a low arch, near a coffee shop.

"Where are we going?" asked Dave, or should that be Ian. Hopefully, I'd soon find out for sure. At least he was respecting my privacy and not looking at my thoughts.

"You'll see."

With the feeling that I might be about to get the answers I'd been looking for, I knocked on the door.

"Come in and sit down," said the lady. She was dressed in normal clothes, a sweatshirt and jeans. "It's nice to see you again. Cup of tea?"

Claire Washford was going to help me find the truth about the voice in my head, one way or another. It seemed logical that a psychic medium would be the best person to tell me if the voice in my head was anything more than that, fate had pushed this one my way.

"What can I do for you, Peta?" she said, as she handed me my tea. I had been determined to tell her nothing, give her no clues, I'd even used a false name. I wanted her to have no chance of fooling me. I needed to see her honest reaction.

"Is it true that you speak to dead people?"

She gave me a strange look. "That's not how I'd describe it, dear, but I suppose that's what I do. I prefer to think of it as sensing the energy that's out there. Everything's a vibration, you know, and some of us can see different ones. I see the vibrations of people who've passed, they like to talk to me and send messages to their loved ones. I listen and pass them on, it helps to reassure the living that everything's going to be OK."

In my head, Ian said to me, "At last, someone who I can talk to, someone who understands."

I ignored him for a moment. "That's good," I said to Claire. "I think I'm in the right place. Something is going on in my head and it doesn't make sense to me and I just want you to confirm what it is. I'm not gonna tell you anything more than that, just see what you think."

"All right then," she said. "I love a challenge. Like I said, I knew there was something about you. I'm quite happy to do that; now if you just sit in the chair and relax. Let me take your hand, we'll see what we can see."

I tried to relax but the anticipation was killing me. I think she sensed it. "Just clear your thoughts," she said, "when you're ready take my hand." She pulled up a chair facing me as I tried to screw up the courage to take this next step.

"Are you ready, Dave, Ian, whoever you are?" I thought.

"Yes," he said, "let's get this done."

I reached out my hands and Claire took them.

I didn't know what to expect, it was like a jolt of electricity. Not as bad as when I'd had the fit in school, this was more like when I'd touched the electric fence, back on the farm. Except it went on and on and on. I had closed my eyes and now I opened them. Claire's face was contorted. Her eyelids flickered, it was like she was blinking in bright sunlight only at a ridiculously rapid pace.

"Slow down," I heard her say, "there's plenty of time. I'm here and I know. What do you want to tell me?"

Gradually the feeling passed and I felt my head relaxing. Claire suddenly let go of my hands and sat back. Her expression was one of shock.

She looked at me. "I see," she said, "why you needed to talk to me. I thought that there was a strange aura around you from the moment I saw you. It was much too strong to be yours. What I just heard was amazing. I've never experienced anything like that before. How long have you had Ian Gisbon living inside you?"

She knew, without me giving her any clues. And it was all true. The voice wasn't a part of me, it never had been. I felt relieved, at least that meant I wasn't crazy. What it did mean was something else. I'd have to come to terms with it, at least I had a starting point.

"All my life," I said. "He's always been there, talking to me, telling me things. I used to call him Dave. He went away for a while; I was on a lot of medication."

"You poor thing," she said. "Let me make some more tea and we can talk about what I've just experienced."

Over tea and biscuits, I told her everything that had happened, since before I had seen the picture. She looked shocked to hear it all. "That's awful," she said, "this must be a real surprise now, on top of everything else."

"In a way," I said, "telling me that he's not a figment of my imagination, or my conscience is a relief. It makes so much sense. Finding out that he's a real person who's somehow got stuck in my head, not so much. That bit is unsettling. I can't help thinking that he's responsible for all the bad things in my life?"

"Except it's not just your life is it?" she said. "Somehow, you have someone else's life force trapped inside you. I don't know how he got there, neither does he. He says he woke up in your head, while you were being born. It's been quite traumatic for him too."

"Are you siding with him? Am I crazy to even refer to a voice in my head as a person?"

"Not at all, I'm just trying to tell you that he's real. He says he was a policeman and as far as he can remember, he died a violent death."

This was a revelation. The hints I'd got over the years, the sudden interest in the picture, the attempt to call his widow, they all made sense. But the voice hadn't been honest, it had been manipulating me, ever since I had been aware of his presence. I was possessed. It was like my father had meant, all those years ago. As well as that, I felt violated and lied to. I also knew that meant I might be about to be used to get revenge, although Ian had called it justice. Would Claire know that too? Ian hadn't told her everything, or had he?

"What does he want?" I had to ask, I needed to see if he had told her what he had told me.

"Justice," she said, "he wants the man he says killed him to pay for his crimes. He says he's sorry to have messed you around so much, he never should have exposed you to his death and expected you to help when you were so young. He can see now that it was too much, how it destroyed you."

"So, what, I do this for him and he'll leave me alone?"

"He says so, it will give him closure and he can move on, to where he's supposed to be."

She had confirmed everything that Ian had told me. I hadn't been imagining him all these years. Now I had to decide if I was going to help him. If I did, how could I possibly do that? I needed some time to think.

"Can I do anything more for you?" Claire asked.

My head was full of questions. I wanted to know more but didn't know what to ask first.

"No, I might be back but at least I know where I stand, thank you."

"That's alright, dear," she said, "it looks like you have an important job to do, good luck."

I left and walked back through town to get the bus. I wanted some answers from Ian, about what it was like to live in my head. There was plenty of time for that. I had plans to make, about how I was going to deal with my new life and the responsibilities it brought.

My first thought was to call Gisbon's wife again. It hadn't gone well last time. Ian must have picked up on that.

"If you're going to call Beth," he said, "you could tell her that you need to see her, that you've found new evidence of who killed me, something that the police missed."

"What, after twenty years?"

"Why not? It happens."

I had the number in my phone, I'd kept a copy of it. When I dialled, a mechanical female voice said it was unobtainable.

"Well," said Ian, "that just means we're going to have to do this the hard way. The important thing now is to get to London, call Peta and get moving."

Chapter 27

Before I got on the bus, I went to a cashpoint and took out as much money as I could on Roy's credit card. I was going to need it. On the journey home, I was so much happier than I had been in a long time. It felt as if I'd achieved something. In a way, it was a relief to finally understand and make sense of it all. Trouble was, while I knew that I wasn't mad, I could hardly explain it to anyone else without them thinking I was. Except maybe Peta, who I hadn't bothered to keep in touch with.

I had to ask Ian the question that had been bothering me the most. "What's it like, being dead?"

"Why are you asking me?" he replied.

"I would have thought that was obvious."

"But I'm not dead, am I?"

I was confused by that. "Of course you are. You're not alive, I am."

"I'm as alive as you are, I can feel everything you feel, see everything you see. How else would you define being alive?"

"But I'm me. I'm in control," I persisted. "You can't do anything without me, you can't move my arms and legs, you can't make me look at something or make me say something. All you can do is just sit there in my head and talk to me, also in my head."

"Well," he said, "I'm certainly not dead because I can't see heaven or wherever else we might be going. I can't see any other dead people around me. I have no thoughts or sight of anything apart from what I get from your senses. I could ask you to let me have control but so far, I've chosen not to."

I wish I hadn't bothered asking him now. "So you don't know where we go when we die?"

"Of course not, like I said I don't feel dead. I feel as alive as I ever felt, just powerless."

I tried asking about something else that had been bothering me. "What was it like when I was under the influence of drugs and alcohol?"

"It was awful, I felt like I was as drugged as you were. I tried to talk to you, I wanted to help. The thing was, I couldn't summon up the effort. I felt bad enough, about showing you my life and the end of it when you were too young to cope with it. I caused you all those problems. And I could see what was happening, it was like watching a car crash in slow motion, you know it's going to happen but you can't move fast enough to stop it. If only I could have broken through the haze, I could have warned you about letting your life spiral down like that. It would have gone some way to making up for all the mistakes that I made."

That was quite a speech and I sensed his remorse. It was clear that he didn't want to be in my head, he seemed to be sorry. It made me feel more like helping him.

"Then why did you do it?"

"I hadn't meant to; it was seeing the photo. It did something to me, made me angry. Before that, I'd decided to wait till you were older before I told you the truth. When I saw the picture, I thought I'd show you the first part of my death as a dream, to see if you were adult enough to take it. When you started getting obsessed and making bits of the dream up, with the imagination that you possess, I realised that I'd gone too far. Then it was too late to stop it."

"So you showed me the rest. How did you think that would help? I was twelve. Of course I couldn't handle it."

He was silent. It was past the time for anger, the years had taken the edge off. "It's no good me raking it all up again," I said. "What's happened is past, I have to look to the future. I'm glad Roy got me away from Donnie, I couldn't see it at the time, I was angry but now it's all so clear. I'm going to help you."

"Thank you. I wish it had been different, all I can do is say how sorry I am, about your dad and moving and Donnie and everything."

"Let's start again then," I said. "Clean slate. One more thing. If you died and yet you're here, in my head, does that mean my dad is in someone else's head?"

"Oh dear," he replied, "that's far too difficult a question for me to answer. Even if he is, how would you know?"

That was true, it set me thinking, was my father stuck in someone else's head, with no way to communicate?

I sat in silence for a while. As we drove past the park, I could see a group over in the far corner, I was well away from them. I knew that I was going to be faced with a mission and I had a fairly good idea of what it would mean. If I ever wanted any inner peace, I was going to have to do what Ian wanted. The question was, how could I sell it to the real people in my life? Starting with Peta.

It had been a long time since we had spoken, we had sworn to stay in touch and, when I had first moved away, we talked just about every day. Over time it gradually became less frequent and faded away so that we only spoke at birthdays and Christmas. Even that stopped as our lives unfolded in separate directions.

It applied to both of us; with no shared friends or experiences we had nothing to say. There were only so many times you could discuss the past.

When I got home, there was nobody there. That was a relief. I made myself a sandwich and ate it while I plucked up the courage. Then I called Peta, this was going to be difficult.

"Hello," she said. She sounded happy to hear from me. "Are you OK? I've been wondering about you. You sounded so down last time, it worried me. I guess I should have called." There was a pause. "You know how it is."

"I'm fine," I said. "I should have kept in touch, things got pretty rough for a while but I'm over it now."

"I'm pleased," she replied. "We will have to speak more." It sounded like this might be easier than I had expected.

"I've got a problem and I need to see you," I said. "Can I come up to London and stay with you for a few days? I'd be no trouble and it's really important."

I heard a man's voice in the background, "Who's that?"

"Hang on, Stringy," she said. I expected her to mute me but I heard her say, "It's a friend of mine, Dunc, she needs my help, she wants to come and see us for a few days."

"Sure," the man said. "It'll be good to meet another one of your friends. Which one's this?"

"Suzan," she replied, while I listened.

"Oh yeah," he said. "I remember you talking about her. Wasn't she the one who moved away, years ago? What can we do to help her?"

"I'll tell you later," she said. They were sounding like an old married couple, was it right of me to intrude?

She was back with me. "Of course you can, Stringy. It'll be good to catch up. We never should have lost touch. Do you want to tell me what it's about?"

"There's far too much to tell you on the phone. You'd never believe half of it, Beano. The big thing is, Mum's got a new boyfriend and he's OK.

There's something that I have to do and I'm going to need some help to do it."

"That sounds exciting, when do you want to come up?"

"As soon as I can. I don't know what you're doing for work though. I haven't got a job, that's another story."

"Why not tomorrow?" she said. "I work really good shifts, so I can be around a lot. Call me on the way, I'll meet you at the station."

We chatted for a bit longer. "I have to go, Duncan's cooked and it's ready. See you tomorrow."

"Bye, Suzan, look forward to meeting you," shouted the male voice.

That was it, I was going. It sounded just like it had before, Peta was still my friend. I had some money in my pocket and a credit card. I would be off in the morning. It was a rush but at least I wouldn't have to hide it from Roy for too long.

When Mum came in from work, followed soon after by Roy, I kept quiet and tried to act as if nothing was happening. I was taking notice of Ian and decided that I wasn't going to say anything about me leaving until it was too late to stop me. I would leave after Roy had gone to work in the morning. Roy asked me how the job hunting had gone, I told him there were a couple of possibilities and I was waiting to hear.

I said I had a headache after tea and went to pack. I wanted to be ready for a quick getaway. I knew that there was a train from Ivybridge to London at ten in the morning and I needed to be on it. That meant I had to leave just after Roy to get there in time.

I hardly slept a wink, my phone warbled to wake me, just before I heard the door slam and Roy's car start as he left for work. I was dressed and ready to go in five minutes. I went downstairs, carrying my rucksack. "Where are you off to?" asked Mum.

I told her that I'd been in touch with Peta and that she had invited me to stay. She was initially suspicious. "It all seems to be a bit sudden, are you sure that's where you're going?"

"Yes." I showed her my phone, with the text I'd sent her this morning, *Beano, getting the train at ten*, followed by her reply, *Stringy, call me with the arrival time xx*.

"That's alright then," she said. "I worry about you, we both do. Seeing Peta will be good for you, after everything. It'll be nice to get away from here for a few days and see her again. You lost touch, didn't you?"

"We did and it was mostly my fault. Anyway, we're all good now."

"Are you going now? You missed saying cheerio to Roy."

"I know, I heard his car and rushed but I was too late. I have to go, the bus is in a few minutes and I've got a train in Ivybridge at ten."

She hugged me. "Look after yourself, I'm so glad that you're getting back to normal, you've been such a worry to us. I know I've not been a perfect mum but I've tried. Say hello to Peta from me. Be careful."

"I will."

As I turned to walk away, she said, "One last thing, before you go. Now your mind is clearing, from all the drugs and the other stuff, has Diana come back?"

I was shocked to hear her ask. "How do you know about Diana?"

"I know all about them," she smiled. "Peta's mum told me, a long time ago."

"Why didn't you ever say anything? I thought that only her and Peta knew."

"We talked about everything, I miss her, just as much as you miss Peta. She was so wise. Anyway, it's not my head. I agreed with Peta's mum at the time. It's just your conscience, your way of dealing with things. I expect you've had all the angst; you could always have spoken to me about it. I had weird thoughts when I was young too, I think everyone does, as they grow and try to make sense of it all."

If only I could tell her the truth.

"Did Dad know?" I had to ask.

She smiled. "He didn't need to, the way he thought, he would have been worried. You know he idolised you. More than me sometimes." She sighed. "To be honest, if your father hadn't died, I'd probably have left him by now. And that would have been nothing to do with you, before you wonder. Roy has shown me how happy I can be."

I felt sad as I walked to the bus stop. Another illusion had been shattered. I just hoped that Ian wasn't right about Roy, that he wouldn't take my absence out on her.

I was at the station, in front of the machine buying my ticket when there was a tap on my shoulder. I turned around to find Roy, looking over my shoulder. "Going to London?" he said. "And why would you be doing that?"

How did he know? Mum must have called him.

"I've been invited to go and see someone from where we used to live," I told him. "The person I was best friends with when I was younger. When my life went wrong, I ignored her, now I'm trying to make it right. Anyway, Mum knows and she's all for it."

He ignored that. I could feel Ian getting agitated. "I don't think you should go," he said. "I'm worried about how you'll cope, so soon after all that's happened."

"But that's why I need to go, I've known Peta since I can remember. I'll be safe enough with her and I can't stay here. I'm frightened that if I see Donnie or one of the gang, I'll get sucked back in."

"I suppose I can understand that," he said. "Just look after yourself and make sure you let us know where you are. Use the card if you need to get anything."

Despite what Ian said, I had grown fond of him. I bought my ticket and hugged him until the train arrived.

Chapter 28

Harold

"What is it, Fitz?" Malvis was trying to remember the last time they had spoken in person, it must have been several years ago, when the call had interrupted Christina. She had been fun but was long gone now, Alejandra, her latest replacement, was currently getting the hang of her duties.

"There's been a problem," Fitz announced.

"I don't like to hear about problems, Fitz, I pay you enough to ensure that there aren't any."

Fitz ignored that. "It's the girl, Suzan Halford, the one who said she knew all about Ian Gisbon."

Malvis could hardly remember, how long ago was it, eight or nine years? He had thought that when he'd heard no more from Fitz, it had all been sorted. So her name was Suzan. As if it mattered.

"That was years ago. I thought you'd have it sorted by now. You've never mentioned it in the meantime. So, what's changed now?"

Fitz ignored that too. "There was a complication. After her father died, she moved away and I got the story buried. I had a job tracking her down."

"Please tell me it's under control now, it'd better be."

"I thought it was, boss, she was living in some one-horse town out in the sticks. There was a bloke I knew, he was keeping an eye on her for me. He told me that she was out of it most of the time. She was drinking and on drugs, it looked like she was progressing to petty crime. Not enough to draw too much attention, it was just enough to discredit her if she ever spoke out."

It would have been easier to kill her, thought Harold, there would have been a fuss but it soon dies down. "Why didn't you just waste her? Sounds to me like you were losing your grip. Is that why you kept quiet, afraid that I might think you'd outgrown your usefulness?"

"No, boss, I thought that it was all under control. It was only a couple of days ago when I found out what was happening."

"The answer's obvious. Find her and kill her this time, no more going soft, cos it's a girl."

"That's as maybe. At the time, I thought I was doing the right thing. Anyhow, it all went tits up. She dried out and gave my man the slip, went to London to meet up with an old friend, someone called Peta, the one she lived next to when she was growing up."

"I don't want her autobiography or her travel plans. Just tell me what you're going to do."

"I've already found her again. My man says he's tracked them down. I'm sending two of my lads, Terry and Bogdan, to take them both out of the game, before they can say too much."

"Christ, Fitz, I don't need to know their names on a bloody phone call, just that they can get the job done. This should all have been sorted out a long time ago. Fitz, I'm disappointed in you."

"I can't afford to make too many waves, there's more going on here than you know." Fitz started to raise his voice. Harold waited for Fitz to spill the beans.

"My situation isn't secure," he admitted. "If I make the wrong move, everything comes out, all the things I've done over the years. I might end up taking you down with me."

"Is that a threat?"

"No, boss, just the truth."

"Text me the number of the bloke who's been keeping an eye," said Harold. "I want to speak to him directly." Malvis ended the call. He paced up and down until he heard the ping of a message arriving. He checked the screen and made a few calls of his own. Fitz was on thin ice.

Chapter 29

On the way to London, I watched the other people on the train. There was a real mixture, of families, singles and couples, all of them busy getting on with their lives. What would they think if they knew I was part of a crime-fighting team, on my way to smoke out and catch a master criminal? A girl on a twenty-year mission of revenge led by the voice of a dead policeman who was living in her head. It amused me to think that they were all blissfully unaware.

"Ian," I said. I was getting used to talking to him again, it was like old times but with the bonus of knowing that he wasn't me and I wasn't crazy, merely different. "Are there any more like us?"

"How do you mean, like us?"

"Well, people trapped in other people's bodies."

"No idea, I'm not psychic you know."

Of course, I knew that. The thing was, the nature of our relationship, what the medium had seen, made me think he was more like a spirit, able to go where he wanted. "But what do you think?" I wanted some reassurance after what I'd been thinking about my dad. It had played on my mind, that he could be inside anyone I saw on the street. What would he do if he recognised me?

"Well, since it happened to me and you, it's possible that it might have happened to other people too. I suppose, there's just no way of knowing."

"What I mean is, there might be people living what they think are normal lives, acting on impulses that they think are their own, but really they have another soul in their brain, directing their every move. Peta's mum thought you were just the voice of my conscience. What if the thing she," I nodded at a girl sitting opposite, eyes closed, listening to music, "thinks is her conscience isn't that at all."

"That's creepy," he said. It made me smile.

"And what you're doing isn't? She could be on a mission. Just like we are. Except she might not know it, yet."

There was silence. "I see what you mean," he said.

The train filled up as we got closer to London and I started to feel uncomfortable, I wasn't used to so many people. It was worse when we finally arrived. The platform was crowded and I felt hemmed in as I went through the ticket barrier. It was like crossing London had been, the day we had moved, all those years ago.

The first thing I saw on the other side was a huge cardboard sign, *Welcome Back Stringy*. It was written in sparkly nail varnish letters and decorated with rainbows. Underneath it was Peta. She didn't look any different to the last time I'd seen her, tall and lean with her hair in the same style. When she saw me, she dropped the sign and ran to me and we hugged for several minutes, not talking, just enjoying the contact. She seemed genuinely pleased to see me, as I was to see her.

We talked non-stop on the way back to her flat, catching up on all the details of each other's lives. She had a job, a good one, working in media relations, running publicity for people I'd never heard of. "I only work half days," she said, "unless someone has a big promo going on, or a tour, then it can get pretty hectic. Fortunately, those are all arranged well in advance, I've got a couple of quiet weeks."

Her place was cool, a spacious apartment, six floors up in a large block. The lounge had huge sliding doors, opening out onto a large balcony, complete with a metal table and chairs. It had a modern kitchen, great views of the city from every window and two bedrooms. I might have been in the spare room but it was bigger than the main bedroom at home, it even had a shower room attached. And the furniture was made out of real wood, not flatpack. What I did notice, when Peta showed me around, was evidence of male occupation.

"The man, I heard him on the phone?" I said, worried that I might be stepping on toes. "Will he mind me being here?"

"No, he won't, it's all pretty casual. He works shifts and only stays over on his days off. His name's Duncan, you heard him on the phone. You'll like him. What about you, any men in your life?"

I thought about Donnie, he didn't count. She must have seen my sad expression. "Sorry," she said, "bad ask."

We sat with wine and takeaway pizza. "I hope that's OK for you," Peta said. "Just help yourself to anything that I've got."

"It's great," I said, "I'll eat anything, except for black pudding." She laughed at the memory. Ian said nothing.

"Tell me everything," she said as we ate. "I want to know all about what's happened to you."

"There's a lot of bad," I said. "My life hasn't worked out as well as yours seems to have."

She shrugged, looked around the flat. "Don't let this place fool you. My life isn't some sort of perfect. Mum's gone, she had cancer and I miss her terribly. The man who replaced your dad on the farm wasn't as nice. My dad's still there but he can't wait to retire."

It seemed like we'd both had some rough patches. "Peta, I'm so sorry about your mum," I said. We hugged and I could feel her tears, hot on my shoulder.

"Tell me everything," she said when we broke apart. I opened up and told her all about the dark times I'd been through. As I told her more, she alternately gasped and shook her head. When I got to the bit about Donnie and the park, she eyed the wine dubiously. "Are you OK with that? I don't want to set anything off again."

"No, I'm cool." I sipped. It tasted good, nicer than vodka ever had.

"Anyhow," she said, "what can I do for you? You hinted that there was something that I could help you with."

"It's about Ian Gisbon," I said and her face fell.

"Not him again, hasn't he caused you enough trouble?"

"Listen, Beano, this is important and you've got to promise me that you won't freak out when I tell you."

"Don't tell me that you've been trying to call his wife again?"

"No, well only once but the number was unobtainable this time. I might be trying to find her again soon." I saw her shake her head. I took a big gulp of wine. "This is hard for me to tell you. Do you remember the voice in my head?"

"How could I forget? My mum said it was your conscience."

"That's right, she did. But it turns out that it isn't." I said it quietly but the effect it had on Peta was anything but. She put her wine glass down and gave me a very serious look.

"What are you on about?" she said. "After everything, I do hope you're not starting with this obsession again. All because of a photograph."

"Listen, Peta, this is serious, it explains everything. I won't pretend that it wasn't a shock to me but I've come to terms with it and I want you to as well. The voice went away, after Dad and the seizure. The drugs were suppressing it. Now I'm clean again, they've come back and they had a strange tale to tell me."

Peta sighed. "Why do you call it they? I suppose you're going to tell me, anyway. Go on then?"

I had to convince her that Dave was Ian, not just a part of me. At least I wasn't starting with her knowing nothing about his presence. "It's best if I give you an update. Do you remember, before I left, that I said that it had gone, or at least was around less?"

"Yes, I always thought it was funny that you gave it a name once, what was it... oh yeah, Diana."

Ian was on at me straight away. "Oh yeah, I wanted to talk to you about that."

"Chill, Ian," I thought. "I did that because I thought using a male name would be even worse. I was only seven."

"Well?" said Peta. I had to tear myself back to the conversation I was having in the world outside my head. "That was a lie, sorry. I called him Dave because he was a man's voice. I thought telling you that would make it sound even weirder. He told me that he went quiet because he knew he had messed up. He said that he had shown me too much of his life when I wasn't old enough to handle it. Now that I'm clean, he's back. And there's more to it than I ever realised. He's not just a voice in my head."

She put her glass down and gave me a puzzled look. "Hang on a minute, what do you mean? *He showed you his life*, are you saying that the dreams weren't dreams, they were real somehow? That would mean the voice in your head is really..."

"Ian Gisbon, the policeman in the picture, that's right."

She nearly fell off the chair. "No, you're having me on. That's crazy. He can't be, you mean like his soul is..." she frowned. "There are just too many questions already. How can it be?"

"Let me explain it properly. When I went to Devon, after Dad died, Dave had vanished completely. I've found out, because he told me, that was due to all the drugs. Because of the fit that I had at school, I was pumped full of them. Anti-epileptics for seizures, antidepressants for grief and feelings of guilt. I stayed on them for years. Then, when I started drinking and doing weed, the effects of them kept him even more hidden. I got clean, thanks to Mum's new partner, Roy, and that's when he came back."

"I think the weed has affected you more than you realise."

"Listen, Peta. OK, it was weird, but I have to believe it. I've gone to a lot of trouble to prove it to myself. I've not told anyone else this. Before I called you, I wanted confirmation of what he was telling me I had to do."

"You should hear yourself. And how did you get that?"

"I went to see a medium. I used a false name. I didn't give them any clues but they got the same story. She told me that the voice in my head was Ian Gisbon."

"Don't be daft."

"It's true, Peta. You know me, why else would I come all this way to see you? You're the only person I can trust. I can't tell Mum, I never could. And there's another thing, Ian doesn't like Mum's new fella, Roy. He says I can't trust him."

"Will you listen to yourself? Ian, the voice in your head, tells you that you can't trust someone that your mum likes, the man who saved you from a life of drunken debauchery, petty crime and who knows what else. Do you have any idea how plain stupid that sounds?"

"Of course I do, but you're the only person who knows about my previous relationship with Ian. I never knew Dave was Ian until he told me, that was only a week ago. Now, thanks to the medium, I know it's true. Ian wants me to find the man who killed him. If you remember, in the papers and all the research we did, nobody was ever arrested for killing him. Ian knows who it was, it was that Harold Malvis that we couldn't find anything out about. Ian wants me to find him and bring him to justice."

I don't know what I expected her to say. Maybe she would throw me out, or explode in fury, call me mad. She was quiet for what felt like several hours, although it could only have been a few seconds, as she picked another slice of pizza and took a bite.

"OK," she finally said. "Only because I know what happened before, I'm going to believe you. Suppose for a moment that I go along with this. If I decide to help you, how are we going to start?"

"I have no idea. But someone can't just vanish."

"The man who killed Ian, Harold Malvis, has." That was true enough.

"So far," I said. "Ian said that he told him he was going to Spain before he stabbed him. Will you help me, please?"

She looked shocked, which I suppose was understandable. "I haven't decided yet. But I'll tell you one thing. I'm not going to Spain. Let's sleep on it."

We cleared away and said goodnight. I couldn't sleep, Ian was excited. "Do you know where we are?" he said.

"Ian, I'm trying to go to sleep, why does it matter?"

"This is my old patch," he said. "I used to work in this area, my old station is just down the road. I bet some of my old team are still here. It's like an omen."

"Good," I said. "Let's think of it like that. Now can I get some rest?"

Chapter 30

I'd only just gone to sleep when I was woken. I could hear Peta on the phone. Before I drifted off again Ian asked me if I thought she would help.

"I hope so," I answered. "I'm doing my best to get you closure. If this doesn't work, then I don't know what else I can try. I don't have much money to stay somewhere if Peta can't or won't help us."

The next time I woke, Peta was knocking on the door, I could smell coffee and the sun was shining through the curtains. "Breakfast," she shouted.

I had a quick shower, dressed and joined her on the balcony. I was ready to hear her say that she wouldn't help me, but she was smiling.

"I hope you don't mind," she said, "but I mentioned your quest to my boyfriend when we spoke last night."

I had a sudden panic. "You didn't tell him about Ian, did you?"

"No, I don't want him thinking I'm as crazy as you probably are. I just said that you wanted my help to try to find someone you once knew."

"That's alright then, what did he say?"

"He wanted to know why you were looking for them. I told him that it was a person from our childhood. I said that it was to do with something that happened when you were younger, before we moved apart. I said that you'd been stewing on it for a long time, how we'd lost contact and now you wanted to find out more."

"He was cool with that?" It sounded a bit of a strange way to describe it all to me.

"He said he would do what he could. He has one more night shift, then a week off. He says that he'll help if he can."

"That's great, I appreciate it."

"You'll like him, in his line of work, he can find out lots of things that we can't."

"What does he do?"

"He's a policeman."

"That could be useful," said Ian. "I'm beginning to feel a lot more positive about this."

We talked while we ate toast. "What's your plan?" Peta asked me.

"I haven't decided yet. Ian doesn't know where to start. I told him that I needed to speak to you and see how you thought we could approach it. I'm so relieved that you've decided to help me. But there is one positive thing."

"What's that?"

"You live where he was a detective, so there may be people at his old station who know something."

"Of course," she said, "the shopping mall from the dream. Or should I say from Ian's reality? It's only a few miles from here."

"It's such a relief, knowing you'll help. Don't worry about how you think of us, it confuses me too. I was worried that I would have to do it all myself. I couldn't go back now."

"Did you think I would leave you hanging like that? It'll be like one of those shows on TV where friends team up to solve a crime. Wasn't there one where a dead detective helped his old partner?"

"I don't remember that one."

"I only vaguely recall it, not what happened, we can look it up on the internet." This was the Peta I remembered, bursting with enthusiasm. "So, what ideas have you got?"

"We need to speak to anyone who remembers Ian," I said. "Maybe we can find one of his old colleagues?"

"No," said Ian. "I've been thinking, I'd been wrong to get excited about talking to my old colleagues. One of them set me up. I'm sure they were protecting Malvis. We have to be careful, use people who weren't on the force then."

"Ian says no, he thought one of them was working for Malvis."

She looked at me. "Is he here now?" She sounded scared.

"Yes," I said.

In my head, Ian said, "Tell her not to be frightened, I'm quite safe. And thank her for believing in me and offering to help."

I repeated it. "I don't know how you do it," she said, "carrying him around like that. Don't you think it's a bit creepy, knowing that he can hear and see everything you do? What about when…, you know?"

It was my turn to squirm. "It always seemed so normal that I never thought about it. He's been gone for years, with the tablets and stuff. Since I found out the truth, I haven't, and after you just said that; I don't think I want to."

Ian had the good grace to refrain from commenting. Peta laughed. "It's going to be a nuisance, hearing him and repeating it all, can't he talk through you?"

"Well, Ian?" I said.

"I could talk," he said, "but then you couldn't, only one of us can be in control at any time. I think the constant switching might harm you, when we're both too active at the same time is when your brain activity is worse. If I tried to take over, or we kept swapping, you might have another fit. I don't want to make the same mistakes again and put you in any danger."

I couldn't be bothered to repeat all that. I just said, "No, it doesn't work that way. I'll manage."

"Fair enough. How about Ian's wife," said Peta. "I know it was a bust before but, well, we know better now. Do you still have the phone number?"

"I've tried it and it's no longer in service."

"Then we need to look for her online, see if we can pick her up that way. When was the last time you looked?"

"It's years; since I lived next door to you."

"When I spoke to Duncan this morning, he suggested some websites to try, as well as a few tips for searching for people." She pulled a laptop from a bag and set it up on the kitchen table.

We searched for Ian Gisbon. It gave me a strange feeling seeing all the results, where before there had been thousands, now, in the intervening years there were twice as many.

Ian was amazed to see just how much things had changed online since I had last looked.

"It's incredible," he said, "just how much information is out there. It would have made my old life so much easier. Before we try to find Beth, can we try Harold Malvis again?"

"Ian says let's look for Malvis first," I said.

"Sure," Peta typed the name into the search engine. The strange thing was, there was still nothing more about Malvis, just the same scattering of random sites that I had seen before.

"Don't you think that's weird, Beano?" I said. "The Gisbon stuff must have doubled, yet the Malvis stuff hasn't."

"I can vaguely remember that you said there was hardly anything before."

"The only explanation is that someone is hiding it all," said Ian. "I thought, back then that Malvis had high-level protection, from police officers on his payroll. Remember the dream, I was told to go home a different way, I'm sure that was to set me up to be killed because I was getting too close."

"But which policeman said it? Whoever it was, they must be the one."

"I'm trying to remember, it wasn't anyone in particular, it was just shouted out as I left, it could have been anyone in the room, or one of them repeating what he'd heard."

"Ian thinks it's been suppressed, he suspected that Malvis had a man working for him in the police," I said, it was easier than repeating everything that we'd just discussed.

"Fair enough. We've got distracted," said Peta. "Let's leave Malvis, just try to find Beth Gisbon."

We started on the most recent results. After an hour or so, Peta went to make coffee. We weren't getting very far. A lot of the new websites just repeated the same stuff, then we had a breakthrough. We found a fifteenth-anniversary appeal for information, it mentioned that Beth had remarried and settled in St Albans, a town north of London. Armed with her new name and using Duncan's suggestions, finding her was easy and we soon had an address for her. Her phone number wasn't listed, so we couldn't call and see if she would be in.

"That's good," said Ian, "we don't want to call her first, remember what happened last time."

"But we might travel all that way and miss her," I replied.

"Then we go back," he said. "This is too important to mess up now."

I told Peta what Ian had said.

"Makes sense, we can go and try to see her tomorrow," suggested Peta.

"Don't you have to work? It's Monday tomorrow."

"I'm only doing mornings this week, six till two. They're early starts but social media and publicity never sleep. It's always daytime somewhere in the world. Next week I'm doing afternoons, two till ten. If you can amuse yourself while I'm at work, we can do it when I get finished. Get to the station after lunch and buy two tickets. I'll meet you there and we'll head on up to her." She looked at her watch. "It's three in the afternoon," she exclaimed, "we've been online for ages. What shall we do for the rest of the day?"

We went out for a late lunch, to a small pub somewhere by the river. It was a warm day and so good to be out and feel normal. I drank sparkling water, not because I was frightened about drinking alcohol, but because I wanted to enjoy the taste of food again without the memories that drinking brought back.

I started to ask Peta about what had happened to everyone I remembered from school, what they had been doing and where they were. To my surprise, the ones I had thought were destined for great things had not always achieved much while others had blossomed. Hearing about them all made me start to well up. I had missed them all so much, their absence was another one of the reasons why my life had taken the course it had.

"What about Bec?" I'd left her till last, although she was the only one I really wanted to know about. After all, it was her that had been the most active in the demolition of my life. I expected to hear that she had blagged her way into a wonderful job with loads of money.

"She left our school, not long after you," Peta said. "Then, about three years ago, we heard that she killed herself."

"What?"

"Yes, news travels, you know. They bullied her at her new school, because of what happened. Her father got the sack from his job, then he was cautioned by the police for harassing you. It never went as far as court. Even so, no newspaper wanted a reporter with a police caution. He was forced to get any work he could. Bec blamed herself, one day they found them together in her father's car. They had ended it together."

I was devastated, it felt like such a waste. I gasped and dropped my glass. It shattered, stopping the buzz of conversation. Everyone looked at me, I felt like they could all read my mind.

"Are you OK?" asked Peta. I was too numb to say anything. I just nodded. A waiter appeared, with a brush and dustpan.

"Are you alright, miss?" he asked as he started to sweep up the fragments.

"I'm sorry," I said, "I just heard some bad news."

He finished cleaning up and departed. My mind was spinning, I heard Ian say, "Don't feel guilty about it, it's not your responsibility, she made her choices."

"Was there a note?" It sounded awful to ask but I had to know.

Peta nodded. "She said that she was sorry, that her lies had ruined everything for her family and yours. Her father wrote one too. He said that he had lost everything through his stupidity and desperation for one big story and this was the only way out."

"Can you see what you've done, Ian?" I said it out loud, though I didn't mean to. The waiter, bringing a new glass of water for me, gave me a strange look, put it on the table and scurried away.

Peta looked at me. "What do you mean?"

"I was talking to Ian," I said quietly. "It sort of slipped out. It's to do with what I was telling him a couple of days ago. It's all about ripples. I wanted him to understand what he did and what he's caused."

Ian was silent. "Think about it for a moment, Peta," I said. "What do you make of it all? Because Ian showed me a dream, my father's dead. Now I find that another two people are dead. I spent nearly eight years on medication, it ruined my life and my mother's life. Here I am, me, Suzan Halford, running around about to catch a criminal and it's all because a voice in my head, the soul of a dead man who hasn't moved on, couldn't wait. If he had only left it until I was eighteen or nineteen like I am now and then told me. I could have done things differently and those people would still be alive."

Peta nodded. "I can see that. What about Ian, though? From what you've said, he didn't want to be in your head, just like he didn't want to be dead. He thought that he was doing the right thing. He's trying to keep people safe, take a criminal out of circulation. He's left a family too, what's happened to them? If it was you, wouldn't you want revenge, as soon as you could get it?"

I thought about it, I'd wanted revenge on Bec for so long, was I pleased now I knew she was dead? Did it make things alright? It was something that I was going to have to get straight in my mind before things got too heavy.

After that, we went home. Peta had an early start in the morning so she excused herself and went to bed. I heard talking on the phone for a few minutes but I sat around watching some TV and had a mug of hot chocolate before I too went to bed.

It was strange how quickly Peta had accepted Ian as a part of me. After her initial shock, she was quite calm about the whole 'other person living inside my head' thing. It was a relief; I'd expected it to be much harder to convince her. I guess our history had a lot to do with it. She had known about Ian when he was Diana. Not only that, I felt comfortable here, with her, it was as if I'd never been away. I was sad about her losing her mother, she had been a lovely lady, so understanding and wise. I could feel myself getting maudlin. I needed to think of something else, be grateful for true friends and prepare for tomorrow's adventures.

Ian hadn't said much since I'd made a fuss about him and ripples, perhaps he was digesting the information. I didn't care. *If you can hear me, you'll have to sort it out, Ian,* I thought, it was how I felt.

In the morning, I didn't hear Peta get up and go to work. I woke late, got up and had a shower. I had nothing much to do till lunchtime, so I had some breakfast, then washed everything up and did a bit of cleaning and tidying around the flat.

I didn't need to be at St Pancreas station until just after two o'clock, the train was at half past. All I had to do was go and buy the tickets. Peta would be there in plenty of time.

I spent the morning wondering what I was going to say to Ian's wife. I decided that it might be better if I didn't mention that I had called all those years ago. She had said she got a lot of crank calls, with luck, mine would be lost among them. I'd never mentioned my name and the number had been withheld. I probably didn't sound the same either.

Of course, I talked to Ian, who was excited about the trip.

"I'm looking forward to seeing Beth again," he said, "even if it's only through your eyes. Hopefully, she won't think it's too strange and I can talk to her through you. I want you to give her a message; tell her how much I love her and miss her and how I'm sorry that I made such a mess of things. Who knows, maybe even I'll see Tommy, see how he's grown."

"There is one thing you should be prepared for though," I said.

"What's that?"

"Well, the fact that she's got someone else. You saw it when we searched for her new address. He might be there."

"You mean like your mum and Roy?"

"That's right, you have to accept that she's with someone else and stay calm. You mustn't do what I did at first and hate her for it. I hated Mum when she found Roy but what I didn't accept was that she was only trying to be happy. I thought it was almost as if she was pretending my dad didn't exist or that he didn't matter but I can see now that that was stupid of me. So, if we go to the house and there's another man with her, or maybe even more children you should accept it and not get angry." I didn't mention the other possibility, that Ian could overload my brain with emotion and I would have another fit.

"Do you know something," Ian said, "you're turning into a lovely adult. You're right and I'll do my best."

Now we had got that out of the way, I asked him the most important question. "Can you give me something I can tell her, something that will prove to her that it's you?" I asked.

"How about the black pudding?" he said. "Beth knew I liked it, she hated it, I had to eat it in cafés while I was at work."

"Don't mention the black pudding, please, I can still taste the stuff. There has to be more than that."

"Let me see her first, I don't want you to freak her out. If what you have to say upsets her, or it looks like she's not going to believe us, we might have to get out. I'd rather not put you in too much danger."

"But I thought this was what you wanted."

"I've learned my lesson. I look after you first. I want Malvis. I know I can get him and I understand that I can't get Beth back. Seeing her, knowing she's OK, even if she doesn't believe a word of it, will be enough for me. If she has more children, I don't think that they should have been mine. As long as she's happy, that's fine."

"And what about your son?"

"He won't remember me, he was too young, he was only one and it's nearly twenty years ago. He might not even be there."

Chapter 31

"What do you want?" Peta asked me. "Or should I be asking Ian that?" We were on the train, it was almost empty and nobody could hear what we were saying.

"I, well, Ian, wants to bring Malvis to justice."

"Is that what he says? If it was me, I'd want to kill him. I'd want to see him die."

"He says he wants him caught and sent to prison for a long time."

"And you're OK with that?"

"I have to be. I've seen his pain, I need to do this for him."

"But do you think it's going to be that easy? It might get violent, what will you do then? It won't be like the fights we had at school. Ian was stabbed, who's to say Malvis won't do the same to you? You might have to defend yourself, could you kill him before he kills you?"

"I don't know, Beano," I said. "It bothers me sometimes but Ian tells me that we won't be going to meet him unprepared. We'll tell the police all about the meeting and make sure that we have backup waiting. Ian says he'll help me organise it and if that's what I have to do I guess it's what I have to do."

"That's all very well and good," she said, "but you do realise that you might end up killing him? Or being killed by him if the police don't get there in time. What about if Ian was right, there's an accomplice of Malvis's who's working to keep him safe?"

"That was years ago; anyway, what choice do I have?"

Peta was silent, I knew she was right. In less than a minute, she'd crystalised all the misgivings I'd had and tried to ignore. The time for putting them off was running out.

In my head, I said, "Ian, you know that you said you'd never get me to do anything bad."

"I'm not," he said. "This isn't bad, what Malvis did was bad, this is good because it's the right thing to do. I agree there's a risk, but if we do it right, it should be fine. Violence would be the last resort, and only what's needed to keep you safe."

"I have to go along with it and trust that it'll all be OK," was all I could say to Peta. "Anyway, you'll be with me, he can't get all of us."

We got out at the station and took a taxi to Beth's house. I asked it to stop at the end of the street. I paid it off and we walked the rest of the way.

The house was modern, in a street where the houses on both sides were identical, built in pairs, with two garages between each pair. There were large front gardens and concrete driveways. A lot of the garages had windows and seemed to have been converted into extra rooms.

With a deep breath and a knot in my stomach, I knocked on the door. There was no answer.

"What should we do now?" said Peta. "We really should have found out if she was in before we came up here."

"We had no phone numbers. Anyway, Ian didn't want to," I said. "Remember he was worried that if she heard my voice it might spook her."

"We'll have to call a taxi and go back," said Peta. "This has been a waste of time and money."

"I know," I said. "We'll have to think of something else before we come up here again."

As we turned to walk away the door next to Beth's opened and an old man came out. "Hey you," he shouted, "what are you up to?"

"We're looking for someone," Peta replied. "Perhaps you can help us?"

"You're not reporters, are you?" he eyed us suspiciously. "You look young but then everyone does these days. There are still a few of them, coming around here hassling Beth. As if she hasn't had enough trouble in her life. Or are you looking for that lad Tommy? He's got girls coming out of his ears."

"Yes, that's right," I said, it wasn't an answer to either question but I hoped he might not notice. "We haven't got the phone number so we just thought we turn up and see if he was about."

He laughed. "He won't give out his number, just in case, reporters again, do you see? They try all sorts of tricks to get the story out of him and worm their way in. I keep an eye out for them."

"We're not reporters," Peta said.

"Well, you won't find any of the family here today," the man said. "They're not about. I know they aren't because I'm looking after the house and the cat for them. If you come back tomorrow, Beth will be here with the baby, after lunch. Helena comes in from school at four. No, she stays with a friend on Tuesdays. Tommy will be here with his dad, around half-past five, when they come home from work. Or," he said, "I suppose you could go and see him there."

He waited to see if we asked where that was. We both kept silent. "Oh well," he said, "if he didn't tell you, then you'll have to come back tomorrow."

He went back inside and the door shut. Five seconds later, he was peering out the window at us.

"We'd better go," said Peta. We walked to the end of the road while I called the taxi. What a waste of time today had been.

"So much for your idea," I said to Ian.

"Never mind," he replied, "it was never going to be easy. At least we know we have the right house, and we have a time when they'll be there."

I relayed that to Peta. "True," she said. "We'll be back tomorrow. We know that she'll be on her own from lunchtime till after five."

We sat in silence on the train, three of us in two bodies, all engrossed in our own thoughts.

"That man," Ian suddenly said, "did you notice how he called Beth's new husband Tommy's dad? That annoyed me, I'm Tommy's dad."

"Ian, you have to chill, I did warn you," I replied. "If Tommy was one when you died, he never knew you. That man has taken him on, brought him up. He's cared for him, he probably loves him too. Of course, Tommy's going to think of him as his dad. Maybe the neighbour didn't know the full story."

"No," he almost shouted it, "he knew, he said that reporters were still coming round and that Beth had lots of hassle, he knew all right."

I could feel a headache coming on, I had to calm him down. "But he didn't say it to upset you, as far as he knows you're not there. Don't get too excited, you'll give me another fit."

"Sorry, I wasn't thinking, it still hurts though," said Ian. "I know you're right but that doesn't change how I feel. And my Beth has two daughters as well as Tommy. We always wanted Tommy not to be an only child."

"You should be pleased for her," I suggested.

"I suppose," he replied, "it's just a shock. I might feel differently when I see her."

I debated talking about it with Peta. Maybe it wasn't a good idea?

As we got closer to home, Peta got more excited. "Duncan will be around tonight. You can finally meet him."

When we got back to Peta's flat, there was the smell of cooking as we opened the door. "Duncan's home," Peta squealed and ran into the kitchen. I left them to it and went to my room to wash my hair and give them some space.

I was drying my hair when Peta called me. "Come and meet Duncan, we're about to eat."

He was a tall, chunky bloke, very handsome. He shook my hand. "Pleased to meet you," he said in a deep baritone voice. "Peta's told me quite a bit, she was so excited when you got in touch. She said that she'd really missed you."

We ate spicy chicken and rice and while we did, Duncan filled me in on his life story. "I'm a police constable," he said. "I've only been qualified for a year but I'm doing OK."

"Can you help me then? Do you know what's going on?"

"Only that you need Peta to help you find someone. It's not officially allowed but I can ask around, off the record."

"I trust him," said Ian in my head, "you can tell him the name. Harold Malvis. Ask him if he knows about him."

"Thanks, Duncan. The man I'm looking for is called Harold Malvis, if you could find anything, it would be a great help."

His face was blank. "Never heard the name," he said, "but I tell you what. I'm over at the rugby club tomorrow evening, there will be a few people there that I can have a quiet word with after the training session."

"Duncan," said Peta, "be careful."

He looked serious. "Sure, what's this guy done, Suzan?"

"We think, well I think, that he might have killed someone, a long time ago, and he got away with it."

"That wasn't what I thought, from what Peta told me," he said. "Where are you getting the information from?"

"It's a long story, let's just say it has to do with what happened when I was very young."

He persisted; it must have been his police training taking over. "Peta said it was something to do with a journalist who killed himself."

I started to feel uncomfortable, I could feel myself going red.

"Duncan, leave it, you're not at work now," said Peta. "Probably best if you don't know too much. There's a lot of death, suicide and angst involved."

"I'd appreciate any help you can give me, Duncan," I added. "I've wasted too much time and this is becoming a bit of a crusade."

"OK," he said, "can you give me a rough date?"

"Around twenty years ago."

"Leave it with me." He smiled.

Chapter 32

Duncan and Peta weren't around the next morning. I had heard them being very active in the night, not that it bothered me. It wasn't the same as Roy and Mum and I was happy for her.

We were ready for another try to see Beth. Once again, I was going to meet her at the station with tickets.

"Did we keep you awake?" It was the first thing that Peta said to me when we had got ourselves settled on the train. "I was a bit vocal, I kind of forgot you were there."

"I heard you, not that I'm jealous or anything. Is that why Duncan wasn't here when I got up?"

She smiled. "I told him, he'd better not be hanging around. I haven't asked, do you have a boyfriend in Devon?"

I thought about drunken fumbles, fending Frog off and always being worried about Donnie's jealousy. Having to do what he wanted, when he wanted. It wasn't a good advert for relationships. "Not exactly, but that's OK, I'm not climbing the walls with unrequited lust."

"He was going to catch up with his mates today," she said, "and ask around this evening. He'll be back tomorrow, maybe he'll have some news for us."

Fortunately, this time there was a car parked outside the house when we arrived. As we walked past it, I spotted the child seat in the back. "I saw it, too," said Ian. "It's OK. I'm not going to go off on one."

The door opened not long after we had knocked. A dark-haired woman stood there. "Yes," she said, "how can I help you?"

"Were you Mrs Gisbon," I asked. Inside my head I could feel Ian's emotions, it felt sad and proud, all at the same time.

"Not anymore," she replied. "I'm Mrs Collins. That was a long time ago. I'm sorry." She started to shut the door.

"Come on, Stringy," said Peta.

"That's a shame," I said to the rapidly closing door. "We had some new information about Ian, sorry to have bothered you." The door stopped closing.

"Wait a moment," she said as we saw her face again. "What new information? Are you reporters? Or are you the two that Len next door told me about, from yesterday? Everyone here looks out for us, they've seen what happens, every anniversary."

Ian said, "Ask Beth about Tommy."

"Beth, please," I said, and she stood back.

"Just because you know my name, why should I talk to you?" she asked. "I have no idea who you are. Len said you were looking for Tommy."

"How is he?" I added. Anger flared in her face.

"Who are you?" She moved towards me. Peta grabbed me and pulled me back.

"Come on, Suze, this was a bad idea."

"Hang on a moment," the woman said. "Are you Suzan, the girl from years ago, you were going to be in the newspapers. You even called me once, didn't you? Perhaps you'd better come in, it's time that you told me what you know. Len said that you were looking for my Tommy, you're not, are you?"

"No," I said, "we're not. We didn't think it was appropriate to tell your neighbour everything. And about before, when I was twelve, I'm sorry about that. I never meant to upset you. After what happened to you over the years, I didn't think you would have remembered one call from a silly girl. Why did you say newspaper? The story was never published, the police told me that they'd stopped it. Perhaps you should know that my father died because of that reporter."

She was shocked. "I'm so sorry to hear that," she said. "The reporter called me, he told me that he was currently unable to print anything but that things might change in the future. He wanted a story ready, just in case. He came to my old house, we did an interview, pictures, the lot. Only I never heard from him again."

"Ripples," said Ian in my head. "It's so strange to see her again after all this time, she hardly looks a day older."

"Are you sad?" I asked him, which was probably a stupid thing to say.

"Yes and no," he said.

We sat in her front room; toys were scattered around on a brightly coloured playmat. "Please talk quietly," she said. "My little girl is asleep, she's only three. Now, what can you tell me about Ian, you look too young to know much."

"What did the reporter tell you?" I asked her, ignoring Ian's emotions, which I could feel so clearly. "Because I suspect that a lot of it was wrong."

"He told me that you had dreams about Ian. He said that you saw what happened through his eyes, that night..." She stopped for a moment and I thought she was going to cry. "I'm sorry, you'd think by now I could talk about it. He's been dead for three times longer than I knew him."

"What he told you is true," I said. "Back then, I was only twelve, that was what I saw. Please believe me when I say that I'm not trying to scam you or upset you. I've lived with this since then. There were times when I dreamed it, every night."

"But how? Why did you start dreaming about my Ian?"

I took a deep breath. "I saw a picture of him, on the front of an old newspaper. He died the day I was born, at about the same time. At first, I thought that the dreams were my imagination, making up a story. But that's changed now. I know why I was getting the dreams and it's going to surprise you. It blew my mind and it took me a lot of effort to prove it to myself."

"What do you mean?" She looked puzzled. "You say a lot but I get no answers. Are you some sort of psychic? Goodness knows I've had enough of them turn up here and try to convince me they were talking to Ian."

This was the big reveal, either she accepted what she was about to be told or I was in trouble. I heard Ian say, "Be convincing."

"Do you believe in reincarnation, the persistence of the soul?" I asked her. She shook her head. "I don't know, I've never really thought about it. What has that got to do with Ian?"

I took a deep breath. "Because Ian is living in my head."

She laughed, not just a giggle, but a full-blown explosion of mirth. She looked at me in the way you'd look at a fool who has just embarrassed themselves and put her hand gently on my arm. "That's the best one I've heard yet. Nobody's ever come up with that idea before. Ian's living in your head? Pull the other one. I'll ask you what I asked all the others. See how you get on."

"Fair enough, just consider this, were the others born at the exact moment that Ian died?"

She gave me a mocking look. "As if that makes any odds, except that you're too young to know what you're talking about. Prove it," she said. "Prove that you're not just another con artist. Don't you think that over the years since Ian died, I've had so many of them? They come here, they've done their research on the internet and they think they know all about Ian. They try and convince me, they've all failed." She was flushed, her voice raised. "To prove it, tell me something that nobody except Ian could possibly know. When you don't convince me, you can get the hell out of my life."

I didn't answer straight away, Ian was whispering something in my head, showing me a memory of him and Beth. I could feel myself going red when I realised what he was showing and telling me. As I remained quiet, she seized on it. "I thought so, what's the matter? Cat got your tongue?"

"Not at all," I said, "since you mentioned tongue." I got up, leaned over and whispered what Ian had told me, in her ear. I wasn't going to say it out loud, not in front of Peta. It was embarrassing enough repeating it, not that I didn't know what he was talking about. It had been a favourite fantasy of Donnie's when he was sober enough to articulate what he wanted.

Now it was her turn to go red, she pulled away and I stepped back. "How could you possibly know about me and Ian doing that?" she said. "Or about my birthmark?"

"Know it," I answered. "I've just seen it. Ian showed me, through his eyes."

The mood changed. I think Peta cottoned on at that point because she started to go red.

Beth looked surprised. "I couldn't imagine how anything you might tell me could be true, but I don't know how you could know that; unless it was."

She slumped in her chair and all the breath seemed to leave her. She looked broken. There was a painful silence and I wondered if I should say anything.

"Ian," she said, "are you really in there? How is it possible?"

"Tell her this," said Ian.

"Beth, this is Ian speaking," I told her, "through me. He's giving me the words."

She nodded. Ian spoke to me and I repeated it.

"My darling, I'm in this girl's head, I don't know how I ended up where I am but I'm sure it's for a reason. I wanted her to come here because I needed to see you one last time. I love you and I've never stopped. I'm sorry that I had to go when I did. Suzan is going to try to help me right some wrongs, I'm sure it's why I'm still here."

Beth started to cry. "Please tell her not to be upset," Ian said. I repeated it. If anything, it made the tears flow faster. Peta went over to her, sat beside her and put her arms around her.

"One more thing," I said. "I'd appreciate it if you didn't tell anyone what we've talked about."

"Are you crazy," she sobbed. "Who would believe me?"

"That journalist did, and it got my father killed. Then he killed himself, with his daughter."

She hardly reacted to that, I suppose after what she'd heard there was nothing else I could say to surprise her. "If it's caused you so much pain," she said, "then why did you come here?"

"Ian wanted to see you one last time. I didn't know who he was for so long. Now that I do, we have an understanding. It felt like the right thing to do."

She took my hand and looked right into my eyes. I found it unnerving.

"Are you in there, Ian?" she said, tears rolling down her face. "Ian, I'm happy now, not because you're gone but because I've got used to the idea and I've built a new life for myself." She seemed to be trying to make a decision. "Tommy is a fine boy, you'd be proud of him. He wants to be a policeman. He has two half-sisters now, Helena and Maeve. My new husband and I..." She stopped and sobbed again. "Wait a moment, I have something for you, let me go and get it."

While she was gone, I looked at Peta. "It's awkward isn't it," I said. "Ian was quite graphic in what he showed me."

Beth returned with a tattered box file, in an old plastic bag. "This is all Ian had from work," she said. "I kept it, never looked inside and never told anyone. Even though some of them asked. Ian said there was a corrupt policeman and I should only give it to someone I trusted. After, well you know, it never seemed to be important, until today. I think you should have it."

Ian was excited. "Tell her thanks. I'd forgotten all about that box," he said, which I did.

Her face lit up. "Do you remember, sitting at our old kitchen table, the one with the wobbly leg, and working on those papers?"

"Tell her I do, and tell her that what's in there is going to help me in what we have to do next."

She listened. "I was wondering about that, what does he want from you? I mean, what does he want you to do? Why is he in your head?"

"I can't answer all that," I said. "Ian doesn't know himself. All he can do is what he thinks is the right thing and that's to find the man who killed him. A man called Harold Malvis."

"I've never heard that name," she said.

"I never told you," Ian said. I repeated it.

"And what will happen, if or when you do?"

"Ian wants me to find Malvis, wherever in the world he is. Then, I have to get in touch with him somehow. I have to spin him a convincing story that makes him come to see me. Meet him somewhere so that the police can catch him. That way, Ian can have some sort of justice, so that he can be where he should be, in peace."

Her eyes widened. I could tell that she was working out what that might entail. "That's incredibly brave of you," she said, "helping like that. It's a risk, meeting him when he's already killed once."

She looked at her watch. "It's time you left. My husband and Tommy will be back soon. I have to protect them; will you go and never say anything about why you were here?"

"Of course we will," I said standing up. "One last thing, I expected you to freak out, call me crazy or call the police, yet you took it so calmly. Why?"

She smiled at me as she went to open the door. "You were so close to being thrown out," she said, "but there was something about you, an aura of kindness. You're not like the others, it's not about you."

"I'm not doing it for me," I said, "goodness knows how much harder this has made my life."

"You know," she said, "I remembered all those people who said that, if anything happened to them, they would find a way to tell their loved ones that they were OK. Ian and I never discussed it but we both knew what might happen. When he'd gone, I wondered if he would be able to get me a message. When people started turning up, claiming to have been in contact, they were all so obviously fake that I thought it wouldn't be possible. I wanted a message so definite that I would have no choice but to accept it was him. All the others who've tried to convince me they were in touch with him could never prove it to me but you, well, let's just say that you were more convincing."

As we left the house, a car pulled to a stop in the drive. "My husband is here," she said, "and Tommy. Not a word, please. Goodbye, and good luck."

Two people got out of the car, a tall, distinguished-looking man, and a younger man who emerged from the passenger side. "What's going on, Mum?" the younger one shouted. I looked, it was Ian, from the picture. No, it can't have been; it must be Tommy.

"These two were trying to convert me," she said. "They're just leaving."

In my head, Ian said, "I kept my promise, look at him, just like me. I'm so proud, thank you, Suzan."

"What did you tell her?" asked Peta, we were back on the train again. "She went red. So did you. Was it something to do with their sex life?"

I avoided answering the question. "Do you know what the worst bit about Ian being in my head is? It's that I can see and feel his memories, what he saw and heard and felt. I mean him getting murdered was bad enough, that felt horrible but what he showed me today, well just seeing it from his point of view was a shock and quite different to being on the receiving end."

Peta looked shocked. "I suppose it's the difference between being male and female," she said. "It's the same thing happening but you see it differently."

If I had thought that Ian would say anything at that point, I was wrong. "Well," I thought, "I know I asked for something that would prove it was you, but did you have to show me that?"

"It got her attention," he said, "so I guess it was worth it. I didn't embarrass you too much did I?"

I thought back, to drunken fumbles and the memories of what I'd done with Donnie. At least Ian hadn't been watching, or if he had, he wasn't mentioning it.

"It's OK," I said, "I'm not a stranger to the idea, it was just having to tell Beth."

There was a second's silence.

"Thank you for what you did today," Ian said. "You don't know how much it means to me, seeing Beth and having her believe that it was me. Not only that, we have the box. I never thought that it would have survived. All my investigation notes are in there, I kept separate copies. All my work on Malvis. I didn't want anyone to see it until I had enough to take it to a senior officer I could trust."

"Does it say who the person you suspect is?"

"No, but there's a list of possibles."

"What about Duncan? Should we show whatever's in this box to him?"

"Wait a bit," said Ian. "Let's see if he wants to get involved first."

"Stringy," Peta nudged me, "I'm talking to you, am I interrupting you talking to Ian?" asked Peta, "you looked as if you were miles away."

"I was, we were just talking about the box. Ian's pleased, he says it's all his notes, from when he was hunting Malvis."

"That's good," she said, "it might be useful. When Duncan tells us what he's found, we can add it all together."

When we got back to the flat, I put the box, still in its bag, in my holdall. I didn't want to see inside it, yet.

Chapter 33

Peta was at work when I woke up. I was excited because Duncan should be around later with news. So was Ian. "It'll be good to talk to a fellow policeman," he said, "if I decide that he's up to the truth. Perhaps, with what he has found out and what I know, we can move forward."

I was in such a nervous state that I decided to go for a walk around the area after I'd eaten breakfast. Peta could do with some milk and I wanted to get out. To be honest, I already missed the countryside. I took the stairs, I needed the exercise. Once I got to the ground floor, I almost wished that I hadn't bothered. Everywhere was concreted, there were gangs of people hanging around and everyone avoided eye contact as they scurried about. It was nothing at all like Tavistock.

I found a shop, bought milk and a few other things and lugged them back to the flat. The lift wasn't working, so I had to carry my shopping up all the steps. It felt like I was being watched or followed but nobody came close. I was relieved when I shut the door behind me.

"It's not nice here," I said to Ian as I put the groceries away.

"Things have got worse since I was here last," he agreed. "You have to be careful, it's not like Devon, walk defensively and try to avoid deserted spaces and alleyways."

What a way to live. It was all very well having a nice flat. If you didn't feel safe using it, what was the point?

Peta arrived home from work at half past two. "Hi Stringy, what have you been up to?"

"I went out to the local shops, we needed milk. I got biscuits and a few other bits," I said. "It's not like home here."

"You get used to it. Did you use the stairs? I forgot to tell you, there's another set of lifts around the end of the corridor. Thanks for the food but you shouldn't have. I get a delivery on Thursdays."

"It's OK, I had to go out. I was so wound up, waiting for Duncan, wondering if he'll have any news for us."

"He should be around soon," she said, "he knows I finish at two." She was putting the kettle on when her phone rang. "That'll be him, on his way," she said. She put the call on speaker so I could hear him.

"I'm sorry, babe," he said, "I have to work an overtime shift tonight, we'll have to leave it till tomorrow."

"What about our mystery man?" she asked. "Did you find out anything?"

"There isn't much to tell. I asked around about Malvis. It seemed like nobody had heard of him and then I found a couple of people who recognised the name. One was a retired inspector; he's always propping up the bar with stories of the old days. He was a bit drunk but he said that apparently, he was a small-time gang boss that just vanished. No one seems to know where he went. The theory was that another gang killed him and disposed of the body. There was a detective, Ian Gisbon was his name."

When he heard that, Ian got excited in my head.

Duncan carried on. "He was also killed in mysterious circumstances. According to the inspector, Gisbon had this theory that Malvis wasn't really small fry, he was behind a lot of unsolved crimes. Rumour was that he had an escape planned to Spain if anyone got close to him. Trouble was, this Gisbon could never find enough evidence to make it stick. He made a bit of a nuisance of himself with his wild theories. He upset a lot of senior people, claiming that Malvis had protection, a man in the police who kept his name out of everything. It's all so long ago. I was talking to him when another man, still a serving officer, a detective chief superintendent, joined in. He was called Fitzsimmons, he told me that he was around at the time and remembered Ian Gisbon, who had an obsession with Malvis. He told me that he would ask around. He said that he had some contacts in the criminal fraternity."

Ian said in my head. "Fitzsimmons? Is he still there? He was there when I was on the case, I liked him. He might know more about it by now, that's very useful."

"Thank you, Duncan," I said, "that's a great help. Maybe this Fitzsimmons will be able to throw some light on things."

"That's a real nuisance, Dunc," said Peta, "having an extra shift tonight."

"Sorry, babe, I didn't have much choice. When the boss calls you, you just do it. The overtime will be useful for when we go on holiday though." She turned the speaker off and went into her bedroom, so they could talk privately.

Ian was in a positive mood. "Fitz was a good bloke," he said, "he saved me more than once. If he's on the case, things will happen. And it's good to hear that there are not that many of the old faces around, less chance of Malvis's man still having influence."

Peta came out, she looked upset. "We were going to take you out for a meal tonight too, we had it all booked. We thought that it'd be nice after we'd spent the afternoon discussing Malvis."

"We can still go, just the two of us, can't we?"

Her face brightened up. "Of course we can, let's go and enjoy ourselves."

We spent ages getting ready, I didn't have any smart clothes with me, just jeans and tee shirts, Peta lent me a dress and shoes, I hadn't worn one for ages and it felt like the start of a new me. I did the best I could with my hair and was feeling quite grand as we went down to meet our taxi.

The cab picked us up at the entrance to the flats and took us away from the estate, into a much nicer part of London. The restaurant was very quiet, the food was superb. Since I had got myself sorted out, my taste had returned and I ate for pleasure now. The weirdest thing was, they had food from Devon on the menu, Brixham fish, Ruby Beef and ice cream from Salcombe.

"This is crazy," I said, "all the food is from Devon."

"I never realised," Peta said. "Duncan said he'd heard that it was nice here. Does it make you feel homesick?"

I thought for a moment. "No, it doesn't. I don't feel like Devon is my home, nowhere is, not since I saw that picture. Home used to be the farm where I grew up but since the day when my dad died there, I just feel like I don't belong anywhere."

We talked about when Duncan would be around. "He'll sleep tomorrow morning and come over after lunch," Peta said. "We can show him the box then and tell him a little more if Ian thinks it's OK."

"Sounds reasonable to me," said Ian. "He knows that Malvis is real now and once you show him my notes, he'll have more to work with. Perhaps he'll have some ideas about what to do next."

Halfway through dessert, Peta got a call. Frowning, she pulled her phone from her bag. "Number withheld, it's probably a scam," she said and cancelled it. Two minutes later it rang again.

"Perhaps you'd better answer it," I suggested.

Peta picked up the call and listened for a few seconds. She went very pale. "What's up, Beano?" I asked.

"It's Duncan," she said, in a whisper, "he's in hospital. He's been attacked."

I signalled a waiter. "The bill, please," I said, "and can you get a taxi for us, quickly? My friend has just had some bad news." I paid with the credit card that Roy had given me.

When we got to the hospital, we found that there was a policeman on guard at the door of his room. Peta hadn't spoken since we had left the restaurant, she was pale and shaking.

"Who are you?" he asked us. In a whisper, Peta told him she was Duncan's girlfriend. "I've heard him talk about you," he said, "but I can't let you in. Sorry but it's family only. You wouldn't be able to talk to him anyway, he's unconscious."

"Do you know what happened?"

"I don't. I wasn't on duty with him. All I heard was the call for assistance, there was trouble at a pub. You'd best speak to one of the others who were working on his relief. Try Shelly, she was attacked as well but she's OK."

"I know her," said Peta. "She's a good person to have as your backup. I've got her number."

We went down the corridor, Peta called her and spoke for a moment. "Shelly was busy, she just said what the man on the door said. But, she'll meet us in the morning, after her shift."

"We were going to show Duncan the box," Peta said. "Should we ask her about it?"

"No, best leave it. Maybe we could let Fitzsimmons see it?"

"What do you think, Ian?"

"That would be no good," said Ian. "Fitz already knows most of what's in there, he helped me compile a lot of it."

With nothing else to do, we went home and tried to sleep. I could hear Peta crying in the room next door. I had a horrible thought, which I shared with Ian. Duncan had raised Malvis's name at a police social club, now he was in hospital. Had I, we, put someone else in danger?

"It's probably a coincidence," said Ian. "People get called for extra shifts all the time. And violence around pubs has always been a thing. It's no use speculating until we have all the facts. We'll have to find out in the morning."

We were up early, Peta looked terrible, red-eyed and pale. "I knew in the back of my head that this could happen," she said. "Duncan told me it does, to others. He was always careful, he said that everyone has each other's backs." I hugged her and kept my suspicions to myself.

We met Shelly in a café, near the police station. She was in civilian clothes, she grabbed tea and we sat at a greasy table. The place was a policemen's haunt, there were pictures of uniformed men on the walls and several of the people sitting around were in uniform. She took Peta's hand and said how sorry she was about it all.

"What happened, Shelly?" asked Peta.

"We were called to a fight at a pub, well before chucking out time," she said. "It was unusual but nothing sinister, just some lads who'd had too much beer. Duncan moved in to stop them from fighting each other and they both turned on him. There were a couple of punches, he fell over and hit his head on the edge of a table on the way down."

Instantly I had a flashback to my dad and gasped. "What's up?" she asked. "You look like you've just seen a ghost."

"My dad, years ago," I could feel myself starting to cry. "He was tripped, he fell, broke his neck, he died," I said.

She put her hand on my shoulder. "I'm so sorry," she said, you could tell she meant it. "It often happens when you try to break up a fight. They forget their differences and attack you together. I was busy with a problem of my own when I saw him fall out of the corner of my eye. Another car turned up and we managed to get the two in the van for a night in the cells. They'll be in the magistrates' court later this morning. Which means I don't get a proper sleep today."

"What were they called?"

She thought for a moment. "One was called Terry. The other was foreign, Bogdan or something, I can't remember the rest."

We left her to her tea. I thought we were going to walk back to Peta's flat.

"I want to go to the court," she said, "see the two scumbags and just hope they'll get remanded. They should, assaulting a police officer is more serious than just a pub fight."

When we arrived, we found that the court wasn't in session till ten, so we went into a coffee shop across the road and had a bacon sandwich and a drink. Peta wasn't saying much and I left her to her thoughts. I was having a hard time; my guilt was bubbling away in my head. The old feelings were resurfacing. I was convinced that, because of Ian, someone else was hurt. I didn't want to talk about it to Peta or hear her say it was all my fault.

We sat in the public gallery, watching all the speeding and drunk offenders, then it was their turn. Terry Dellor and Bogdan Problido were brought up and charged with drunk and disorderly conduct and assault on a police officer.

To my surprise, they both pled guilty. The evidence of what they had done was not presented. Then their defence solicitor went into a long-winded ramble about how they were sorry and ashamed of what they'd done while under the influence of drink. He said that they had disagreed and fought each other. When the policeman intervened, they had not realised who he was and hadn't meant to hurt him. The solicitor said that the injury had been caused by a fall, not a punch and as such, was accidental and was much regretted, in the cold light of day.

The two men, in nondescript clothes and slightly threatening in appearance, both looked sorry. They both apologised and were given fines. As Terry was being led away, he looked up and caught my eye. I'm sure he winked at me, then he was gone.

Peta was fuming as we got up and left the court. Her hands shook as she pushed the door open. "Bastards," she said. "How did they manage to swing that?"

Outside we saw Shelly and she came over to say hello.

"Can you explain that?" said Peta. "What just happened?"

"They were very well advised by someone," she said. "Pleading guilty automatically means a lighter sentence. And no need to give evidence either; since an admission invites automatic sentencing. Showing contrition helps too. Makes me wonder why we bother sometimes. Trouble is, the system is so backed up that they try not to remand if they can help it. They let you go unless you've killed someone. Anyway, I'm off home to bed. I've another shift tonight. I'll check in on Duncan later."

"They won't tell me what's happening to him, 'cos I'm not family," Peta said.

Shelly smiled. "I can get around that for you," she said, "don't call the hospital, call me."

"It's not right," Peta said. "My Duncan's lying in a hospital bed and all he's trying to do is help people. I don't like it, there must be something we can do."

I took her for another coffee and cake to try to get her to calm down. While we were there, Shelly called, she said that she was just going to sleep but had called the hospital first. There was no change in Duncan's condition, he hadn't regained consciousness but he hadn't deteriorated either.

"What if he never wakes up? Will they be re-arrested for murder?"

There was no answer to that. We finished up and left. I was going to suggest looking at the contents of the box when we got back, but it seemed a little insensitive.

As we got in the lift, a man came in and stood with us by the control panel. He had a hoodie on, well pulled down and he kept his face turned away. Even so, by the way he stood, he looked vaguely threatening.

The man asked us what floor. "Six, please," said Peta. "Me too," he answered, pushing the button. "I'm seeing a couple of girls today. I've been looking forward to it."

Ian whispered a warning, "Get out, now, don't argue, just go."

I grabbed Peta's hand. "Come on," I said. We were too late; the doors had started to close. I reached for the door button but the man was standing in the way.

"Where you off to then, ladies?" he said, his voice quiet but full of menace. "Forgotten something have we?" He had a distinctive accent and I realised where I had heard it before.

"Get ready," said Ian. "It's about to kick off."

Chapter 34

I held Peta's hand all the way up to our floor. We exchanged worried glances, she had sensed the tension I felt that something was very wrong. The man was silent, standing in front of the alarm button and avoiding eye contact. He exuded confidence, you could tell that he knew that he was in control of the situation. As the door opened on our floor, we saw that another man was standing in the corridor. Peta let go of my hand and tried to move past him, she was grabbed and spun around to face the wall.

As I moved forward, the man in the lift pulled my arm up behind my back. He pushed me forwards. "To your flat," Peta's assailant hissed. "No noises, no trouble." He had a foreign accent, everything was starting to add up. I didn't like it one bit.

I wanted to show him that I was aware of the situation. "What's going on, Terry?" I gasped as I was forced along, following Peta but not close enough to kick out at the man holding her.

"Clever girl," he answered. "What do you think? You've been asking questions, poking your nose in. It means the end for you, but before that, you need to tell us what you know. Then we have to make it look like an accident."

I heard Ian in my head. "Don't worry, I'm going to help you in a moment, just let me take over control of your arms and legs when I say. Meanwhile, play dumb."

When we unlocked the door and went into the flat, Peta was released and pushed towards the balcony. "Open it," Terry shouted. She slid back the door. "Now get out there, both of you."

I realised what was going to happen. Terry let go and shoved me towards her. When we both turned, two knives filled our vision.

"Hand over your phones," the foreign one said. They had to be Terry and Bogdan, the two men that had attacked Duncan. They were dressed differently from when we had seen them in the court. Peta must have realised it by now. In silence, we handed our phones over. Terry put them in his pocket.

"My boss," he said, looking at me, "he wants to know why you're having the dreams."

I did what Ian had told me. I played dumb. "What are you on about? You've got the wrong person here."

He smiled. "No, we haven't. You're Suzan Halford, this is your friend Peta. We've dealt with the bloke, Duncan wasn't it, now it's your turn. Before you take a short step off the balcony, my boss wants answers. What do you know about Ian Gisbon and Harold Malvis? Oh yeah, and where's the box?"

Everything was connected. I could see Peta going red, she was getting angry. Good, that might be a help. We were the same height as the two men. Peta used to be handy in a fight, as many a boy had found out. I had Ian to help me, the question was, did she still have it?

I looked at Peta. "I don't know anything," I said as Peta shrugged.

"Same here," she said. "I saw you in court, is that why you hurt my Duncan?"

Ian said in my head, "Get Peta ready to create a diversion. I'm going to want her to move to her left as if she's going to climb around the partition."

"How do I make her do that?"

"I don't know, use your imagination."

"Well? Is it?" Peta was wound right up, I could hear it in her voice. She would never climb over the railing and swing across to the other balcony in time. Unless I stopped both of them. How could I do that?

"Lousy plan, Ian," I thought.

Terry was talkative. "Yeah that was us, we needed to make sure he was out of the way before we got closer to you two."

While Terry had been talking, Bogdan had gone back inside. Now we could hear him wrecking the flat. "You were seen, carrying a box from Gisbon's wife and my boss wants it. Gotta make it look plausible, he said. Like you was burgled by... I don't know, addicts or something," he said. "My boss said you'd know about that, wouldn't you, Suzan?" The noise stopped, a door slammed and it started again.

This was worrying me, how did these two and their boss know about me in Devon? Unless someone had been watching me. I thought of Roy, was Ian right about him? I had no time to ask, Terry was still talking and I wanted to concentrate on what he was saying.

"Don't worry, if it's here, he'll find it," Terry continued. "Dan is thorough, he loves his work. Tell you what, before you go, as it were, maybe the burglary could include a bit of fun? Bonus for us, give you some happy memories. Even if you are both skin and bone."

He turned. "Hey, Dan!" he shouted. There was no reply. "Don't go away, ladies," he said and went inside, leaving the door open. There was the mutter of conversation, followed by laughter.

"What are we going to do?" asked Peta. "These are the two who attacked Duncan, who are they working for, is it Malvis? It has to be."

"No idea, Ian says he's got a plan, he said something about climbing around the partition."

She looked at me and shook her head. "Has he forgotten we're six floors up? No chance."

"I don't know then, just go along with me."

"Shut up." The two men had returned, looking excited. "I found it," said Bogdan. "It's on the settee, ready to go."

"Well done. That's business over, now for pleasure. Which one do you fancy first, Dan?" asked Terry.

"Neither," he said. "I like my women with a bit of meat on them."

"Beggars can't be choosers. Ugly bloke like you, this is the best offer you'll get today."

He laughed. "OK, her," he said, pointing at me.

Without me thinking I said, "There's nothing wrong with skinny women, we have lots of stamina. Anyway, there's no need for you to *fight each other* over us, is there, Peta?" I tried to emphasize fight each other, I hoped she got it. It was what had happened to Duncan, this would be revenge. Never mind Ian's idea, this was my plan.

"What are you on about?" asked Terry. "Just shut up and get your gear off. Dan, you go first, whichever order you like. I'll make sure they don't try anything."

Bogdan put his knife down and approached us, leering. He fumbled with the front of his trousers. Before he could grab either of us, I went for Peta. As we got close, I whispered in her ear, "Play fight, distract them. Then we act together when I say."

"OK," she said and we started to wrestle. She was wound up, so was I and it didn't feel like playing. She hadn't lost any of her strength, it almost turned into a real fight between us. That was good, our lives depended on the performance.

"Stop that," Bogdan shouted and tried to separate us as Terry called out for us to stand still. The three of us moved into the corner of the balcony, by the partition and against the railings. As we moved, I kicked one of the metal chairs back towards Terry, it hit him in the shins and he howled with pain.

"Now, grab him," I said and we changed tack. We stopped fighting each other and each got one of Bogdan's legs. I hadn't thought about what we were going to do next, before I realised what we were doing we had lifted him off the ground and heaved him over the balcony. There was a long scream, followed by a squelching thud. Terry was hopping around, clutching his shin. He had dropped his knife. I ran and picked it up.

"What have you done, you crazy tarts?" he shouted and made a move back inside. Peta pushed past me and Rugby tackled him. He fell to the floor. He tried to get up, but the sight of my blade stopped him. That and Peta's foot in his back.

"Well done," said Ian, "just make sure he doesn't leave."

"Shut it, Terry," Peta said. "Give us our phones back, and yours."

"Get stuffed," he said. She pressed down on his spine with her foot, just below his ribs. "OK," he said. "I can't breathe." He scrabbled around and pulled three phones from his pockets.

"Lay still, unless you want to follow your mate," Peta said. "Hands behind your back. Stringy, if he tries to move, stab him."

I stood between him and the door, well away from his hands and pointed the knife at his face, Peta took her foot off his back and ran into her bedroom. Terry watched the blade and didn't move. She returned with a pair of handcuffs. We made Terry shuffle on hands and knees out onto the balcony, where we secured him to the railings. Underneath us, a small crowd had formed around Bogdan's body. I could hear sirens. "We're going to call your boss," I said, "and tell him we need to meet."

"I can't do that. Help!" he shouted. "Up here! Help!" I waved the knife in his face, nicking his cheek, that shut him up. But was it too late?

"Do you want to join your mate?" He shook his head. "The police will be here soon; you've got some explaining to do."

"So have you." He sounded smug. "Help me," he shouted again.

"We acted in self-defence, especially when they find out that you were the ones who attacked my boyfriend."

He smirked. "I've got protection. I'm fireproof with the police. Didn't you notice, I just got away with what I did to your fella."

We exchanged glances. "Who's protecting him?" asked Ian. "I always knew that Malvis had someone looking after him, that was why I could never make anything stick. We need a name."

"You call your boss now, tell him." The police had arrived below, they were looking up.

"We have to go," said Peta, in a daze, I followed her inside. She shut and locked the sliding door. She put the key in her pocket. "That'll slow them down," she said. Terry started to shout for help, we ignored him.

She picked up all three phones. "Grab your bag and that box," she said. She went into the bedroom; I could hear her opening drawers. I picked up the box, went into my room and pushed it back into my holdall on top of my gear. I hadn't unpacked much; it only took a few seconds to shove everything back into my bag. We met in the lounge; Peta had a rucksack on her back.

"Ready?" she asked. I nodded.

We left her flat, with Terry chained to the balcony, still shouting his head off and headed past the lifts, pushing the call buttons on the way. We went up the stairs to the seventh floor. There we walked back to the lifts. According to the indicator over the door, both of them were stuck on the sixth floor.

"That's why I came up here," she said. "I remember Duncan telling me about a bloke who did it to evade capture."

"It didn't work for him though, did it?" I said sarcastically. "Or you wouldn't know."

"No, he got clean away. They found out what he'd done after he'd gone, from the CCTV and the witnesses who saw him."

"What do we do now, then?"

"Follow me," she said. We walked down the corridor until we came to the other lifts. Peta pushed the call button. "Now we act innocent." The lift arrived at the sixth floor, stopped for a moment and then came up to us. The doors opened.

It was empty.

We rode to the ground floor, left the lifts through a deserted foyer and headed into the street.

"That was crazy," I said as I allowed myself to breathe. That had been too easy. "Why weren't they covering all the exits?"

"In a couple of minutes, they will be," she said. We could hear more sirens approaching as we headed towards the bus stop.

"Where are we going?" I asked. I had little idea where I was.

"We'll get the bus to Victoria," she said, "get a train or a coach somewhere. I don't know where we can go after that yet. There's something I have to do first."

While we waited, Peta found and turned off the location tracking app on Terry's phone. "It wasn't even locked, whoever sent them is using amateurs," she said. "They won't be able to find us now. Do yours too, and I'll do mine."

I'd just done it when the bus arrived. There was so much we had to talk about, it felt like everything was getting out of hand.

"That was pretty intense," Peta said as we sat in the back seat. The enormity of what we had just done was starting to sink in, I felt myself shaking. I gripped Peta's hand, it was doing the same.

"Never mind that, Beano. What have we just done? We killed a man."

She nodded, "I know and it scares me too. But we have to remember, he would have done the same to us, we must have got someone really rattled. Those two weren't professionals, it had to have been set up in a hurry."

"Handcuffs?" I said. "You just happened to have them lying around?"

She had the grace to turn red. "NO! Duncan leaves a full set of gear at mine, in case he goes straight to work. Good job, if you ask me. Anyway, it means that I got this." Peta showed me a stab vest in her holdall. "I thought it might come in useful. And you have the box that they were after, it must have something really important in it."

"We need to get somewhere where nobody would think of looking for us," I said. "When we're safe, we can give Terry's boss a call. There must be a number on Terry's phone. I'm pretty sure what just happened is connected to Malvis."

"Should we call the police?"

"Not yet, I've been thinking and it's pretty clear that a policeman's involved."

"How do you get to that?"

It was time to share my suspicions. "Well, the day after Duncan mentions to several policemen that he's looking for Malvis, he gets called in for an extra shift, where he happens to get beaten up. Remember, Ian said that he thought Malvis had protection. The two who did it plead guilty, with a sob story, knowing that they'll get off. Then they come for us. One of them saw me in the court and winked. At the time I thought it was just bravado, now I'm not so sure." She was nodding, she could see my logic. "And Terry confirmed that he was fireproof, it all fits." I'd neglected to tell her my suspicions about Roy because that was all they were. From what Terry had said, the thing that set it all off was our visit to Beth.

Peta looked devastated. "So we sent Duncan into danger. We should have told him more, instead of keeping it to ourselves."

"No, it was a fair guess that any protection Malvis had was twenty years ago, before he vanished. It would have to be a senior man then, so he probably would have retired by now. Just unlucky that we rattled his cage."

Ahead of us, the bus stopped at Victoria Station. "Come on," she said, "let's get out of this city, to a place where they'll never find us."

Whereas Paddington station had felt crowded and overwhelming, the crowds at Victoria were comforting and made me feel safe. We sat in the rear corner of a bustling bar, drinking soft drinks in ice-filled glasses while we planned our next move. People flowed in and out, if anyone had managed to follow us, we'd never know.

"What does Ian have to say about all this?" Peta asked.

"He's not there at the moment, he does that, comes and goes, ever since I was on the tablets, the booze and the weed didn't help, it weakened the connection somehow. He's been around a lot, I guess it's tired him out."

"But where does he go? This gets weirder by the minute."

"He doesn't know, says it's like sleeping but he never knows how long it'll be for."

"Well, we'll just have to do it without him." She looked at her phone. "Shit," she swore, "I just connected to the café Wi-fi." Frantically she pushed at the screen. "The police could track us by seeing where we logged into Wi-fi, turn your phone off."

I did, then Peta turned Terry's back on. "I'm assuming his is pay-as-you-go," she said, "harder to track. I'll use that. I'm looking for a place we can stay, out of the way but handy," she said." Maybe a chain hotel, near a station." She looked for a few minutes, "Here's one; we need tickets and trains to West Malling in Kent."

"I've never been to Kent," I said.

"Neither have I, it's perfect." She called them to book a room. "A family room is all they've got," she said, "there's a restaurant in the pub next door and it's five minutes from the station." She ended the call and turned Terry's phone off. We finished our drinks and went to get tickets.

After an hour or so on a train, full of homeward-bound suits, and a short taxi ride, we were sitting in a hotel room, near a place called West Malling. The box was residing in the hotel safe. Neither of us wanted to take the next step and look inside it. The room was large, with a double and a single bed, a decent bathroom, a TV and a kettle.

I called Mum, on the hotel phone. Roy answered. "She's in the shower," he said. "Are you OK?"

"Yes, we're fine."

"Where are you?" I remembered what Ian had said and told him a lie.

"We've gone away for a couple of days, back to where we used to live growing up."

"Oh right, I'll tell your mum you called. Have a nice time. Make sure you keep in touch."

"What are we going to do now?" said Peta. "We can't just hide in this room. Why did you tell Roy a fib?"

It was time for honesty. "Ian warned me about Roy, he doesn't like him. I don't want him to know where we are."

"Why? Do you think he's connected to it all?"

"No, I think seeing Beth triggered this. I'm just being cautious."

"Right," she said, "I'm calling Shelly." She dialled; it went to voicemail and she left a message.

"Now we can start to fight back," I told her. "We're safe. If Roy has anything to do with this, he'll be looking for us in the wrong place. We need to call Terry's boss to get the ball rolling."

She turned his phone on and scrolled the list of contacts. "Which one is it? Do we have to try them all?"

"Take a look at his call history," I suggested. "Try the last one he called or maybe the last call he received."

"That's a good plan," she said. "Was that Ian's idea, or yours?"

"I can function without him you know," I said. "Anyway, he's still not around."

She was looking. "The last call was from a mobile, there's no caller ID so it could have been anyone."

"Call it then," I said and she pressed the button.

She handed the phone to me. "You'd better speak."

It picked up. "Is that you, Terry, is it done?" said the male voice that answered. It sounded distorted, like a robot.

"Terry can't answer that," I said.

"Who is this?" He sounded puzzled. It was time to put some pressure on.

"I'm the person Terry and his mate Bogdan were sent to rape and kill," I answered. "Me and my friend. Just to let you know, Terry can't come to the phone, he was tied up the last time we saw him. As for his buddy, well let's just say he didn't bounce too well."

"What do you want?" The voice was flat and unemotional. You wouldn't think I had just told him someone was dead.

"I want Malvis, face to face." There was a laugh.

"That's not going to happen."

"Then it's the newspapers for me," I said. "With what I know, his new life, wherever it is, won't be worth living. I've still got the box, the one your two amateurs were unable to get. There must be a few secrets in there. I want to see Malvis, not someone pretending to be him because I'll know if you try to fool me. Tell him it's his call."

There was a click. He hadn't even said goodbye.

Fitz ended the call with a sinking feeling. He didn't want to hear any more. He'd assured Harold that he had things under control. Up to that moment, he was looking forward to restoring himself in Harold's eyes by announcing that the problem was solved. How could his men have screwed up so badly? He needed to compose himself. He had to get people looking for the girls, he wasn't going to phone Harold until he had something positive to tell him.

Chapter 35

Haold

Harold had always read the English newspapers; they were a day late arriving in Spain but he liked to keep in touch. That morning, the headline in one of them caused him to miss breakfast. "Tony!" he shouted. "Get Fitz on the blower, now."

"Fitz," he said, when Tony handed him the phone, "I need an explanation. I'm looking at yesterday's headlines. Man dies in fall from policeman's balcony, it says. Was it a robbery gone wrong? There's a couple of names in the report that I don't like the look of."

"What do you mean, boss?" Harold thought that Fitz sounded guilty, so he should.

"Don't try to fool me, Fitz. I know that Bogdan was one of yours. You told me yourself. And the name of the owner of the flat, Peta. It's an unusual name, isn't it? One coincidence too many, don't you think?"

There was silence.

"Well, are the girls dead, or just one of your goons?"

Fitz spoke quickly. "I don't know how it happened, we found them, they went to visit Gisbon's widow. They got some papers from her, something she always denied having. I discovered that Peta's boyfriend was a policeman. He was asking questions. My men got him out of the way and moved in on the girls. Then it all went quiet. Until I read the paper, I thought it had gone according to plan."

"This is starting to get annoying, Fitz. You told me not to worry. I think it's about time you told me the truth."

"I am, and I still mean it."

"I'm guessing that whatever they did, it didn't work."

"That's right. One's dead and they got away from the other. Pretty slick, they left him handcuffed to the balcony. He was arrested but I managed to smooth things over. They took his phone and called me."

"What? Can I be traced?"

"Not from the phone they have, it leads to a forwarding number, then to me. It's anonymous. There's a filter I use to disguise my voice."

Harold was not convinced. "Better change all the numbers anyway."

"Can't do that, Harry. How will we get in touch with her? We're gonna have to get her somewhere alone to deal with her. We tried to track her but she's done something to her phone and the one she got from my man, so we can't. When she called, she told me that she wants to meet you."

"I hope you told her to piss off, Fitz. Even better, pretend to be me and go yourself, she'll be annoyed but who cares, it'll be her last emotion."

"I was going to, but I thought better of it. She knows a lot more than she should about Gisbon, and she has the papers that his wife swore she never had. That makes three people who know. If any of them talks, it might be hard to keep a lid on things. Plus, she says she'll know if we try to fool her, said she knows what you look like. I have no idea how but can we take the risk?"

"It's her word against mine, and you're police. Can't you find something on her? You said she was hanging with people who were getting her stoned. Can't you arrest her for supplying drugs? With your clout, you could get her locked up. My people inside can sort her out. As for Gisbon's lady, perhaps she needs a lesson. But that's for another day. The first job is to get the girls and the papers, then we can mop things up. Find them, use everyone."

"I don't know where to start, she's not daft, she's got us all running around looking for her. Her credit card has only been used once since she left Devon. In a restaurant, they said she left in a taxi, the driver dropped her at a hospital. She's not gone back to her friend's flat, or her home in Devon. I'm worried that she might have recorded her story already and made copies of whatever was in that box of papers. I've sent men back to where she grew up, figured that might be where she was headed but nobody there has seen her. Her friend could have the same information, she's vanished as well. They might not even be together any more, we just don't know."

"Fitz, you're the bloody police, it's your job to know. Sounds like you've made a real mess of things."

"It all happened so quickly. Trust me, Harry, I'm working on it."

Malvis sighed. "I suppose that means I'm going to have to come over and sort it all out for you."

"I think you might have to," Fitz admitted.

Harold thought for a moment and let Fitz sweat in the silence. He came to a decision. "This is what you're going to do. Call off your men, I don't want to risk hurting either of them before I know how much they have on me. Get in touch with her on Terry's phone and give her my number here. Tell her to call me and I'll set up a meeting. I'll make it at the old warehouse; quite poetic don't you think? I'll tell you when I'll be there but I'm not stopping in England a moment longer than I have to. Tony can fly me in and wait for me."

"Good plan. I'll show up and nab them. They won't suspect me if I come in uniform."

"Brilliant, Fitz, it's all going to work out."

And I want to deal with you when I've dealt with her, he thought as he put the phone down. It was time to call Fitz's man in England again.

Chapter 36

Suzan

Ian returned that evening. We were in our room, drinking the complimentary tea and deciding what to do about eating. I didn't know about Peta but I felt exhausted by the events of the last twenty-four hours. So much had happened since we had sat in the restaurant.

"I'm back," he suddenly announced, "what did I miss?"

"Where have you been, Ian?" I asked him.

"Having a rest," he said. "What's happening? Where are we?"

I got him up to speed. "That's good," he said, "that'll draw him out."

"It's turning into quite an operation," I said.

"I know, I thought it would be easy, just get Malvis to England and get the police to pick him up. Now I'm not so sure."

"Why? Is it because of what Terry said, that he was fireproof with the police?"

"Partly, I figured that after all this time, with no Malvis around, his protection from the police would be long gone."

"Unless he hasn't gone, perhaps he's still running his crime business, just not from here."

"That's a very good point." He suggested a few things to me, which made me gasp and laugh.

"Are you alright?" asked Peta, she was sitting on the bed, watching me. "You went a bit strange there."

"Just Ian, he's back and we were just catching up."

"I need to talk to him," she said, "he wanted me to climb over my balcony. You can tell him from me—"

I interrupted her. "Just tell him yourself, he can hear you. I only need to repeat what he wants to say."

"OK," she said, "that has to be a dumb idea, Ian."

"He says that it was the best that he could think of. But that you did well in the end."

"Let's hope you're on better form when Stringy goes to meet Harold for you then," she said.

In the end, we ate from room service and decided to have an early night. I wanted to watch the evening news, to see if there was anything about us on there. I watched the whole bulletin, our escapade wasn't even mentioned.

"Maybe the police are keeping it quiet?" suggested Peta. "If there is a crooked copper, he might have pulled strings." It was food for thought as we prepared for sleep.

The next morning, we woke late. I felt better; more relaxed. Then I remembered what we still had to do. We had no idea when or even if Terry's boss would call again, or if he had changed his number after our last call. Surely he would be bothered enough by the potential we had to disrupt Malvis's life to keep in touch.

When Peta turned Terry's phone on, it buzzed to let her know that a text message had been received.

"Who was that?" I asked.

"It's from Terry's boss," she said. "It's a phone number. It looks like an international one. The message says, 'call this'. There's nothing more."

"It must be a number for Malvis. I'll call it after we've had breakfast."

We ventured over to the restaurant for a late breakfast. It was practically deserted; if anyone was interested in us, they would be easy to spot. Even so, we didn't hang around. I was feeling nervous and found eating difficult, I managed to force some toast down and had a cup of coffee. I just wanted the next part to be over.

Back in the room, I was shaking as I called the number. "Is this Harold Malvis?" I asked the man who answered.

"No, I'm Harold James, who the hell are you?"

I took a deep breath, in my head, Ian said, "That's him, I'd know that voice anywhere." I could feel his anger, I was relieved that he was back, now things were getting critical. "Tell him what we agreed," he said.

"Don't insult me," I said, "you're Malvis, your man gave me this number."

There was silence. "Carry on," said Ian. "Well?" I said.

Malvis laughed. "What if I am? My advice to you is this, don't be stupid, you're just a girl. I know about you, you're the one with the crazy ideas, you should have been killed years ago. There's been someone keeping an eye on you, they are supposed to have stopped you before you got this far."

It wasn't Roy then, he had let me go at the station. I realised that he must mean Donnie. He was a criminal. Donnie had used the same words, he said that he was keeping an eye on me. At least I had got away from him. Better than that, he couldn't stop me now. Which meant that Roy was in the clear.

I ignored his insults and carried on with my prepared speech. "Ian has a message for you," I said, "but he needs to see you in person to deliver it."

"What bollocks are you talking? How can a dead man have a message for me?"

"You know where would be a good place to meet, don't you? The warehouse where we met last time. It's a shopping centre now. Just tell me when you'll be there. You can find out all about it then."

"Or else? Look, love, it sounds convincing but I'm a busy man, I run a business. I haven't got time to come and see you, just tell me what it's about."

"No, face to face, or else the whole story goes live."

He laughed again. "You're deluded, it must have been all the weed you were smoking in that park. I know about you, nobody will ever believe a crazy junkie."

"You think? There're enough facts to make it irresistible to the media. Remember, what one girl thought she overheard years ago was enough to get my father killed. And get your attention. How much more is there now? Attempted murder, police corruption, people falling off balconies?"

"Nothing ties any of that to me. I'm Harold James, reputable businessman, whatever name you might use for me."

"Can you take the chance? Especially now I know the name you're using. I have a very interesting box of evidence that's just come to light. Text me on this number when you have a date and time. I'll be waiting."

Without giving him a chance to answer, I ended the call.

"I'm proud of you," Ian said, "well done."

"Now what do we do?" asked Peta.

"We wait, it's up to Malvis to get in touch."

"You said he'd know the place, is it Hendrix's old warehouse?"

"That's right, Ian wants it to be there."

"I can understand that."

"When we get a time, we need to let Duncan's boss know. What was his name, Ian?"

"Fitzsimmons," he answered, "he was a DC when I was a DS. He transferred in. He was a good detective. He always seemed to be the one that believed me."

"As soon as we get a time, we can get him there with the cavalry."

Chapter 37

The next two days felt like two weeks, as we waited for the message to say that Malvis had agreed to meet us. We were hardly leaving the hotel room, we didn't want to take the risk of being spotted now that the end was so near. I turned Terry's phone on to check for messages every couple of hours.

Peta phoned Shelly twice a day for updates. To her relief, she was told that Duncan was awake, he'd had surgery on a blood clot in his head and for some internal injuries. Despite our situation, she wanted to go and see him or at least talk to him on the phone. Shelly told her that she couldn't do either yet, he was still in intensive care and too weak. But he was alive. It helped my feelings of guilt to settle down, knowing that he would recover.

We ate our meals in the adjoining pub, or from room service. All this waiting was getting to me and I started to worry about how much it was costing Peta. I asked her how we were going to pay for it. "I've got a bit of money," I said, "but I know it's getting expensive and I haven't got that much."

"Don't worry about it, Stringy," she replied. "It's all going on my credit card. It's important we get this finished, we're a team, remember."

Then, on the third day, the phone had another message when Peta turned it on. *Next Monday at 8:00 PM. Service entrance. Come alone.* It was a relief to finally know that the end was near.

"That's great," said Peta, "now we know what we're doing, we can turn the phone off and dump it."

I wasn't so sure. "Shouldn't we keep it? It's evidence."

"OK, I guess. Anyhow, all we have to do is call the police and let them know what's happening."

And be there, I thought. "Don't worry," said Ian. "We're nearly finished now."

Peta called the police station where Duncan worked and asked for DS Fitzsimmons.

"Can I ask who's calling?" said the person who answered.

"It's Duncan Swift's fiancée." I never knew they were engaged; she hadn't said and wasn't wearing a ring.

Fitzsimmons came on the line; Peta spoke a few words about Duncan and I could hear him sending his best wishes for his recovery.

"Can you have a quick word with my friend?" said Peta, handing the phone to me.

"Good morning," he said. "This is Fitzsimmons, what can I help you with?"

"Hello, my name is Suzan Halford." I felt Ian's elation, *"Fitz,"* he said, *"I'm pleased to hear him again."*

"How can I help you, Suzan?"

Knowing that Ian trusted Fitzsimmons meant that it wasn't as daunting as when I'd spoken to Beth. "I have information about a criminal," I said. "I know where he'll be at a certain time."

"Really," Fitzsimmons said, "and how do you know this? Think carefully before you answer, as it may incriminate you. I should inform you that this call is now being recorded and may be used in evidence."

"Are you cautioning me?"

"No, it's just a reminder, if you know where criminals are, it could mean that you are involved with them. How do I know you're not a criminal yourself, or setting a trap for my officers?"

I thought that sounded like a strange thing to say. "I'm not, I'm just a girl, a friend of Peta's. I heard an interesting conversation recently, where doesn't matter. A criminal, who's been living in Spain, will be in England, at the Hendrix Gate Shopping Mall. He'll be there next Monday at seven p.m. If you're waiting, you'll be able to arrest him."

"I see. Thank you," Fitzsimmons said, "and what name do you have for this criminal?"

I took a deep breath. "Harold Malvis."

"That's an interesting name," he said, "one I haven't heard for a while. Where did you say you got it?"

"I didn't, just be there." I ended the call.

"Do you think he'll be there?" said Peta.

"He was one of the few that believed me about Malvis," Ian said. "I'm sure he will."

"He'd better be," I said. "My life depends on it."

"I think we should move on from here," said Peta, "now we've done that. We can get a bit closer to the mall and keep watch on it before the date."

Chapter 38

It was Monday evening, just before eight. We were in the main car park at Hendrix Gate Shopping Mall, watching the service entrance from a seat in the bus stop. The box and most of our things were safe in a nearby hotel, where we'd spent the last day and a bit. There was nobody about. We watched the main doors close at six. The car park had emptied and then a stream of workers had come out of the service entrance and departed. All the lights in the shops went out and then, just before eight, the service door opened and half closed.

"That's our way in," said Peta. "Come on."

I stopped her. "He said I was to come alone, you wait here for Fitzsimmons and the cavalry."

She rummaged in her rucksack. "Here, take this, put it on under your jacket." It was Duncan's stab vest. "If Malvis killed Ian with a knife last time and he tries it again, you'll be protected."

"Thanks," I said. I put it on; it was a bit loose but my jumper underneath padded it out. With my jacket zipped up over it, you couldn't tell I was wearing it. The feel of it made me more confident.

"I'll wait outside and come in with them," Peta said. We hugged. "Good luck."

I slipped through the open door and walked along the deserted corridors. Although they were lit by ornate globes hanging from the ironwork, all the lights were out in the shops. I shivered, despite my layers; it felt eerie.

"It's so different," said Ian, "none of this was here, it was just a shell, filled with old dusty shelving."

"I know," I said, "don't forget that I've seen it too."

A man was sitting on one of the benches in the middle of the walkway with his back to me. It was so similar to what Ian has shown me in my dreams, all those years ago.

"So you're here then." The man must have heard me, he stood and turned. He had a hard, tanned face. An older version of the face from my dreams.

"He's a lot older than I remembered," Ian informed me. "But it's definitely Harold Malvis."

"Hello, Harold," I said.

"You're the girl that's caused me all this trouble," Malvis said.

"If you say so," I answered. "You look older than the last time I saw you."

He ignored that and looked at me. "I haven't been here in so long," said Malvis. "I hardly recognised the place. But I can't stop. In about two hours, I'll be on a flight back to Spain. It seems to be getting a little hot for me in this country again. I'd rather be out of it."

"You won't be going anywhere," I said. "The police will be here in a minute and you'll be under arrest."

He laughed. "No, they won't. You're on your own, there's no backup, my man would have told me. I'm walking out of here. You should have kept your mouth shut and stayed drunk in the park."

I moved towards him. "I can't let you go."

He pulled a knife, the blade caught the light and flickered. "I'd rather you had never got me to come over here. But we're where we are. Whether you try to stop me or not, only one of us is leaving." The blade swished, catching the light again. The reflection flashed across my face, making me blink.

"Like last time, you mean?"

He stopped and looked at me. "Mind games, I don't think so, is that all you've got?"

"You have no idea what I've got," I said.

"Well, I know that you've been stupid, getting involved in things that happened long before your time. I've been keeping an eye on you."

Perhaps he would tell me who it was, Martin, Donnie or Roy. My money was on Donnie, whatever Ian thought. "What do you mean?"

"After the incident with your father, I heard that you had this wild idea about Ian Gisbon. So I got one of my associates to keep an eye on you. It all went quiet for a while, then he told me you'd given him the slip. I was expecting you to call. I knew, sooner or later, it had to be this way."

Ian was getting very agitated in my head. "Just let me speak, let me use your voice," he said.

"It's all yours," I answered, without speaking.

"It's not the same, is it, Malvis?" The words were in my voice but not from me. It was weird, I could see what Ian meant, having presence but no control was strange. I wondered why he had never done this before.

"What do you know?" Malvis said, he still thought it was me talking. "You're just a kid. How could you know?"

"I remember it all. You were sat on a metal stool, just over there, in between all the rows of shelving. You were younger and thinner then, blue shirt, light trousers."

He frowned. "You can't know that, you're too young. Who have you been talking to?"

"You said I was unlucky, told me to be sensible, to go home to my family."

His mouth dropped open. "How can you know that? Tell me right now!" There was a trace of fear in his voice.

Ian carried on. "You told me my wife's phone number, *oh-eight-three-six, seven-four-four-two-one-eight.* Are you getting the picture yet? There's one thing more you need to know. Suzan might be too young to know it all but there's one important thing about her. She was born the night you killed Ian Gisbon."

He seemed to be struggling for an answer. He shook his head. "No, it's all a trick." He was trying to sound brave and unconcerned but the fear was there, and there was worry in his expression. "I suppose you're going to tell me that Ian's in your head. Like that reporter reckoned."

"If she did, would you believe her? She's already told you enough to prove it, things that she can't have known from the papers, that she can't have known any other way than if Ian Gisbon was here with her, right now."

"You're trying to frighten me."

"I am. Is it working?" He took a step back. The knife was still pointing at me; did I see it tremble, just a little?

"Why are you here, doing this?" he asked. "Why stir it all up, how can it benefit you?"

"Why do you think? Ian wants revenge, he wants justice so that he can rest in peace."

"And that's coming from you?"

"From us would be more correct. Why not?" He didn't answer.

I heard the noise of a door opening and felt relief. The police had arrived. Malvis heard it too.

"Over to you," said Ian, "my work is done." I felt control over my speech again.

"Looks like your time's up," I said. "My backup's here. Unlike last time."

He didn't answer, just smiled. The knife was steady now. When it shouldn't have been.

Peta appeared; she didn't look happy.

"Thank goodness you've arrived, Beano," I said, sure that everything was going to be OK. "Where are they?"

"They're not coming." A man's voice grunted, "Move, bitch, go and stand with your friend." As she stepped forward, I saw that a man was standing behind her. Then I saw the gun in his hand. It was pointed at her.

"I'm sorry, Stringy," she whispered.

"It's OK," I said, even though I had a horrible feeling that it wasn't.

A policeman, it must have been Fitzsimmons, walked into view, in uniform. I should have been relieved, now that the police were here. Except that I knew what was about to happen. I think Ian did too, his initial surge of pleasure at seeing the policeman had gone, replaced by puzzlement.

The policeman went to stand between Malvis and me.

"Is this your reinforcements?" asked Malvis dodging to one side so I could see him.

"He's a policeman." It was all I could think of to say. Wasn't it about time Ian took over again?

"Yes," said Malvis, "and he's mine. Hello, Fitz, you've made me come to this bloody place again, just like last time."

Ian was angry, I could feel it. "Fitz," he said. "Malvis's man on the inside was Fitz. Now I've seen him I've remembered a bit more about that night. He was in the group who told me about the accident. That made me come home this way. He might not have said it, but he probably started the story. It was a setup, it all makes sense, Malvis hinted at it back then."

"What's the matter, little girl?" said Fitzsimmons. "No clever repost?"

"Ian says hello, Fitz," I said. He looked around with a confused expression on his face.

"Ian says? I don't see him here. I'd call for him to come forward, but it would be pointless, he's dead. He was getting too close, he had to go. I set it all up, then, when Harold told me it was done, I reported it."

"I know," I said. "Ian died at twenty-oh-eight, on October the fifteenth. Do you know what else happened at that exact instant?"

"Of course I don't."

"I was born, me, Suzan Halford. I entered the world. But I wasn't alone when I did."

"What are you going on about?" said Fitzsimmons. "Gisbon's dead and you soon will be. So will your friend. She can go first, you can have that as a last thought, that she's dead because of you." He turned to Malvis. "Do you understand what she's going on about?"

"She says that she's channelling Ian Gisbon's spirit or some nonsense," said Malvis. "Bet you weren't expecting to hear that. Looks like I'm going to have to kill him again."

Hearing our fate, although I'd known it was always his plan, sent a chill up my spine. I think it was the casual way he said it. Like it was nothing to him.

Ian told me not to worry. "I'm sorry that it's come to this. I never wanted you to get hurt. It's not over yet. I can help you, and you have the stab vest, he won't know about that."

"Ian's here," I said. I was surprised at just how calm I felt. "I can assure you of that, he told me he always knew a crooked copper was protecting Malvis and now he knows who it is. He's disappointed and upset, he thought you were his friend."

Fitz laughed, "That was the idea, he was getting too close. I fed him misinformation. I became his friend, it was the best way to keep him close. I knew everything he was up to. I thought I could make him give up and when I saw he wouldn't let it rest, he had to go."

"He says you're a bastard," I spat the words out with as much feeling as Ian had given them to me with.

Fitz ignored that. "Where's the box?"

"What box?"

"Don't be stupid, you know what I'm talking about. The one you got from Gisbon's wife, the one she always denied having."

"I don't know what you mean."

"You were seen, coming away from her house with it."

"Is that what you're so worried about?" said Malvis. "Some evidence that Gisbon had?"

"Yes," said Fitz. "It was everything about you and me, all the clues. Gisbon collected them. I managed to delete it all officially. Gisbon always said he had an ace up his sleeve, which meant there had to be a copy somewhere. That was what I meant, Harold, when I said this was bigger than you thought."

"I've seen it," I said, even though I hadn't. "There's enough in there to bury both of you."

There was a moment's silence. Peta held my hand. We knew what was going to happen, the wait was gut-churning.

We heard the door open and close again. Everything seemed to stop. I had a sudden feeling of hope and then I realised. Nobody who could help us knew we were here, it had to be another one of Malvis's men.

Roy suddenly stepped out of the shadows. What was he doing here?

"Suzan, there you are," he said. "I've been looking for you."

"Someone else comes to join the party?" said Malvis. "Who's this?"

"He's Roy, my mother's boyfriend," I said.

Fitzsimmons laughed. "Is that what you think? How much do you know about him? He's working for me. Tell her, Roy."

Roy couldn't look at me. Fitzsimmons spoke again. "Roy's the man I got to keep an eye on you, he said it would be a good job, fringe benefits and all that. We've been speaking on the phone regularly, haven't we, Roy?"

"I told you not to trust him," said Ian.

"You bastard," I said to Roy. It hadn't been Martin after all.

The three of them stood facing us. Peta gripped my hand like it was all that was keeping her alive.

"That was the original plan, to keep an eye on you, keep you from drawing attention." As Roy said it, my heart sank. I had two people I thought were on my side, two who were going to help. It had turned out that both of them were useless. "Then I got new orders," he added.

"Will one of you two useless articles just do what you've been paid for and solve my problems," said Malvis.

Roy pulled a gun from his waistband. Now there were two pointed at us. One each. "Ian," I thought, "will this stab vest stop a bullet?"

"No, I'm so sorry," he said.

Time seemed to stand still as I heard the sound of a single shot.

Chapter 39

Fitzsimmons coughed. He stepped back and sank to his knees, a red stain spreading across his chest. "That wasn't supposed to...," he muttered and fell forward. Malvis smiled.

"Good," he said. "He was starting to get on my nerves." He still held the knife. "Time for part two, let's get on with it, my plane will leave in an hour or so."

Roy stepped towards me and swung the gun, but not towards us. Instead, it was now pointed at Malvis. What was going on?

"Drop the knife, Malvis," said Roy.

Malvis looked at him. "You're making a big mistake," he said. "Remember whose side you're supposed to be on."

"I know whose side I'm on," said Roy. "It's all become very clear to me, now drop the knife."

Malvis didn't move. Roy fired a shot. The bullet chipped the floor by Malvis's feet and whined away into the distance. There was the sound of breaking glass. "I won't ask you again." He came over to stand beside us.

Malvis dropped the knife and it clattered to the floor. "Now kick it towards us," Roy said.

It spun across the tiles and ended up by my feet.

"Good," said Roy. "Now we're getting somewhere. You see, Harold, I had no problem at first. I was just doing what I was told, keeping watch on Suzan. To begin with, I just kept an eye, from a distance. She had a normal life, went to school, took her tablets and seemed to be getting on with things. She had her ups and downs but nothing out of the ordinary, her life was just like anyone else's. She never talked about her dreams or mentioned you. So, I left her alone. Then, when she left school, she went off the rails a bit. I was keeping in touch with Fitz, he said that if she got into any sort of trouble, she might get arrested and spill the beans. He told me to make sure that didn't happen. I thought the best plan was to get close to her mother. If I became part of the family's life, I might be more able to stop her from doing anything silly."

So it had all been an act, my mother would be devastated if I ever got the chance to tell her.

"You're a bastard, Roy," I said it again. "She told me that she loves you."

"Just cut to the chase," said Malvis. "Are you on my side or hers?"

"I'm coming to that," said Roy. "Where were we, oh yes. Suzan's mother was a fine woman and I thought it would just be a perk of the job sharing her life but I genuinely fell for her. I could see what Suzan meant to her and how much she hated what had happened. I was determined to keep Suzan alive, save her from the losers she was hanging around with and get her back from her addiction. That means you can relax, Suzan, you and your friend. I'm not going to hurt either of you."

"That doesn't explain why you killed Fitz," I said, although it was Ian who made me say it. I didn't look at him, I couldn't stop looking down at the knife by my feet.

"There was a reason for that," said Roy. "Firstly, it was because things were getting out of hand. Do you know what Fitz's solution was? He wanted me to kill Suzan, her mother, her aunt, the kids in the park and just about anyone else who had anything to do with her. All of them. I thought that was getting a bit much. Then, as Suzan came to London, Fitz wanted me to kill Beth and her family as well as her friend here, oh, and her friend's boyfriend. Not only that, I had to ransack his widow's house, looking for a box of evidence. It all seemed a little over the top, just to keep one man safe. Then I realised, Fitz wasn't interested in saving your skin, Malvis. He only wanted to save his own."

"Then I called you," Malvis said.

"That's right," he waved the gun at Fitzsimmons' body. "This was the result."

"So, now everyone knows everything," Malvis said. "Great. Will you finish it? Just two to kill? Not the bloodbath Fitz wanted. Then you can go back to the mother if that's what you want. I'll get someone else to take care of Gisbon's wife, find the evidence and destroy it. We'll be even. Just point the gun away from me and shoot them."

I could feel the pressure to act building in my head. Ian felt different, stronger than he ever had before. "This is crazy," he said, "it's not what I wanted. It'll never be over until Malvis is dead."

"What are you going to do, Roy," I asked, "isn't it time we called the police?"

He shook his head, "I'm in too deep. In case you didn't notice, I've just killed one of them.

"But he was working for Malvis."

"Can you prove that, when we don't know who else he has on his payroll?"

"Like I said," Malvis repeated, "you'll have to let me walk away. But, if you don't kill those two, I won't forget you went against me. You'll spend the rest of your life looking over your shoulder."

Ian was talking to me again, "Malvis has to go, kill him and all the police on his payroll won't matter anymore."

He was right, I could see that there was only one option that got Peta and me out alive. I wasn't bothered about Roy, he didn't seem inclined to kill me at the moment. "The knife," said Ian, "look at the knife." I felt his will trying to overtake mine, like a creeping headache, advancing over my mind.

I knew that I had to pick the knife up. I bent down and touched the handle. As I did, I felt another sensation, not just in my head.

My legs buckled and I started to fall, it felt like I was losing control of my body. Was I having another fit? I tried to speak but no words would come out. Suddenly, it felt as if I was just watching someone else who was in control of me. I heard Ian, out loud. He wasn't just using my voice, this time he had taken over my body as well.

"This is the knife," his words came out of my mouth with Ian's voice, a deep voice. "This is the knife you killed me with."

Malvis looked genuinely worried now. "Come on, girl," he said. "Why are you mucking about? Stop pretending to be someone you're not. Last chance, Roy."

"I'm not Suzan anymore," I said. "Do you know who I am?"

I, he, took a step forward, it felt really weird. I couldn't stop him. This must have been how it had felt for Ian, for all those years.

"Perhaps you believe me now," Ian said. "Isn't it ironic, the knife that killed me is going to do the same to you? In the same place. Let me tell you how it will be. It's going to slide in, between your ribs. It's going to feel strange. Like an injection with a hot needle, the biggest injection you've ever had. In an instant, your mind will know that it's the worst thing that could ever happen to you. Then, quite quickly, you'll start to lose feeling. Quickly, so quickly, you'll be gone and I'll be free."

Malvis took a step back. "You're crazy," he said. I felt my body move towards him and he took another step backwards, his hand reaching around the back of his jacket.

"Look out," said Roy. I realised that I was in his line of fire. At the same moment, Malvis's hand reappeared, with a knife in it. His wrist jerked, I saw it spinning across the gap between us in a blur and I knew Ian couldn't move me quickly enough. Even if I had been able to, it was too late for me to move. I heard Peta scream, "Stringy!"

The knife hit my stab vest and bounced away, my body kept walking towards him. Ian was still talking through me. "That was your last play, Malvis, now you're going to die. This is the only way it can end. There's nowhere left to run."

My body started walking faster. Malvis looked confused. "How did that happen? It bounced off you?" He panicked, turned to run and crashed into a rubbish bin. He got up and ran. I chased him to the end of the mall, up against a shopfront. He turned to face me. In a reflex, he put his hands up. "Can't we just talk about it?" he said.

Ian didn't answer. I felt my arm moving forwards. I felt the resistance as the knife entered his body. Malvis looked down at the blade. "I never thought of it like that, you're so right," he said. His eyes rolled and he fell.

I stood over him and he looked straight at me, the eyes were glazed and unfocused. "Goodbye, Malvis," Ian said.

"Is that you, Gisbon?" he whispered. "I can hear you but I can't see you."

"Yes," Ian answered. "It's Gisbon, I'm here."

Malvis was silent, the eyes staring. I don't know if he had heard Ian before he died.

Peta and Roy ran towards me, I felt her gently touching my shoulder. "Are you OK?" she said. I could feel pressure in my head, almost like a headache coming on.

Then a voice said, "Thank you, Suzan. Goodbye."

"Why are you saying goodbye, Ian, where are you going?" I said it to myself, just like I had so many times before.

"I'm already there," the voice in my head faded out.

It felt like a weight was lifting off my shoulders. My legs suddenly gave way, it went dark as I fell to the floor.

Chapter 40

I woke up and didn't know where I was. As I looked around, I could see that I was sitting on the back seat of a car. Peta was sitting next to me, holding my hand. Roy was in the driver's seat. We were parked outside an all-night burger restaurant. I looked at my watch, I'd been unconscious for three hours.

"What happened?" I said.

"Don't you remember? You killed Malvis," Peta said. "You stabbed him. Neat trick, by the way, speaking with a man's voice. Were you talking to Ian, just before you collapsed?"

"Yes," I said, "he's gone now."

"What do you mean, he's gone?" asked Roy. He looked puzzled.

"I can't hear him in my head anymore, it's a long story."

"Let's go inside and get a burger," Roy said. "You can tell me all about it."

Peta and I sat at a table. The place was quiet. Roy didn't ask what we wanted, he just left us there and went over to the counter. I was feeling bereft, there was so much I'd wanted to ask Ian. Now it was too late.

"So it's all over?" said Peta. "I thought I was going to die."

"So did I. What happened when Fitzsimmons turned up?"

"I had a sinking feeling," she said. "He was in an unmarked car, on his own. He got out. I asked him where everyone else was. He said they were on the way but it didn't feel right. He asked me to show him where you were. As I went through the door, I heard a click."

"That was the gun?"

"That's what he said, he told me to keep quiet and walk in front of him. Has Ian really gone?"

Before I answered, I asked him myself, "Are you there, Ian?"

There was no reply, my head felt empty but it also felt very strange. "I think he has," I said. I can't believe it, after all this time."

"Isn't that a good thing?" she said. "He kept his word. He did what he had to, he said he would leave and he has."

"I don't know, I've been wanting him gone for so long but now he has it doesn't feel right."

"He got his justice," she said. "Now he's gone to be at peace somewhere."

"You're right. I guess he's where he should be now."

"And this man, Roy, what about him?"

"I don't know. I'm confused, he was a good guy who turned out to be a bad guy. Now he's good again. Ian said don't trust him, does that still apply?" I was going to have to work that out on my own. I hoped that whatever happened, Mum didn't get hurt.

Before she could answer, Roy returned with a tray, piled with food and drink. I realised just how hungry I was.

"Do you want to talk about it?" Roy asked, as Peta and I grabbed at the food.

"How much do you know?"

"Not a lot. Look, I'm sorry that I deceived you. I was working for Malvis. I knew all about his past, how he killed Ian and how you came to his attention. I followed you up to London."

"Did you set those two on Duncan and us?" Peta asked.

"No," he said. "I wasn't involved in what those two thugs got up to. That was all Fitz. What I don't get is what I just saw."

"Can I trust you?" I said. "What do I have to say to Mum? You misled her, she's going to be devastated."

He looked at me. "What you tell her is up to you. But I would ask you to consider this. I meant what I said to Malvis, I've fallen for her. I want to go back and be with her, for a long time. You can tell her all about it; if you want to spoil her happiness."

He must have seen my look of disgust. "I'm not trying to blackmail you," he said, "you have to do what you think is right. Malvis told me to kill Fitz, then you both. I'd already decided to do what I did. It wasn't a whim." He thought for a moment. "I'm just as implicated as you are, we both killed someone. Your defence wouldn't convince anyone. Mind you, neither would mine."

Roy and I looked at Peta. "You're the only witness," we both said, at the same time.

"I don't intend to tell anyone what happened," she said. "I was waiting outside when Fitzsimmons arrived. I thought it was strange, how he was on his own. When he produced the gun, I knew we were in deep trouble. There was no way to warn you."

"There will be no CCTV," Roy said. "I disconnected it all, on Malvis's orders. He didn't want any evidence. I was there before the mall closed. I guess Malvis was there too, I didn't see him."

"Ian took over at the end, didn't he?" asked Peta.

"He must have, but he didn't warn me. He only asked me if he could use my voice."

Roy was looking puzzled. "Fitz and Malvis both told me you were some sort of psychic, getting messages from Ian. It was more than that, wasn't it?"

"Much more," I said, around a mouthful of burger. "Hang on." I chewed, swallowed and took a drink. "Ian's soul, for want of a better word, was living in my head, it always had been. I never knew how much power he had until he picked up the knife."

"Go on, pull the other one," said Roy. You could tell that he found it hard to believe. I couldn't blame him for that.

"Whatever," I said. "When I picked up the knife, I felt Ian take full control of my body. I felt what it must have been like for him all those years, while I was doing everything. It must have been what he meant, when he said that I shouldn't worry about whether I would be able to help him. He knew that I wouldn't have to. I couldn't stop him, it was his will that moved my arm and stabbed Malvis, not mine."

"I still can't get my head around it," said Roy. "So you were possessed?"

"Not in a horror movie sort of way. Ian was benign until then. Where's the knife? It'll have my fingerprints on it."

"Don't worry," said Roy. "That's all been sorted, the knife has been wiped clean and is currently residing in the River Thames under Kew Bridge. If anyone ever finds it there will be nothing to tie it to you. I locked up when we left the shopping mall; in the morning people will go in and find two bodies there and they won't have a clue how it happened."

It seemed like he'd thought of everything. We were in the clear. "What's next for you, Roy?" I asked.

"I'm going to go back to your mother now," he said, with a smile. "I want to be with her, always. What are you going to do?"

I hadn't thought about it. "I think I'd like to spend a few days with Peta. If that's OK with her. Her flat needs a tidy." She laughed. "Plus," I added, "I need to get my head straight before I come home."

"Of course you can," Peta said. "You can stay as long as you want."

"At least until I can see Duncan. I need to apologise for putting him in danger."

"And explain?" he said.

"I don't think so, not everything," I said.

"Finish your burger," said Roy. "I'll drop you two off at your hotel before I head out."

He didn't ask where it was, I suppose he didn't need to.

Afterword

I hope that you have enjoyed this book.

As an independently published author, I have no huge marketing machine, no bottomless budget.

I rely on my readers to help me gain attention for my work. And next to the readers who love my work; reviews, either by word of mouth or online remain one of my most important assets.

Talking about my books, telling your friends and family and reviews on websites help bring them to the attention of other readers. If you've enjoyed reading this book, please would you consider leaving a review, even if it's only a few words, it will be appreciated and might just help someone else discover their next great read!

Find out more about me and my worlds at www.richarddeescifi.co.uk, where you can see details of my other novels and short story collections.

Thank you very much.
Richard Dee.

Printed in Great Britain
by Amazon